MIND GAMES

THE WITCHES OF WHEELER PARK: BOOK 4

CHRISTINE POPE

MIND GAMES

ISBN: 978-1-946435-36-1

Published by Dark Valentine Press

Cover design by Lou Harper

Book formatting by Indie Author Services

1

JEREMY WILCOX SHOT AN ANNOYED GLANCE AT HIS phone, which sat on the table next to the computer where he was working and had just started to buzz. His first instinct was to ignore the call. After all, everything in the witch world had been basically quiet as a tomb for the past couple of months, ever since his brother Jake had settled in with his girlfriend Addie, and all of the "orphan" witches they'd liberated from a government facility in Virginia had either been united with the clans they belonged to or had been given a place to live in Flagstaff. There hadn't been a single ping in the system Jeremy had set up at Trident Enterprises to locate clan-less witches and warlocks, not even the slightest blip on the radar to indicate there might be more of them out there somewhere in the world.

No, the call was probably from Jake, who'd taken advantage of the gorgeous September weather to take the afternoon off and hike around Aspen Corner with Addie, and who had probably just gotten back into cell phone range and wanted to make sure he hadn't missed anything important.

Right. Like there was anything to miss, important or not.

Their cousin Laurel, who made up the remainder of the Trident team, was also playing hooky. She hadn't provided any real excuse for skipping out on work, except to say she was tired of sitting around and doing nothing, and so she'd gotten together with a couple of other Wilcox cousins to go down to Jerome for the day and hang out.

In other words, shop and eat and probably hit all the wine-tasting rooms. Jeremy hoped they'd at least picked a designated driver.

Most people probably would have understood their restlessness. Flagstaff in September tended to be near perfection—mild temperatures, fresh air, skies so serenely blue, they could have been carved from a vast block of lapis. Jeremy, on the other hand, couldn't help being a bit irritated with his brother and his cousin. They needed to treat Trident Enterprises like the serious business it was. Hadn't they already located fourteen "orphans" in pretty much one fell swoop? So, they were currently going through a bit of a dry spell. That didn't mean everyone had license to go off and do whatever the hell they wanted.

Scowling, he picked up the phone. His irritation lessened slightly as he read the number on the screen.

It wasn't Jake's.

No, it was Dan Begay calling.

Dan wasn't a member of the Wilcox clan—he was Navajo—but the local branch of the tribe knew all about the Wilcoxes, knew there was a lot more to them than appeared at first glance. While the witch clans in general did whatever was necessary to conceal their natures from the rest of the world, the Wilcox family had had dealings with the Navajo from pretty much the very moment they'd settled in Flagstaff in the 1870s, and so there weren't many secrets between them, not after spending almost a hundred and fifty years around one another.

Although Dan's family lived out near Cameron on the Navajo reservation, he'd gone to high school in Flagstaff, which was how he and Jeremy had become friends. And while they didn't see each other much anymore—Dan had been working at the Twin Arrows casino about twenty miles east of town for the past few years—Jeremy knew his friend wouldn't be calling unless he had a damn good reason.

One more ring, and it would roll over to voicemail. That seemed to decide things.

He picked up the phone and swiped the screen. "Jeremy here."

"Hey." As usual, Dan sounded calm and easygoing,

as if he didn't have a care in the world. However, Jeremy doubted he would be calling unless something was up.

Which turned out to be exactly the case.

"We've got a situation here," Dan went on. "At least, we think it's a situation. Maybe it's nothing."

"At the casino?" Jeremy asked.

"Yeah. A weird pattern of wins."

Jeremy's mind immediately went to the most plausible explanation. "Someone counting cards?"

"We're not sure."

That reply didn't make much sense. After all, casinos trained their dealers to look for signs of card counting, and Jeremy doubted the management at Twin Arrows would have overlooked something so fundamental when it came to making sure their staff members were on top of any situation that might arise at their gaming tables.

"You have someone in particular you're watching?" he asked.

"No." A pause, and Dan added, "I know I'm not giving you much to go on. This is probably more a hunch than anything else. But you told me to keep an eye out for anything that seemed out of the ordinary."

True enough. As they were ramping up Trident Enterprises back in the spring, Jeremy had suggested to Jake that they might have a few select people in the Navajo nation lend their own assistance when it came to finding any orphaned witches or warlocks. No, they couldn't tell someone was a witch just by looking at her, of course, and neither would they experience the subtle tingle or twitch or ringing in their ears that happened whenever a witch or warlock met one of their kind for the first time, but at the very least, they could provide more sets of eyes and ears in locations where traffic cameras and other official means of surveillance were in short supply. Jake had gone along with the plan, mostly because he knew as well as anyone else that the Wilcoxes didn't have many secrets among the Navajo, and he figured having some extra help couldn't hurt.

"Well, I can take a look," Jeremy said, even though he had a feeling this was all probably a wild goose chase. "But you'll have to give me access to your security system."

A brief pause, and then Dan said, sounding diffident, "I thought you could get in without anyone's help."

His friend had him there. In school, Jeremy had tried to keep his talent with computers somewhat in check, mostly because he hadn't wanted to freak out his teachers with the true extent of his abilities, but Dan knew his friend's magic allowed him to hack just about any computer system in the world. "True," Jeremy said. "But it'll take me some time." He paused as another thought occurred to him. "Or is it that you don't want anyone to know you've reached out for help?"

"Something like that. Let's just say this isn't an official request."

Fair enough. Dan had been working security at the casino for a couple of years, but it wasn't as though he was head of operations or anything. He'd been recently promoted to a position of more responsibility—at least, Jeremy had a vague recollection of getting a text invite to a party to celebrate the promotion. Not that he'd gone; he didn't see the point in hanging out with a bunch of people he didn't know, fending off questions as to why he wasn't getting wasted with everyone else. Sure, he liked to crack open a beer every once in a while, and he drank wine at the Wilcox Christmas potluck, that sort of thing, but he'd never been a fan of killing off brain cells in mindless pursuit of supposed "fun."

Anyway, he could see why Dan wouldn't want anyone at the casino to know that an outsider was inside their security system and taking a look around. This might be nothing…or it might not. If someone really was taking advantage of the casino by counting cards—it technically wasn't illegal, but it could still get you booted if you were found out—then Jeremy figured he'd be doing them all a favor by locating the culprit.

"No problem," he said. "It shouldn't take me long to get in, and then I'll poke around and download the footage so my algorithms can take a hack at it."

Dan made a noise that might have been a sigh. "Hey, man, I know you have this crazy talent for computers, but do you have to make it sound like you're cracking someone's locker combination?"

"I could lie, but what would be the point?" Jeremy paused for a second, then added, "But don't worry—I'm sure your security is perfectly adequate to most situations. It's just that I'm not 'most situations.'"

"No, I guess not."

Another thought occurred to him. "Hey, if I see some obvious holes in your security, I'll write up some notes, show you guys how to take care of any issues I find."

Apparently, Dan wasn't as enthralled by that offer as Jeremy thought he would be, since he said, reluctance clear in his tone, "Uh…sure. I could take a look and pass on any recommendations."

Meaning that his friend would probably take the credit for those insights and carefully avoid mentioning that it was someone else who'd formulated the analysis. Which was fine. Jeremy honestly didn't care one way or another if anyone at Twin Arrows knew it was his work and not Dan's; it wasn't as if he planned to become the casino's cyber-security boss or something like that. Anything he offered would be as a favor and nothing more.

"Whatever works," he said. "Anyway, let me get into it, and I'll text you if I find something."

"Thanks, man. I appreciate it."

Jeremy made a noncommittal noise and ended the call, then absently set the phone down on the table so he could return his attention to the computer in front of him. When Dan called, he'd been debugging the latest tweaks to what Jeremy referred to as his "search and destroy" algorithm, although of course, it didn't actually destroy anything. No, it just went about the business of slicing through untold gigabytes of data from servers the world over, looking for any anomalies that might indicate the presence of an individual with supernatural powers.

At any rate, the debugging routine could wait. He had something far more interesting to work on now.

A crack of his knuckles, and he got to work.

Sloane Kennedy paused at the entrance to the Twin Arrows casino's gaming room and allowed herself a quick survey of the interior. Not to familiarize herself with the place—this would be her third visit—but to take a look at who was manning the poker tables and make sure she didn't go to one operated by a dealer who might recognize her.

Not that there was much chance of that, even if she went back to a table she'd played at before. Today, a blonde wig covered her chestnut-brown hair, and she wore lots of mascara and glittery pink lip gloss in a bubblegum shade she would never have chosen for herself. Thank God it was so easy to get human hair wigs on eBay; she had a collection of eight of them now, all in various colors and cuts, and she rotated through them on a regular basis. Yes, sometimes it got old, having to pretend to be someone else, but she needed to make sure there was little chance someone would recognize her before she'd collected her winnings and moved on.

Moving on was the important part. The longer you stayed in a place, the greater the risk of getting caught.

She immediately recognized the dealer at one table, a Navajo man probably in his late thirties, sharp-featured and handsome, shining black hair pulled back into a severe ponytail. He'd flirted with her a little bit when she played at his table two nights earlier, and she'd enjoyed the back-and-forth even as she guessed he probably did that with all the attractive customers. Yes, he was way too old for her—even if she'd been considering a relationship, which she wasn't—but it had been an amusing diversion, if nothing else. Probably against the rules, but she certainly wasn't going to rat him out for trying to make his job a little more interesting.

Still, that table was out of the question. Another glance told her that the one just beyond wouldn't work, either, because the briskly efficient woman working that particular location, also Navajo and probably only five years or so older than Sloane's twenty-three, was another person she recognized.

However, neither of the other two dealers was familiar, so Sloane decided to go to the one manned by a guy who looked around her own age. Not because she wanted someone to flirt with, but because she'd learned over the years that the younger dealers didn't tend to be as sharp-eyed as the ones who been dealing hands for decades.

She wasn't going to cheat, though. Or at least, she didn't consider what she did to be *exactly* cheating, although she had a feeling her strict Mormon parents might have a few words to say on that particular subject.

Don't think about them, she told herself, even as William and Susan Kennedy's disapproving faces swirled through her mind. She'd long ago given up trying to please them. They got a phone call at Thanksgiving and cards at Christmas and gifts on their birthdays so they'd know she wasn't dead, but she didn't see the point in trying to pretend she was the ideal daughter they wanted…and expected to have. That ship had sailed ages ago.

Settling an expression of excited anticipation on her features, she headed toward the table she'd selected. An older man was the only one playing there; he wore an expensive watch and a gold ring with a diamond on the pinky of one hand, so obviously, he could afford to lose some money. However, Sloane knew she didn't have to worry about taking his cash, because the game they'd be playing was Head's Up Hold 'Em, a variant of Texas Hold 'Em where you played against the dealer rather the other people sitting at the table.

Most of the time, the house won.

But not when Sloane was playing.

She came up to the table and said, in a breathless voice that didn't sound much like her own, "Is it okay if I play?"

The older man shot her an interested look, gaze moving downward to the tight pink T-shirt she wore and the amount of cleavage it revealed. He smiled, eyes almost obscured by the deepening wrinkles around them. "Sure thing, darlin'. Take a seat."

Texas? Maybe. His accent sure sounded like it. What he was doing here, gambling in a casino on the outskirts of Flagstaff, she had no idea. Just passing through, probably. He was heavyset, shirt straining at its buttons. He didn't look like the kind of guy who'd come to the area to hike, that was for sure.

Not that she really cared. He had a half-drunk glass of what appeared to be whiskey on the rocks by one elbow, and she hoped it was his first. She might have had a lot of practice dodging half-drunk guys who'd decided to get handsy, but that didn't mean she enjoyed it.

The dealer—also Navajo, like just about everyone else working at the casino, with a round face that made him look barely young enough to be working someplace that was restricted to people twenty-one and over—acknowledged her with a nod, but he didn't seem to react to her presence otherwise. Well, maybe he didn't like blondes.

"You've played before?" he asked politely.

"Oh, yeah," she responded. "I went to Vegas a few months back for my bestie's bachelorette weekend, and we played everything—blackjack, Texas Hold 'Em, pai gow poker, baccarat. It was awesome."

His neutral expression didn't shift at all as she told him that pack of lies. Well, all right, she'd been in and out of Vegas multiple times, always making sure to stay away for at least four or five months before she went back to make the rounds again, but she definitely didn't have a "bestie," let alone one who'd had a lost weekend with a bunch of her bridesmaids. But the story fit the blonde wig and the pink T-shirt she wore, so it was one she often recycled.

"Great," the dealer said, then picked up a deck of cards.

Sloane kept smiling, although inwardly, she couldn't help tensing. Sure, she'd done this hundreds—if not thousands—of times before, but she still hated the feeling of knowing that sometimes the cards were against her no matter what she did, that sometimes she'd lose some of the money she'd worked so hard to earn. It didn't happen often, and yet there was always the chance that she'd be dealt a hand so crappy, there wasn't anything she could do except fold and wait for better things to come along.

The dealer placed two cards in front of her face down, and she picked them up to take a look. Two jacks, one of hearts, one of spades. Not a bad start. She kept smiling, just because the persona she'd adopted was not the sort of woman to maintain any kind of poker face. Besides, suddenly turning serious would have been much more of a tell than keeping that stupid smile plastered on her mouth.

Two more cards were placed in front of the guy from Texas, and he gathered them up as well. By that point, his expression had gone stony, and Sloane could see he was doing his best not to allow any betraying tells to creep across his features.

Unfortunately for him, it wasn't his face that he had to worry about.

It was always like flipping a switch in her mind. Back when she was a kid, and this gift or curse or whatever you wanted to call it had descended on her, it had felt like being bombarded by the sounds of a hundred TVs or radios at once—voices babbling away in her head, threatening to crush her with the weight of their words. Except she'd figured out soon enough that what she was hearing wasn't a television or a radio or someone's phone, but people's damn thoughts, beaming straight into her brain. And not long after that, she came up with a way to create a barrier in her mind so she wouldn't be forced to listen to other people's garbage all day long. Now, when she wanted to use her gifts, she imagined that barrier dropping and then turned her focus on the person in question, and suddenly she could see what they were seeing, hear what they were thinking.

In this case, she saw that Tex had a couple of garbage cards—a three of clubs and a six of diamonds. If she'd been holding those cards, she would have gone ahead and folded, not bothering to wait to see what the dealer would put down for community cards.

But apparently he'd decided to stick it out...mostly because of her presence.

Hot little thing...wonder if she'd mind if I bought her a drink. A couple of those, and she might not care that I'm twice her age.

More like three times my age, grandpa, Sloane thought in some derision. All right, maybe not exactly, since he looked to be in his early or mid sixties, and she was twenty-three, but still.

Yuck.

She backed out of his mind and directed her attention toward the dealer, who'd just dealt himself his two hole cards. A pair of eights.

Okay, things were looking up. He could still maneuver around her if he managed to get a third eight, or, less likely, a trio of new cards to fill out a full house, but at the moment, she was definitely doing better than either of her opponents.

All the same, she wasn't going to blow it by getting cocky. Her cash reserves were looking pretty good at the moment, since she'd been winning steadily ever since she got to the Flagstaff area—not in huge amounts, a couple hundred bucks here, a thousand there. She could afford to lose some, even though she guessed she probably was going to emerge the victor in this particular go-'round. However, she knew the empty-headed college girl she was pretending to be wouldn't bet aggressively.

She slid a couple of ten-dollar chips toward the

center of the table. The dealer noted their movement, as did Tex, who bet the same amount.

Of course he did.

Next came the first three community cards. King of diamonds, ten of spades, two of spades. Nothing that any of them could do much with, which meant she was still on top with her pair of jacks.

The hand played out just as Sloane had imagined it would, with her winning a modest pot of a little over a hundred bucks. She acted surprised and startled, lying through her teeth as she exclaimed that she'd never won anything before in her life.

"Beginner's luck, I guess," she said to Tex, who smiled back at her, not looking too upset by the money he'd just lost.

"Can I buy you a drink to celebrate?" he asked.

Damn. She'd really been hoping he wouldn't go there.

"Oh, um…thanks," she responded, mind working furiously. A quick dip into his thoughts told her he truly was just passing through, and actually had to be in Scottsdale that evening for a business dinner. Some kind of real estate deal.

That information sent a surge of relief through her, since now she knew she could stall a bit and be safely rid of him. He wasn't staying at the casino, and he didn't have enough room in his schedule to loiter around for hours, trying to soften her up.

"But some friends of mine are meeting me here

later," she went on. "We're planning to party, you know, and so I don't think it's a good idea for me to start drinking this early in the day. But that's really sweet of you."

Disappointment flickered in his watery blue eyes. To her relief, though, he didn't press the issue, but only said, "Well, that's real responsible of you, miss. You have a good time with your friends—I need to cash out and get going anyway."

With a nod toward the dealer, he gathered up his remaining chips and headed toward the cashier's window. Sloane reached for the glass of water by her elbow and took a sip, glad that she never consumed alcohol while gambling, and therefore her claim about waiting to drink until she met up with her mythical friends would have sounded plausible enough.

After swallowing the water, she looked over at the dealer, who'd watched her exchange with Tex, expressionless the whole time.

No point in smiling at the guy. Some people you could get around, and some people you couldn't. And she wasn't going to peek into his mind to see what he thought of her. What difference did it make? He was here to work...and so was she.

Voice level, she said, "Hit me."

2

THE SECURITY MEASURES IN PLACE ON THE TWIN Arrows casino's computer and surveillance systems were pretty decent, all things considered. Still, they were child's play compared to the firewalls that had once protected the Special Enforcement Division of Homeland Security. Those barriers had taken him nearly forty-eight hours to penetrate, whereas Jeremy was inside the casino's security system within an hour of ending Dan Begay's call.

Some would have said tact wasn't Jeremy's strong suit, but even he knew it probably would be better if he didn't mention to his friend how easily he got inside.

Everything on the security footage looked pretty normal to him…but of course, it would. Your standard gaming rooms, with tables for blackjack and poker, roulette and craps, and banks and banks of slot machines. The place was probably a little ritzier than a lot of Indian casinos, since the facility wasn't even ten years old yet, and a lot of money had been spent to ensure it would be a showplace. Not that Jeremy could know for sure; he definitely wasn't into gambling, and although some of his Wilcox cousins went out to Twin Arrows on a regular basis to go eat someplace different from the usual batch of restaurants in Flagstaff, or to visit the night club, or even simply to have a quick getaway to someplace that was still in the clan's territory but not too distant, he'd never cared much about going, and so he'd never actually been there.

At the moment—a little past four on a Thursday afternoon—the place didn't seem all that crowded. Some people playing slots, a few more at the poker and blackjack tables, but it probably was pretty thin compared to the kind of traffic the casino would get on a weekend.

Anyway, he wasn't all that concerned about eyeballing the current group of patrons. Maybe Randall Lenz, formerly with Homeland Security and now hanging out in Wilcox territory, would have been able to survey the crowd and detect any patterns of behavior that seemed off, but Jeremy knew he didn't have that kind of training.

No, he had a different kind of analysis in mind.

Because things had been so quiet at Trident Enterprises lately, he'd been spending most of his mental energies on creating his own facial recognition software. He knew the government had employed several versions of the technology, but he wanted to write his own code and see what he could come up with. True, it probably wouldn't help much with Trident's main goal of locating orphan witches and warlocks, since by definition, he and Jake and Laurel didn't know exactly who they were looking for and therefore couldn't know anything about a particular witch or warlock's appearance, but he still thought the program would be something handy to have in his toolbox.

Because Dan had said this was a recent occurrence, Jeremy downloaded the last seventy-two hours' worth of security footage to Trident's servers, then had his facial-recognition program go to work on it. He figured at the very least, it would pick up on anyone who spent a lot of time in the casino or had an unusual pattern of activity when it came to moving from table to table or coming and going from the casino itself.

While that project was humming away in the background, he went back to work on the debugging routines he'd been focused on when Dan called. Maybe not the most glamorous task in the world, but it was something to do. At least he could say he was earning his keep, unlike Jake and Laurel.

All right, that probably wasn't entirely fair. After everything Jake and Addie had been through together, they deserved some time off. If anything critical had come down the pike, of course Jake wouldn't have taken the afternoon to go hiking. Laurel, on the other hand, hadn't really put in enough hours to justify blithely heading off to Jerome with several of their cousins, but since Jake hadn't seemed to care one way or another about her playing hooky, Jeremy knew it was better for him to keep his mouth shut.

Most of the time, he preferred to work alone anyway. He hated interruptions, hated it when he got into a good flow state and then had to stop abruptly because Jake had a question or Laurel wanted to chat, or whatever. Honestly, it was better that they were both gone.

A soft chime came from the Mac Pro he'd been using to analyze the security camera footage from the casino. Frowning slightly—he hadn't thought it would get through the analysis that quickly—Jeremy rolled his office chair over to the Mac's big cinema display and took a look at the screen. Six individuals had been flagged, although he could tell right away that the first two had attracted the attention of the algorithm simply because the people in question had spent what seemed like a ridiculous amount of time wandering around the casino before deciding on a game to play. One man, one woman, both of whom looked to be in their late forties or early fifties, although they didn't seem to have any connection to one another beyond their similar ages.

The third person was, Jeremy realized after a moment, a plainclothes security guard for the casino. The guy never even sat down at a gaming table, which meant the algorithm shouldn't have pointed him out in the first place. Something Jeremy would have to fix the next time he went in and fiddled with the code. He'd included the parameter of being an actual gambler when he set up the specs for the scan, but obviously, something had glitched.

The fourth and fifth and sixth people were a trio of women in their early or mid-twenties, one with blonde hair set in loose waves down to the middle of her back, the second a redhead, hair around the same length but straight, while the third woman had mid-brown hair cut in a choppy bob that didn't quite hit her shoulders. The blonde wore a tight pink T-shirt and similarly tight jeans, while the redhead had on a flowy flowered dress, and the one with the brown hair was wearing jeans and a sleeveless chambray shirt. They seemed to be roughly around the same height and build.

No, wait…they were *exactly* the same height and build. Eyes narrowing, Jeremy enhanced each image, removing the blur the security cameras had given the still shots. He lined them up next to each other, and gave a satisfied nod.

Those three women were all the same person. When viewed side by side, it was hard to miss the way they all shared the same full mouth, the same heavy arched eyebrows and rounded nose. And okay, in each "version," the woman's makeup was different enough that it did a decent job of playing down those features and making them harder to detect, but they were all still unmistakably the same person. Probably, no one at the casino had detected anything unusual about her because they'd never had the opportunity to see those three different disguises placed next to one another…which Jeremy was sure had been the woman in question's intention all along.

Now that he'd narrowed things down to this one woman, it was easy enough for him to go back and scan through the raw footage again, tracing her movements. In each separate disguise, she went into the casino and played a number of games at the poker tables, each time walking out with a decent amount of cash. Not crazy lottery amounts of money, but definitely hundreds or even thousands of dollars.

And at the end of each session in the casino, she went to the cashier and cashed out her chips, then left, exiting through the lobby to the parking lot.

So, she wasn't staying there.

Actually, that made a lot of sense. If she'd stayed at the Twin Arrows hotel, she would have run a much higher risk of someone noticing that the woman coming and going from a particular room kept radically changing her appearance.

He went back through the footage and paused to watch her playing poker—this time, in her guise as the redhead. Nothing seemed that strange about the way she conducted herself during the game; she seemed serious, intent on her cards, but she also appeared to talk to the others at the table, and looked relaxed enough while doing so. Could someone count cards and also hold a conversation at the same time? He supposed so, although he thought that must take a hell of a lot of mental focus.

Once or twice, though, he caught her going still, face blank as if she was concentrating on something. Counting cards, he assumed, except she wasn't even looking down at the cards in her hand or the ones laid out on the table. Instead, it almost seemed as if she was staring at the other people who surrounded her, although those frozen moments never lasted very long, and he couldn't tell from watching the videos whether anyone at the poker tables had even noticed.

However, he thought he'd seen enough. Maybe the woman on the video just liked to play with her appearance as a sort of hobby, but he kind of doubted it. Much more likely that she kept switching things up so no one would notice how often she'd come to play at the casino…or how much she won.

Jeremy took a series of screen grabs of the woman, then quickly edited the photos to make them a manageable size for sending electronically. Since he didn't have Dan's email address—they always communicated via text—he figured he'd email them to himself, then text them over to his friend. Then Dan could do what he wanted with them.

Except…something about the whole scenario didn't feel quite right. If asked, Jeremy probably couldn't have explained exactly what had sent his spider sense tingling. He certainly wasn't psychic; computers and code were his gift, not reading people's minds.

Reading people's minds....

He wanted to shake his head at himself. Talk about jumping to conclusions. Just because the woman with the constantly changing appearance paused in the middle of game play to stare off into the middle distance didn't mean she was doing so in order to probe the thoughts of the people around her.

But what if she was? Mind reading would be a hell of a useful gift to have if you were trying to support yourself on poker winnings. No wonder Dan had mentioned counting cards—he'd guessed something was up, but he couldn't have known that the casino had a psychic poker player doing her best to accumulate a nice pot of winnings before she moved on to the next place.

If that was even what was going on.

Damn it—Jake had picked a real great day to go AWOL. If he'd been at Trident like he was supposed to, Jeremy could have shown him the footage and asked him what he thought. In general, his brother had better instincts about those sorts of things.

But since Jake was off hiking around Aspen Corner with Addie and probably wouldn't head home until the sun started to go down, enlisting his help wasn't an option. From what Jeremy had been able to tell, it looked as though the mysterious woman preferred to gamble in the afternoons and rarely hung around much past six before disappearing to wherever she went when she was done for the day. It wasn't quite five now; if he left right away, he could be at Twin Arrows by five-thirty.

And do what? Confront her? That sounded like a recipe for disaster, especially since he didn't have any evidence of wrongdoing. The smart thing to do would be to send the photos to Dan, tell him what he'd seen, and walk away. There was no reason to get involved beyond that.

Unless, of course, the woman in question was far more than the card shark she appeared to be.

And wasn't Trident all about tracking down people with unexplained abilities?

Jeremy hesitated for a moment, staring at the images on the screen. Then he muttered, "Screw it," and got up from his office chair. The keys to his truck were in his hand before he even got to the door.

Because if there was one thing in the world he really hated, it was unanswered questions.

Sloane knew it was time to cash out. More people had come along after "Tex" left, and she'd been careful to lose a couple of hands, but her daily winnings were now up to almost twelve hundred dollars, and the dealer was starting to give her the side-eye. Anyway, she'd been playing for almost three hours, and she never allowed herself to do more than that, figuring she was tempting fate if she hung around that long. Besides, they'd just finished a hand, and there was no point in sticking around for another one.

A little start, as if she'd felt her phone buzzing in her jeans pocket. She pulled it out and glanced down at the screen. "Oops—my friends are here," she said. "Gotta go."

Flashing a smile at the dealer, who seemed singularly unmoved, she scooped up her chips and then got down from the stool where she'd been sitting. Once again, the familiar tension knotted her neck and shoulders. Every time she went through this procedure, she expected to feel someone's hand descend on her and yank her back, to hear a casino worker tell her they knew what she was doing and to hand over her chips.

So far, that had never happened.

Well, not exactly. There had been that one strange incident in California, when she'd been approached by a good-looking Hispanic man at the Morongo casino just outside Palm Springs. She hadn't been playing for more than an hour when he came up to her and told her that she needed to leave, that she was infringing on another clan's territory. What that was supposed to be about, she had absolutely no idea, but she hadn't argued, had only taken her chips and left. He hadn't stopped her from cashing out, at least, and yet she could tell he wasn't going to put up with any loitering, either.

As odd as the encounter had been, it still hadn't ended in disaster. She'd simply left and gotten in her car, then driven south to the Pechanga casino down in

Temecula. No one had bothered her there, and she'd had a very profitable few days rebuilding her reserves before she decided it was time to move on.

That was the real trick, after all. Just keep moving.

And she needed to move on now. Most of the time, she spent around four or five days in a given place and she'd only been in the Flagstaff area for three, but she could somehow feel in her bones that it wouldn't be smart to linger. She was almost four grand richer, and when she added those winnings to the cash she already had on hand, it would be enough to keep her alive for at least another two months, maybe more.

Because that was the other trick: don't take more than you need to keep going. She lived out of inexpensive hotels and had won her car in a bar bet years before, so her expenses were minimal. Every once in a while, she'd replace one of her wigs when it started to look ratty, and she had to buy clothes and food, but she didn't have rent or utilities or credit card bills. No bank accounts, just prepaid Visa cards for the places that didn't accept cash.

The system had been working pretty well for her so far. The one thing she really hadn't wanted to face was what she planned to do with herself once life on the road palled and she didn't want to spend the rest of her days fleecing casinos—or their patrons—out of their money.

She pushed the unwelcome thought away as she waited for the cashier to count out her chips and exchange them for a bunch of twenty-dollar bills. Once that transaction was handled, Sloane headed for the exit. The sun was nearly to the horizon, but she was used to driving in the dark.

And she wanted to get out of Flagstaff.

When she'd come to town, she'd thought she would head east and hit one of the casinos just over the New Mexico border, but then realized that was a risky proposition, if only because the largest one near Gallup—Fire Rock—was also run by the Navajo. The last thing she wanted was them comparing notes on who'd won big at their casinos recently.

Instead, she decided it would be better to double back and go to Laughlin. She'd stayed out of Nevada for nearly half a year, figuring a cooling-off period was probably a good idea, but enough time had elapsed that it should be safe. During the intervening months, she'd replaced most of her wigs and would have an entirely new set of personas to use to cover up her identity. Every once in a while, she thought about what it would be like to live life as herself, and not as an endlessly changing lineup of women who didn't truly exist. Problem was, she didn't even know if she could pull off being just Sloane Kennedy and no one else.

Anyway, Laughlin would be a test run of sorts. If no one recognized her, and if everything went well, then she'd feel better about going on to Las Vegas. And once she was in Vegas...well, the sheer number of casinos in the city guaranteed that she'd be able to work for at least a couple of weeks before it was time to move on.

After that? Maybe Tahoe. Or maybe she'd just take a break for a while. A good run in Vegas would allow her to go pretty much anywhere she wanted. She'd always wanted to visit San Francisco as an adult; a childhood trip to San Jose really didn't count. A week or so in wine country sounded like fun, too.

Anything to maintain the illusion that she was doing all this on her own terms, that her desperate quest for freedom from a restrictive past hadn't turned into a prison of her own making.

Mouth tight, she guided her CR-V out of the Twin Arrows parking lot and onto the westbound I-40.

Always moving.

3

JEREMY HOPED TO HELL THAT HIS FRIEND DAN wasn't working that afternoon, or at least was off somewhere else in the casino and wouldn't spot him as he loitered near one of the exits. He already felt like enough of an idiot for following an irrational hunch and driving all the way out to Twin Arrows. The whole time, he'd been berating himself for going off halfcocked like that...and yet he hadn't pulled off the highway and turned around. No, he'd kept driving, even as he attempted several times to call Jake and let him know what was going on.

But the calls had rolled over to voicemail, telling him that Jake and Addie were still out hiking in a spot without a good cell signal. Or maybe they were already back in town, and Jake was ignoring his phone because he didn't want to be bothered. Normally, Jeremy would have said that wasn't very Jake-like behavior, but he had to admit that his brother could be a little crazy when Addie was involved. The guy had lost his mind over that girl.

All right, that was possibly a bit of an exaggeration, and it wasn't as if Jeremy didn't like Addie...far from it. But it just seemed to him that Jake, having gone through so much to find Addie and make sure she was safe, wasn't about to lose any opportunity to spend time with her. They weren't in each other's laps as much now that she'd gone back to school full-time, but her class schedule still allowed them to get out and about, like they'd done that afternoon.

Which in a way was the thing that annoyed Jeremy the most. If Addie had been in one of her classes, then Jake would have been at Trident, and he could have helped Jeremy figure out whether this casino trip was a worthwhile errand or just a wild goose chase.

Well, there wasn't anything he could do about it now. He was at Twin Arrows, without backup, and he supposed he'd find out soon enough if he'd just wasted a bunch of time and gas.

In the next moment, though, his heartbeat sped up. Wait—was that her? For a second or two, he couldn't be sure, and experienced a wave of annoyance at all the various disguises and getups the woman in question used to conceal her appearance.

No, it was definitely her. She was wearing the pale blonde wig and a pink T-shirt, along with tight jeans and platform thongs that had rhinestones on the straps.

The stones sparkled in the light from the chandeliers overhead as she stepped away from the cashier's cage and headed toward an exit...but not the one where Jeremy was standing.

Damn it.

He moved in her direction, walking quickly but doing his best not to look as if he was in a hurry, which was harder than it sounded. Had she spotted him? He didn't think so; her stride was also fast, but at the same time without any true sense of urgency, as though she had someplace she wanted to be while at the same time not being too worried about exactly when she got there.

Since he was a good bit taller than she, Jeremy began to close the gap between them. Luckily, the casino wasn't very crowded, and so he didn't have to dodge too many people as he cut his way across the floor. Now she was barely a yard away, improbably pale blonde hair swinging against her back with each step. She'd seemed taller in the surveillance videos because of the confident way she carried herself, but he realized she was actually on the short side, despite those ridiculous platform flip-flops she was wearing.

What to say to her? His brother Jake had all sorts of speeches worked out for these sorts of occasions, but Jeremy had never worried about that sort of thing, since he hadn't really expected to be out in the field and approaching a strange witch on his own. No, he was supposed to be safely in front of a computer back at Trident HQ.

Too bad real life rarely worked out the way you expected it to.

And there it was—the buzzing he got in his left ear whenever he met a witch or warlock for the first time. A surge of triumph went through him. This hadn't been a wild goose chase after all…his hunch had been proven to be correct.

She was almost at the door. Jeremy was so focused on her, concentrating so hard on the most diplomatic way to say, "Hey, don't want to freak you out, but did you know you're actually a witch?", he wasn't paying enough attention to his surroundings. Before he could stop himself, he barreled right into a chubby older woman carrying a couple of suitcases who was probably headed toward the bank of elevators off to his right.

"Watch where you're going!" she snapped as he stumbled away from her, reeling a bit from the unexpected collision.

"Sorry," he mumbled. The woman looked more pissed off than anything, so he didn't think he'd caused her any permanent damage.

No, the real damage was to his pursuit of the unknown witch. His eyes strained to find her, but she appeared to have exited the building while he was regaining his balance.

Shit.

Well, there was really only one place she could have gone. Jeremy hurried toward the exit and emerged into the parking lot. Holding up his hand to shield his eyes from the westering sun, he quickly scanned the area.

There she was. Two aisles down, climbing into a white CR-V. Almost immediately, she was inside with the door shut, the backup lights coming on.

Great. And his own truck was parked on almost the opposite side of the lot. Still, there wasn't much he could do now, not with her already backing out of her parking space. Cursing under his breath, he ran toward the spot where he'd left his Dodge Ram. It actually wasn't as far away as he'd feared, but he knew he'd already lost valuable time.

Then again, there weren't many places you could go when leaving the casino. It was pretty much out in the middle of nowhere, which meant the only real choices were either eastbound or westbound on Interstate 40.

He jumped in the Ram and pressed the ignition button. To his relief, no one was parked in front of him, which meant he could pull through rather than having to waste time backing out. Within a few minutes, he was on the feeder road that led back down to the interstate.

And there was the woman's CR-V, just pulling onto the westbound on-ramp.

Maybe there was a God after all.

Jeremy headed in the same direction, figuring he'd follow her to her destination and then…what? Corner her and explain he wasn't a stalker, just a guy who also happened to be a warlock?

That would go over really well.

Worry about that later, he told himself. *First, you have to catch up with her.*

Which actually didn't seem like it would be all that difficult. Her little CR-V hummed along at a couple of miles an hour above the speed limit, but she certainly wasn't speeding excessively. Nothing about the way she drove gave any indication that she knew someone was following her. Otherwise, Jeremy thought she would be going a lot faster.

Actually, just following her was the real problem. He didn't want to be too conspicuous, but on the other hand, he didn't want to hang so far back that he ran the risk of losing her if she made a sudden maneuver. It probably would have been easier to escape notice if they'd been driving through crowded city streets rather than out on I-40 east of Flagstaff, where traffic was pretty light on this late Thursday afternoon. Unfortunately, they weren't in downtown Phoenix, so he'd have to do the best he could, considering his current surroundings.

At least he was close enough to get a look at her license plate. From Nevada, with a desert sort of landscape as the background. He thought the first two numbers were "55," but with the setting sun blazing almost directly into his eyes, it was hard to see for sure.

They were both driving in the fast lane, since a long line of semi-trucks occupied the right-hand lane. But even as Jeremy was wondering whether to risk pulling closer, one of the semis abruptly hove into his lane, obviously intent on passing one of the slower trucks in front.

Damn it. Jeremy immediately lifted his foot from the gas and dropped back a bit, muttering another curse under his breath. Of all the rotten timing....

But if the guy was just passing, then he'd be back over in the right lane soon enough, and Jeremy would be able to apply some gas and get caught up with the unknown witch.

Or that was the theory, anyway. To his annoyance, the trucker didn't seem inclined to pull over once he was done passing the U-Haul truck that had originally been slowing him down. No, he continued to tool along in the fast lane, going seventy miles an hour and not a bit more.

Fine, then. Jeremy ground his teeth and eyed the right lane, wondering if there was enough room to slip into the spot the semi-truck had previously occupied, floor it, and then cut in front of the bastard. Maybe. His Dodge Ram had plenty of torque, but it wasn't exactly what you could call nimble. Even so, he probably would have risked it—despite the attention that kind of maneuver might attract—except that the person behind him, in a late-model Mustang, apparently had the same idea. The guy darted out from behind him, speeding past the truck, then slid into the fast lane just ahead of it.

Making the trucker lay on his brakes. Jeremy had to

hit his brakes as well, or he would have ended up smashed into the truck's rear end.

This was just getting better and better.

At that inopportune moment, his phone chose to start ringing. Usually, he would have put the phone in one of the cupholders while he drove, but he'd been in such a hurry to catch up with the unknown witch that he hadn't pulled it out of his pocket. And he didn't dare risk retrieving the phone now, not when he'd already come a little too close to ending up in the semi-truck's cargo container.

Whoever was calling would just have to wait.

After an agonizing couple of minutes, the semi finally pulled back over, but the damage was done. Jeremy didn't see any sign of the white CR-V he'd been pursuing. He tried to tell himself it wasn't that big a deal—after all, until you reached the eastern city limits of Flagstaff, there weren't a whole hell of a lot of places to pull off around there. The little town of Winona if you needed gas, maybe, or Walnut Canyon National Monument. He remembered the witch's sparkly footwear and guessed she probably wasn't planning to go hiking any time soon. Besides, it was nearly sunset, and Walnut Canyon would be closing soon anyway.

No, she had to be going to Flagstaff…or someplace even farther down the highway.

He applied more gas, speeding up to eighty-five miles an hour. The woman hadn't been driving too fast, and so he figured that would be enough for him to catch up to her, even with the couple of minutes he'd lost thanks to that truck driver's stupid maneuver.

But...she wasn't anywhere to be found. He got almost all the way to the Country Club Drive off-ramp at Flagstaff's east end without spotting the white CR-V, then debated with himself whether he should get off there and take a look around. After all, that was where the mall was located, along with a bunch of other stores and a couple of hotels. For all he knew, she was staying at one of them.

That decided it. He got over into the right lane and pulled off the highway, then headed south. Almost immediately on his left were a Hampton Inn and a Fairfield Inn and Suites, and he drove slowly through the parking lots of each one, searching for that elusive Honda SUV. He spotted a couple of CR-Vs, one of them even white, but it had California plates. A bit farther down the road was a Sonesta Inn, and he headed there, hoping against hope that he'd see the vehicle he sought.

Naturally, it wasn't there, either. This time, the hunch he'd followed had turned out to be a dead end. He'd wasted at least ten minutes, and if the strange witch in her white Honda had remained on the westbound I-40, she was now far out of his reach.

Scowling, Jeremy pulled the iPhone out of his pocket and glanced down at the screen. The missed call had been from Jake.

Naturally.

Well, at least now Jeremy had something concrete to tell his brother. That ringing in his ear had let him know an orphan witch had been right on their back porch, so to speak.

And he'd lost her.

Holding back a sigh, he lifted the phone and touched the screen to have it return the call.

Sloane didn't bother to stop and get something to eat. She always carried a few protein bars in her purse, and she knew one of those would tide her over until she got to Laughlin and could have something a bit more substantial. Once upon a time, she might have worried about eating dinner at nine o'clock at night, but she'd been living on an irregular schedule for long enough now that she knew it wouldn't make any difference.

And the drive itself was no big deal. She spent so much time behind the wheel that three hours was barely more than a blip. Besides, she'd gone back and forth over this stretch of I-40 enough times that it was very familiar to her; she didn't even have to think about jogging north on I-93 in Kingman and then to the westbound 68, but guided the Honda by instinct, mind humming away.

Something strange had happened to her back at the Twin Arrows Casino. She honestly wasn't quite sure exactly what was going on, only that she'd just been about to walk out the door when she felt this odd tingle running down the back of her neck. If it had been the first time she'd experienced that sort of sensation, she might have simply chalked it up to nerves or anxiety or whatever.

But…it hadn't been the first time. No, the first time she had that strange zing at the back of her neck had been when that stranger confronted her at the Morongo casino in Southern California, almost six months ago now. At the time, she'd thought she was simply overreacting to having a man she'd never seen before walk up to her and deliver such an odd request. Now, though… now she didn't know what the hell to think.

The man from California definitely hadn't been at Twin Arrows. Her memory for faces was very good, and she knew she would have recognized him if she'd seen him again. Honestly, no single individual in the place had really jumped out at her. The Twin Arrows casino hadn't been all that crowded, and the people who were there were the sorts you'd expect to see at that kind of place on a weekday afternoon—lots of retirees, maybe a few college-age men and women who either were off for the day or possibly playing hooky. Sloane didn't know for sure, since when she was attending the University of Utah in Logan, she sure as hell hadn't played hooky. No, she'd attended classes full-time and worked fifteen hours a week at a local restaurant as a hostess, and had hated every minute of it. The place was owned by a family friend, and supposedly Bill Redfield had given her the job as a favor to her parents.

That wasn't the real story, though. It had been a setup to have her work closely with Bill's son Rob, who Sloane had done her best to avoid during high school and who worked at the restaurant as a waiter. The guy might have looked like Mr. All-American boy next door, but she'd seen enough of his thoughts to know he was a total creeper. Being stuck working with him had made her flesh crawl.

Maybe that was what had made her finally realize she needed to get the hell out of Logan. She'd already chafed at all the restrictions her parents had put on her —no drinking, no smoking…well, okay, that one wasn't so hard…no dates unless she was with a big group of people. And the "modest" clothes they'd made her wear, and…well, everything. Being forced to spend chunks of her time working next to Rob Redfield had just been the cherry on the hot fudge sundae of suck that her life was turning out to be. Even worse was the underlying expectation that they really didn't expect her to graduate. For a lot of Mormon girls, college was just a way to get your "Mrs." degree and nothing more.

No, thanks.

With almost a physical effort, Sloane pushed away those painful recollections. At least she'd made her escape, unlike most of the other girls she'd known. While she never posted anything too personal on her Facebook wall, she still checked in from time to time to see how her high school friends back in Logan were doing. Almost all of them were married already, and more than half had kids.

Double no-thank-you.

Sloane would allow that maybe someday, if she met the right person, she might be okay with settling down and having a family. A *small* family. Like, a kid and a dog. A house with flowers in the yard…she'd always wondered what kind of house her biological mother lived in, whether it had a pretty garden, whether she'd gone on to have other children or if she'd considered Sloane a mistake she didn't want to repeat.

And since Sloane rarely spent more than a few days in one place at any given time, she had to admit that her chances of meeting someone promising were pretty much nil…especially since the type of guy she tended to meet while hanging out in a casino wasn't exactly the sort of person she'd want to spend the rest of her life with. Or even a week.

Frowning, she tried to remember what was going on at Twin Arrows when she'd felt that strange twinge again. There'd been some kind of commotion behind her—she'd been walking fast, but she recalled hearing a woman give someone grief for bumping into her, and a guy's mumbled apology.

Actually, Sloane realized she *had* looked backward to see what was going on. Briefly, just a quick glance over one shoulder as she kept walking toward the exit. There'd been a guy—tall and handsome, around her own age or maybe a little older, with dark hair. Or at least, the brief glimpse she caught of his profile told her he was handsome, although she hadn't been able to make out much detail.

Had he been the source of the twinge?

That didn't make any sense, though. It wasn't as if she got a funny little tingle every time she saw a good-looking guy with dark hair. She doubted there could be any connection between the two men; they were both dark-haired, true, but the man in Southern California had been clearly Hispanic, while she didn't think the guy back at Twin Arrows was, despite his near-black hair.

Oh, well. The world was full of weirdness, things that didn't quite add up. Like her own ability to read minds, actually. She'd never mentioned the strange gift to anyone, guessing that her parents would only have forced her to go to a shrink to see what was wrong with her if she claimed to have psychic powers, or worse, made her talk to the bishop to see if he could help shake loose whatever demons were plaguing her. Better to keep it to herself, especially when the talent had come in useful on so many occasions. Where it had come from, she had no idea. Something she'd inherited from one of her birth parents? That was the theory which seemed to make the most sense to her; her birth records had been sealed and she hadn't been given even the barest description of her birth mother beyond her age, and so she knew absolutely nothing about the woman who'd given her up for adoption. Supposedly, she'd been young, barely twenty, and that was the extent of Sloane's knowledge. More than once, she'd contemplated hiring a private investigator to see if he could dig up any more information for her, but she'd never gotten around to following up with those plans, telling herself she was too busy to pursue something like that.

Unless it was more that she simply was afraid of the truth. She wanted to know what had happened, why her mother had given her up, but at the same time, she had to wonder if she might discover something she would have preferred not to know.

Better not to think about that, either. She replayed in her mind the words the stranger at the Morongo casino had spoken to her.

You're infringing on another clan's territory.

The way he'd said "another" seemed to indicate there was more than one of those "clans." Who even talked about clans in California, anyway? It wasn't the Scottish Highlands, for God's sake. And "territory"? Was there some kind of weird gambling turf war going on that she hadn't heard about? If that was the case, though, you'd think the man would have been a little more forceful about making sure she left the casino. But he hadn't done anything except watch quietly as she collected her winnings and got the hell out of there.

She wished the guy she'd glimpsed at Twin Arrows had gotten close enough for her to pick up some of his thoughts. That was the one serious limitation on her ability—if someone was more than a yard or so away from her, she couldn't get a damn thing from them. Even if he'd been within range, though, she honestly didn't think she would have peeked into his mind. It was one thing for her to use her talent to help her out at the poker table; she wasn't in the habit of randomly digging around in people's brains just for shits and giggles.

Still, he'd been cute. Probably too cute. She didn't need that kind of distraction right now.

Fingers tightening on the CR-V's steering wheel, she headed west toward Laughlin, and put all thoughts of Flagstaff behind her.

4

"You're sure she was a witch?" Jake asked. His tone was frankly skeptical, but at least he seemed willing to hear his brother out.

"Yes," Jeremy replied, practically biting off the single syllable. The way she'd given him the slip still rankled. His first chance to find an "orphan" on his own, and he'd royally blown it.

Then again, it wasn't his job to be out in the field, chasing down random witches and warlocks. Jake's afternoon of R&R with Addie—and Laurel's little shopping expedition—had forced him to go running after the woman by himself.

They all sat at the dining room table at Jake's house, a long oak piece that could seat up to twelve people, although at the moment, only four of them were clustered at the end near the window, which overlooked a dark backyard. Jake and Addie were both a bit wind-burned but cheerful, while his cousin Laurel sat off to one side, watching as the two brothers discussed the current situation. Jeremy honestly hadn't wanted to wait for his cousin to get back from Jerome, but Jake had said she was already on her way and that it was no big deal to postpone this meeting by a half hour or so.

Jake had ordered in Thai for everyone, a gesture that made Jeremy feel a bit better about the situation. True, they hadn't sat down to eat until after eight, but late food was better than no food at all.

"As soon as I got close enough, I got that buzzing in my ear," he went on, then reached over to snag a wonton from the container in the center of the table. "It was obvious what was going on."

"Did she react to you at all?" Laurel asked. As usual, she was wearing a bright-colored top—this one an almost neon green—and the color made her nearly amber eyes stand out that much more. Her long brown hair had been pulled carelessly back into a silver barrette.

"I don't think so." Frowning slightly, Jeremy tried to recall the moment as best he could. Thanks to the way he'd crashed into that tourist, the situation had been chaotic at best, but he didn't think he'd noticed the strange witch doing much more than pausing ever so slightly to look back over one shoulder. Considering how the tourist had snapped at him after he bumped into her, he had a feeling it wasn't so odd that the witch in question might have taken a second to check out what was going on. Besides, after that one backward glance, she'd kept going full steam ahead. "But I have no idea whether that was because she honestly didn't feel anything or because she was trying to get out of there before I confronted her."

Jake considered those words as he scratched the stubble on his chin. "Maybe you weren't in range. I know that when you get the 'twinge,' it can vary from person to person."

"Wait a second," Addie said, a frown of her own pulling at her brows. "What I don't understand is how this woman could be in Wilcox territory without Connor knowing about it. Didn't you say once that the leader of a clan can feel it when a stranger enters their territory?"

For a second, Jake and Jeremy's eyes met. A shrug, and Jake said, "Well, that's the theory, but just like with a lot of things about witches and warlocks, it varies. Connor's brother Damon could do that, but Connor can't. We don't know if that's because he wasn't born to be *primus,* or whether there's something else going on with his abilities. Angela can do it, but only in McAllister territory, not up here. And Connor mentioned to me once that Zoe—she's the *prima* of the de la Paz clan down in the southern part of the state—has the ability, but only for the immediate Phoenix area, whereas her grandmother supposedly would know the second a strange witch or warlock crossed state lines."

"Oh," Addie said. Her frown relaxed slightly, but it

still pulled at the smooth skin between her eyebrows. She was the only one sitting at the table with light-colored eyes—an unusual gray-green—although her long, straight hair was nearly the same shade of brown as Laurel's. "So, you could have strange witches and warlocks coming and going all the time, and you wouldn't know anything about it?"

"Up to a point," Jeremy told her, not sure he liked the implied condemnation in her words. The clan got along just fine, even without a supernatural security system. "I mean, there are a lot of Wilcoxes in Flagstaff, so if an interloper crossed paths with any of them, they'd know right away that the person in question wasn't meant to be here."

Laurel set down her fork and smiled across the table at Addie, as if doing her best to soften her cousin's rough tone. "Honestly, it's not really an issue most of the time. But as someone who grew up outside a clan, you know better than most how someone might break that rule and have no idea they were doing it."

Addie nodded, and Jeremy said, "Honestly, the witch being here in Wilcox territory isn't the issue. It's where she went. We need to track her down."

"She was heading west, right?" Jake asked. "Since she likes to hang out in casinos, I think it's a pretty safe bet that she's headed to Las Vegas."

That thought had crossed Jeremy's mind as well, but he knew better than to make any assumptions. "Maybe," he allowed. "Or she could be going to

Reno…or Lake Tahoe…or Laughlin. Gambling's legal everywhere in Nevada, you know."

"Yeah, I know," Jake replied, looking slightly irked by the insinuation that he didn't know such a basic fact. "It just seems like Vegas would be her logical destination."

About all Jeremy could do was lift his shoulders. He didn't feel like getting into it with Jake right then. Most of the time, they didn't argue that much, since they both recognized that they each had their individual strengths and weaknesses, and generally tended to stay in their own lanes. Sometimes, though, Jake could get a notion in his head, and it would take a hundred pounds of C-4 to dislodge it.

"I'm running a trace on her plates," Jeremy said. "We'll see if that turns up anything. And I've got one of the computers doing a scan of the traffic cams along I-40. That should help, too."

"You can do a trace when you only have two numbers off a license plate?" Laurel asked, expression halfway between skepticism and wonder.

He nodded as he reached for another wonton. Those things were way too addictive. "It'll take longer, but since I have the make and model of her vehicle, it's not impossible."

Jake was frowning. "What if it isn't her license plate? I mean, it sounds like she's pretty good at disguises. For all you know, she's got a bunch of different license plates and switches them around on a regular basis."

That same thought had already crossed Jeremy's mind. After all, the witch in question was obviously pretty cagey. He recalled the way she'd been driving—a little fast, but definitely not fast enough to catch the attention of anyone except the most over-zealous state trooper. Was she being careful because she couldn't risk getting pulled over and having her plates reported as stolen, or simply because she didn't want to create any additional complications for herself?

Either possibility seemed equally plausible.

He munched on the wonton, then said, "If she's doing that, then yeah, the license plate isn't going to help. Which is why I'm also looking at the traffic cams. They're pretty widely spaced along I-40, but they should still catch her."

"At night," Laurel said dubiously.

"In a white SUV," he reminded her, and she gave him a nod of acknowledgment.

"Any idea what clan she might be from?" Addie asked then.

Jeremy had a feeling he knew why she was asking. Almost as soon as Jake had met Addie, he'd noted something familiar about her, mostly because her eyes were almost the exact same shade as Connor's. Connor, who'd turned out to be her half-brother. And while of course there were tons of variations in every clan, the individuals in each clan also tended to have distinguishing characteristics in common with each other—most of the Wilcoxes had dark hair and dark eyes and tended to be tall, while the McAllisters were much fairer.

The woman Jeremy had seen didn't look like a McAllister to him, although obviously, he had no idea what her true hair color might be. She definitely wasn't a Wilcox or a de la Paz…or a Castillo. He hadn't met anyone from any other clans, so he couldn't begin to guess who the strange witch might resemble.

"I have no idea," he said. "The plates on her CR-V are from Nevada, but, like Jake said, that might not mean much."

"The Delmonicos are in Nevada, right?" Addie asked.

Her question surprised him, because he honestly had no idea that she knew anything about the various witch clans and their home territories. Jeremy had always thought of himself as sort of an anomaly when it came to that field of expertise, since most of his fellow clan members didn't seem to care one way or another about the other witch families scattered around the United States. Out of sight, out of mind; witches and warlocks tended to stay in their own territories, and generally only bothered with the other clans that directly interacted with theirs.

And although the Delmonicos claimed Nevada as their territory, they tended to live up near Reno and Lake Tahoe, abandoning Las Vegas to the civilian— nonmagical—tourists of the world. Still, just because most of them lived elsewhere didn't mean there weren't still some of them hanging around down in that part of the state. It made some sense for the strange witch to have been born in Vegas if that was part of the reason why she'd decided to use her talents to manipulate card games. Maybe her mother had been a showgirl or something. The woman he'd seen had been almost spectacularly curvy. For all he knew, part of the reason he'd walked right into that tourist without seeing her was because his attention had been fixated on the movement of the strange witch's hips and rear end in those tight jeans she'd been wearing.

Jeremy didn't want to believe that about himself. Not because he was indifferent to women, but more that he really didn't want to think he'd been so distracted by the witch's amazing anatomy, he'd made the colossally stupid blunder that allowed her to get away.

Except he had a sneaking suspicion that was exactly what had happened.

"Yes, the Delmonicos are the Nevada clan," he said. "I don't know why there's only one clan in the state—that doesn't usually happen."

"It's like that in New Mexico with the Castillos," Laurel pointed out, and he expelled an irritated breath.

"That's why I said it *usually* doesn't happen, not that it doesn't happen at all." Jeremy reached for his glass of water and took a swallow, wishing he hadn't declined Jake's offer of a bottle of Tsing-Tao. At the time, he hadn't wanted to make himself even the slightest bit blurry, just in case he got a ping sooner than he expected and needed to get on the road right away. Now, he had the feeling he'd shot himself in the foot.

"When you locate her," Jake said, mollifying his brother somewhat. At least he hadn't said *if*. "Do you want Addie and me to go after her? She might be a little less skittish if she's approached by a man and a woman."

That would be the logical plan, since Jake was supposed to be the guy in the field, and it made sense to add a female into the mix, just to seem less threatening. However, Jeremy had already hashed that conundrum out with himself. He'd located the unknown witch, and so he wanted to be the person who talked to her…even while he had to admit that sometimes his communication skills could be just a bit deficient.

"I'll do it," he replied. Was his tone too casual? He didn't know for sure, but he couldn't take the words back now.

Jake lifted an eyebrow. "You're sure?"

"Yeah, I'm sure."

To Jeremy's relief, Jake didn't push it any further. Maybe just the slightest sidelong glance, as if doing his best to assess what his brother's motivations for wanting to handle the errand actually were, but he only said, "Okay, it sounds like we have a plan. I guess now we just have to wait and see what you can find, right?"

Jeremy nodded. "It's a waiting game at this point."

Which was part of the reason why he'd agreed to come to this meeting in the first place. Jake just loved to have these "councils of war," and while Jeremy agreed that sometimes it was better to hash things out in person, he wouldn't have been willing to commit the time if he hadn't already known there wasn't much else he could do until his algorithms produced the actionable data he needed.

"Well, hopefully, we won't have to wait too long," Laurel said. "But you're sure you don't want one of us to come along? I can ride shotgun."

His cousin's voice was a little too deliberately casual. Jeremy had a feeling she really wanted to come with him on the chance that they actually did end up in Las Vegas. She'd never been there—neither had he, actually —and she was probably hoping she might have a chance to see some of the sights.

This wasn't a vacation, though. Whenever he was able to determine where the unknown witch had gone to ground, the trip to find her would be clan business, and nothing else.

"No, I'm good," he said, and then wanted to chuckle at Laurel's crestfallen expression. However, since he knew she probably wouldn't appreciate his amusement, he managed to hold it in.

"I guess that's it, then," Jake said. He probably hadn't missed the subtext to Laurel and Jeremy's exchange, but he also wasn't going to call attention to it.

Addie looked thoughtful. When she spoke, her gaze was fixed directly on Jeremy, as though letting him know she wanted her words to penetrate. "We don't know anything about this girl—where she came from, what her plans are. But if she's been dealing with this gift since she was a kid, just like I had to, then she's probably processing a lot of different things. It's not like it was for the rest of you. This is hard stuff to deal with on your own."

"I know that," Jeremy responded, a little offended that she would waste time pointing out something so obvious.

"Maybe," Addie said. For a second or two, she was silent, as if trying to decide whether to say anything else. When she spoke next, her tone was earnest, her gaze direct. "Just…be kind."

Nothing much seemed to have changed about Laughlin in the six months since Sloane had been there last. She put on her red wig—it was a fairly recent purchase, so she knew no one local would have seen her in it—and got herself a king room at the Tropicana. Right then, she wasn't sure how long she planned to stay in town, but she told the clerk at the front desk that she'd be staying for three nights. If it turned out she needed to leave before then, well, they had a pretty flexible cancellation policy, so she wasn't too worried about it.

After the drive, she wasn't in the mood to face people. The next day, she'd have to put on a new face and a new wig—and go gambling somewhere other than the Tropicana—but in the meantime, it was enough to order a club sandwich and some iced tea from room service, to put her feet up and watch TV while she ate, not even caring what she was watching, only wanting the background voices to help relax the little knot of tension that had formed at the back of her neck somewhere between Flagstaff and Laughlin.

Since she was used to hotel beds, she didn't have any trouble falling asleep that night, and she woke up late the next morning after being passed out for nearly ten hours. Good; she felt much more refreshed and ready to face the day.

No one had seen her enter her room the night before, so she figured it was safe to put aside the red wig for the day and wear the shortish brown one. It was her most unobtrusive piece, and the one that would attract the least attention. She remembered the thoughts she'd seen in the mind of Tex, the older guy at the poker table at Twin Arrows, and repressed a shudder. Looking mousy wasn't always a deterrent for anyone who was a hardcore lech, but she figured she might as well do what she could to avoid any unwanted attention.

As she carefully braided her own thick, chestnut-brown locks in preparation to stuff them under a wig cap, she wondered yet again if she should just save herself the trouble and chop her hair off. After all, hardly anyone actually got to see her natural hair. But she'd always been proud of it, proud of how healthy and luxuriant it was, and she couldn't quite bring herself to take that drastic step. Maybe someday she'd decide she really didn't care, but for now...

...for now, she'd spend a lot of time braiding it out of the way. What if one day she wanted to be just plain old Sloane Kennedy, and she'd cut off all her hair? She didn't like that scenario very much. Vanity, probably, but there it was.

With the brown wig, not much makeup, just mascara and some gloss. Jeans and a plaid sleeveless shirt, flat sandals. Although temperatures had been just about perfect in Flagstaff and its environs—mid-seventies at the most—she knew it would be blazing hot in Laughlin. Which was fine. She wasn't planning on spending much time outside anyway.

No room service that morning; she couldn't take the risk of having the same bellboy drop off her food and notice that her appearance had changed drastically overnight. Instead, she took the stairs down to the lobby, then slipped out a back entrance to go to her car. A breakfast sandwich and coffee from Carl's Jr. got her going for the day, and then she headed to the Aquarius Casino. It hadn't been one of the casinos she'd frequented the last time she was in Laughlin, so she figured she was fairly safe going there.

Whenever Sloane went to a new casino, she allowed herself to wander a bit, to check out the gift shops, to play some slots for a while to give herself time to ease into the vibe of a place. One could say all casinos were alike, and on some level that might be true, but they also each had their own personalities. She could tell that the clientele at the Aquarius seemed a bit younger than it was at a lot of the other casinos in Laughlin—or at Twin Arrows, actually. In a way, that was a relief, because then she wasn't quite so obvious as she roamed the casino floor, playing nickel slots for a while, then surprising herself by winning a hundred bucks with a random quarter she'd put into another slot machine.

She never won...not when the results were left purely to chance, anyway.

But after that—and after she got a Coke from one of the waitresses circulating on the casino floor—Sloane knew it was time to go to work. They didn't have Head's Up Hold 'Em at the Aquarius, which wasn't optimal because she'd be playing against the other people at the table as well as the dealer, but she'd make do. No huge pots, nothing that would cause the other players to lose large amounts of cash. Using her talents to win the casino's money was one thing; taking money from people who probably couldn't afford to lose it was quite another.

By that point, it was a little past one in the afternoon, and weekend travelers were starting to trickle in, wanting to jump-start their Friday afternoon partying. The tables began to fill up, and she figured it was time to stake her claim and get started.

The table she chose had two couples around her own age seated at it, which was much better than having to deal with single men who might be looking for a hookup. When she climbed onto the one stool that remained, the people already sitting at the table barely gave her a second glance. Good. The less they looked at her, the better. She wanted to be as unmemorable as possible.

This time, the dealer was a woman, older, probably in her late fifties. She had the kind of stern expression that reminded Sloane of her eighth-grade P.E. teacher, making her think she'd have to be doubly on her guard. That woman didn't look like she'd put up with any shenanigans.

And "shenanigans" is exactly what Mrs. Baker would have called what I'm planning to do, Sloane thought. *Good thing she's not around to see what I've made of myself.*

Oh, the hell with that. She wasn't going to let her mind wander down those paths. When she'd settled on poker as a way to make a living with her odd talent, she hadn't scrupled at what she knew most people would call dubious practices at best. What else was she supposed to do? Set herself up as a psychic? That would have involved far more intimate contact with people than she felt comfortable with. She'd spent enough time in forced sociality already, thanks to her upbringing in the Mormon church. Seminary in the morning before school, work projects on the weekend, dances so she could meet someone from the small group of boys her parents found acceptable. At least with what she was doing now, she called the shots—and most of the time, the only people she was really hurting were the casino owners.

They could afford to take the hit.

The first two times, she was dealt crap from the beginning, and could easily excuse herself from play without having to even dip into the minds of those around her. On the third hand, she got a pair of aces at the beginning, and so made herself stay in. One of the other couples was clearly just playing to get free drinks, and they made beginner mistakes, betting too much on hands that weren't worth it, thus increasing the pot but also digging themselves deeper and deeper into a hole.

The other couple—well, the woman didn't know exactly what she was doing, but at least she knew to fold before things got too grim. Unfortunately, the guy she was with had obviously played a lot of poker, and he proved to be a tougher opponent. Also, his mind was one of those rare few that were nearly opaque to Sloane; she came across those sorts of people from time to time, but it meant she had to really focus her own brain on his to even catch a glimpse of the cards in his hand. In a way, though, she was glad of the effort, if only because it made her feel she'd had to work harder for the win. And because his mind was so closed off, all she'd seen was his cards, and nothing else of what he might be thinking.

"Good game," he said to Sloane, hazel eyes narrowed ever so slightly as he slipped his arm around his girlfriend's waist and helped her off the stool where she sat. He was probably in his middle or late twenties, with longish light brown hair and a scruff of beard covering his strong chin.

"Thanks," she replied. Cool customer. He'd just lost nearly a grand and was acting as if it was nothing.

A brief nod, and the two of them wandered off toward the bar. The other couple also got up and left, their thoughts signaling that they'd lost enough for one day and wanted to do something more relaxing, like play slots for a while.

Sloane couldn't blame them. If she'd found her wallet a couple hundred bucks lighter after only an hour or so of play, she'd head off in search of other pursuits, too.

The dealer was giving her a narrow-eyed look. A quick peek at her thoughts told Sloane that the other woman sensed something was off, even if she couldn't quite put her finger on it. Which was fine—she could feel hinky all she wanted, but as long as she couldn't come up with any real evidence for why she felt that way, she probably wouldn't do anything about it.

Still, the woman's suspicion was a sign that she needed to go. Laughlin wasn't as packed full of casinos as Vegas, and Sloane knew better than to gamble at the Tropicana's gaming rooms, but there were still plenty of other options available to her.

She cashed out, nearly two grand richer for the afternoon's play. The sun beat down on her as she left the Aquarius, and she paused for a moment. No need to go running off to another casino right away, after all.

She'd brought a bathing suit with her, so she figured she might as well get some time in by the pool.

A few hours later, she went back to her room to change, this time into a close-fitting, low-cut black dress and the blonde wig. Much more makeup this time— liner and shadow and actual lipstick instead of gloss. No need for false eyelashes, not when her own were so long and thick.

Dressing like that was always a calculated risk, but Sloane wanted to make sure her appearance was pretty much the polar opposite of how she'd looked earlier in the day. After several years of doing this, she knew what types of people she should try to avoid, and if the tables at the casino she chose were full of guys on the make, well, she'd simply go to another one. She'd already made enough that afternoon to call her trip to Laughlin a success, so worst-case scenario, she could pack it in and head to Las Vegas next. Or maybe Reno. She hadn't been there for more than a year, so possibly that was a better plan.

But her luck seemed to hold. Although some of the men she encountered gave her searching glances, none of them seemed inclined to act on the lascivious thoughts swirling around in their heads. She played carefully, doing her best to lose consistently enough so as not to arouse suspicions. Her gains that night were modest, and yet by the time she decided to call it quits around nine-thirty, she'd won nearly eight hundred dollars.

After collecting her winnings, she headed out to her car. The high-heeled sandals she wore had begun to hurt, the narrow straps biting into her feet. Right then, all she could think about was tearing off the damn things and walking around her hotel room barefoot and in the oversized tank top she wore to sleep in.

But, just as she pulled out the fob to unlock her CR-V, a man with over-long brown hair came around from the other side of the vehicle and stood there, arms crossed. He seemed oddly familiar...and then Sloane realized he was the man who'd been playing poker at the Aquarius casino earlier that afternoon. His date was nowhere in evidence, and the smile he sent her, somehow murky in the orange-hued illumination from the parking lot's sodium vapor lights, looked anything but friendly.

Her fingers closed around the slender strap of the purse she had slung over one shoulder. Inside was the can of pepper spray she carried with her at all times, and she began to slide her hand down, hoping to unobtrusively unearth it from beneath her wallet.

"Nice hand of cards you played this afternoon," the man said, his tone too casual. "Want to tell me how you managed it?"

"I don't know what you're talking about," she said, even as she wondered how the hell he'd recognized her. She'd been a mousy brunette when she encountered him at the Aquarius. "I wasn't playing anything before tonight—I was lying out at the pool."

And since she'd gotten a touch of sun while doing so —a warm flush that the neckline of her gown clearly displayed—she figured her story should sound plausible enough.

However, the stranger didn't seem convinced. He took a step toward her, still smiling—a smile that was more a threat than anything that looked remotely friendly. "Oh, you look a lot different now, that's true," he said. "But you can't quite hide that pretty face of yours. So…tell me how you did it."

A pause, and then he added a single syllable, one her brain didn't quite want to absorb.

"*Witch.*"

5

ALL DURING THE MEETING AT JAKE'S HOUSE, JEREMY had hoped he would be interrupted by a ping from his phone, an automated signal he'd set up to let him know if any of the computers back at Trident HQ had found something worthwhile. But they'd broken the convo up around nine, and he hadn't heard a damn thing.

Still, he swung by the converted Craftsman house across from Wheeler Park that served as their witch-finding operation's headquarters rather than go straight home. When he checked in, everything seemed to be operating correctly, the algorithms he'd put in place doing their job of sifting through all the data within a particular set of parameters, but obviously, they hadn't found anything.

He spent a restless night and was back at HQ early for him, around eight. Still nothing. Or rather, he had a list of Nevada license plates starting with "55" that had been issued to people who owned Honda CR-Vs, but the list wasn't that long, and none of them were white.

Maybe Jake was right, and the witch in question kept a collection of plates she could switch out whenever she thought one had gotten a little too hot. If that was the case, then he'd have to rely on the traffic cameras...and that would be much harder, given their crappy nighttime resolution.

In the midst of his brooding, Jeremy realized he'd been so wrapped up in the problem of the unknown witch that he'd never gotten back to his friend Dan. He knew he couldn't tell him the truth about what he'd actually found, but on the other hand, the woman in question had left Twin Arrows and probably wouldn't be back any time soon.

So he got out his phone and texted, *I took a look around the surveillance videos but couldn't find anything that seemed strange. If you keep having the problem, let me know.*

There. He hoped that would take care of the situation, and that Dan wouldn't ask too many questions.

Jake and Laurel came in around ten, took one look at his expression, and wisely decided not to bring up the subject of the strange witch. Instead, they chatted about inconsequential topics, such as whether they should convert one of the upstairs bedrooms to a meeting space, since the dining room was now the PC lab, and it would require a ton of effort to relocate all those computers and the peripherals attached to them to a different room.

Jeremy listened to all this with half an ear. Disgusted with the progress of his so-called algorithms, he hacked into ADOT's highway camera system himself, scrolling through hours' worth of data in the hope he might find something that his carefully crafted programs had missed. While he caught glimpses of a couple of white CR-V's, none of them had Nevada plates…which didn't mean much, if the witch he sought had stopped at a gas station or simply pulled off the road somewhere and switched them out.

Late in the afternoon, both Jake and Laurel left, while Jeremy remained hunched in front of a computer screen, eyes starting to burn from all the hours of staring at it in the hope that he might at last catch of glimpse of that elusive CR-V.

And then one of the PCs in the lab beeped. With a blink, he glanced away from the cinema display he'd been scrutinizing, then realized what that beep must mean.

Nearly knocking over the office chair where he sat, he got up abruptly and hurried into the next room. Frozen on the screen was a clear shot of the witch's white Honda, Nevada plates still clearly visible.

And below it, the time and location stamp: *Laughlin, NV, 14:28, 9/18*. Hours earlier, but at least it was the same day. Could have been worse.

He grabbed his phone, sent a quick text to Jake—

She's in Laughlin—and then hurried out, almost forgetting to engage the security system before he left.

Maybe it was crazy to run off like this, without even pausing to stop by the house and put on a clean T-shirt or run a comb through his hair. Then again, what the hell did it matter what he looked like? What mattered was getting to Laughlin before she disappeared again.

Now that he had a lock on her, the algorithms would readjust and begin tracking her vehicle. Sure enough, he got another ping as he was pulling onto the westbound I-40.

Her vehicle had remained stationary in the parking lot of the Laughlin Tropicana for several hours. Was she gambling there, or was the Tropicana the place where she'd decided to stay?

He supposed he'd find out soon enough.

In Kingman, he drove through a McDonald's and got a Big Mac to stave off his growing hunger, but that was the only stop he allowed himself. Good thing he'd filled up the truck just the day before and didn't have to waste valuable time getting gas. As he went, the sun dropped lower and lower in the western sky, making him squint against the glare until at last it mercifully disappeared behind the horizon.

At a little before nine, he reached Laughlin's town limits. Another ping from his phone, letting him know that the witch's CR-V was parked in the lot at the Riverside Resort and Casino. He pulled in, driving slowly around and straining to catch a glimpse of the vehicle he sought, while at the same time trying not to look too suspicious. Maybe it would have been smarter to go inside and start looking for the woman right away, but Jeremy figured it would be better if he determined she was actually on the property before he began wandering around in the casino, which looked huge.

But there it was—a white CR-V with Nevada plates: 558 NOA. To his surprise, she was standing next to the vehicle, wearing the same pale blonde wig she'd had on when he spotted her at the Twin Arrows Casino. And in the next second, he realized she wasn't alone, that a tall man in a brown leather jacket—way too warm for the eighty degrees Jeremy's truck reported to be the temperature outside—was standing close to her. Was beginning to reach out toward her.

At first, Jeremy figured she must have met the man in the casino and that he'd walked her to her vehicle. Immediately after that thought passed through his mind, though, he noted her wary stance, the way her hand was scrabbling inside her purse, as though reaching for something.

No, that definitely didn't look like a friendly encounter.

He didn't stop to think. One foot mashed down on the brake, and he put the truck in park directly behind the open space next to her CR-V. Then he flung open the door and hopped out, brain surging with "fight" impulses even as he realized that he'd never had a physical confrontation with another human being in his life and that his computer hacking talent wasn't nearly as much use in this sort of situation as his brother's powers of telekinesis.

Well, too late for second thoughts. Besides, just as he was about to shout out a warning, the unknown witch pulled a vial of pepper spray out of her purse and shot the guy full in the face with it. At once, he let out a bellow of mingled pain and rage and staggered back a pace. Without waiting for a further response, the witch lifted one stiletto-clad foot and kicked the guy straight in the groin.

Ouch.

She whirled around and seemed to catch sight of Jeremy, her eyes widening. "Who the hell are you?"

I'm Luke Skywalker—I'm here to rescue you, bubbled up in his brain, but Jeremy knew better than to let his inner geek loose at that particular moment. "A friend. Who's that guy?"

Her fingers tightened on the vial of pepper spray she held, and he uttered an inward prayer that she wouldn't point it at him next. However, she only said, "I don't know."

The man in question stirred on the ground and let out a labored groan—but he also looked as though he was ready to push himself back up to his feet. No time to waste. "We need to get out of here," Jeremy said, and the witch shot him a dubious glance.

"What makes you think I'd go anywhere with you?"

Good question. While he was driving, he'd tried to

come up with the best way of opening this particular conversation and had several plans in place, but none of them had involved getting the witch in question away from a guy she'd just stilettoed in the nuts.

"Because I came all the way from Flagstaff to help you."

For just the barest second, her eyes narrowed. "Okay. You get five minutes. Not here. Follow me."

Without waiting for a response, she climbed into her CR-V and started the engine, then backed out of her parking space, narrowly missing the rear bumper of his Ram truck.

Well, hell. Jeremy ran for the driver-side door of the truck and got in, then started it up. The woman was already at the end of the row, turning toward the road that ran parallel to the resort and the Colorado River. Hands clenched on his steering wheel, he followed— but not before he allowed himself a quick glance in his rearview mirror to see what was going on with the man she'd just pepper-sprayed and kicked. He staggered to his feet and stared at the two vehicles for a second before he turned and disappeared, presumably heading for his own car.

Not good. About all Jeremy could do was hope he and the unknown witch would get far enough away that the stranger wouldn't be able to see what direction they were going.

He was surprised to see her turn onto Highway 163, crossing the river—and the Nevada/Arizona border—

and then turn again, this time onto Highway 95. She didn't go very far, however, but only drove a couple of blocks before she guided the CR-V into the parking lot of a Home Depot. Since it was past nine-thirty, the place was closed for the night, the lot deserted.

Somehow sensing that she wanted to call the shots here, he waited inside his truck while she got out of her Honda SUV and came toward him. He'd rolled down the window, and the night air smelled dry and dusty, with barely a hint that a river flowed just a few yards away from the spot where his truck was parked. The witch's high heels clacked against the asphalt as she approached.

She didn't walk all the way up to his truck but stopped a few feet away, one hand resting on her purse as it hung from its shoulder strap. No words, but her intent was clear enough—if he tried anything, he'd get a face full of pepper spray, just like the guy back at the casino parking lot.

"All right," she said, and now he got a clearer sense of her voice, a little lower than he'd expected. Throaty.

Sexy.

He swallowed. "This is probably going to sound crazy—"

"Try me," she broke in.

The way she stood—one hip angled out with her left hand planted on it, chin lifted—was probably meant to be challenging, but it was more provocative than anything. Yes, that was a good word for her.

Provocative, with those full lips and the lush curves of a body that the black knit dress she was wearing did very little to conceal.

Had he ever met anyone who looked like that? Most of the girls in Flagstaff were what he thought of as "crunchy granola" types—jeans and flip-flops in the summer, Ugg boots in the winter, not much makeup. This woman—girl, almost, since he guessed she was probably a year or so younger than he, despite her outward sophistication—was so far outside his experience, she might as well have come from a different planet.

"You have a special talent, don't you?" he asked quickly, knowing even as he spoke that he probably sounded like a madman. "It probably developed when you were around ten or eleven. You never told anyone about it because you didn't want them to think you were crazy. But you use it to help you win at poker."

Her heavily arched brows drew together. Maybe a slight shiver passed over her...or maybe Jeremy was imagining things.

For one long, awful moment, she didn't say anything. He forced himself to sit still, somehow guessing that any movement might make her bolt. Honestly, he expected her to shoot him down, to tell him he didn't know what the hell he was talking about.

But then she moistened her lips, and she pulled in a breath. "How do you know that?"

"I know because I got a ping off you at the Twin

Arrows Casino. I felt it because I'm a warlock…and you're a witch."

A slight tilt of her head, unnaturally pale hair sweeping against the dark fabric of her dress. "You're that guy."

"'That guy'?" he echoed, not sure what she was talking about.

"The guy who made the commotion in the lobby at Twin Arrows. You bumped into someone."

"Yeah, that was me." So, she had noticed something. Clearly, though, she'd either been far enough away not to get the same ping, or she had felt something and had decided to ignore it.

Or, more likely, she hadn't even known what it was.

A long pause. Then she let go of her purse, and Jeremy allowed himself to relax slightly. If she'd really meant to get him with the pepper spray, she probably wouldn't have done that.

"Why did you follow me here?"

Well, that was an easy enough question to answer. "Because I needed to let you know who you really are."

"A witch."

"Right."

Another silence. Her gaze tracked away from him, moving back toward the highway, which really wasn't much more than a frontage road in this part of town. "Okay," she said at last. "You've told me. Thanks, I guess."

And she turned and started walking back toward her little SUV.

What the hell? It wasn't supposed to work like this. He was supposed to tell her about being a witch, and she was supposed to smile and thank him for explaining why she'd felt different all her life, and then she'd follow him back to Flagstaff and—

Well, he had to admit he hadn't quite gotten past that part. Still, he knew it wasn't supposed to end this way.

His fingers grabbed the handle, and he pushed the truck door open and got out. As soon as his feet hit the pavement, she swiveled back toward him, suspicion growing in her expression.

At once, he stopped and lifted his hands. "Hey," he said. "I'm not trying anything. But you need to hear me out. We—witches and warlocks—aren't supposed to be out in the world on our own. We all have clans—I'm from the Wilcoxes in Flagstaff. We're looking for people like you…people who're without a clan, for whatever reason."

She watched him, face impassive. Then she said, "What you've told me doesn't change anything." One hand reached for the door handle of her CR-V.

Desperately, Jeremy said, "You were adopted, right?"

That question stopped her. She dropped her hand and turned back toward him. "What, are you a mind reader, too?"

He didn't miss the way she'd said "too." A small

crack in the wall, but better than nothing. "I don't have to be," he said carefully. "It's a common pattern among what we call 'orphan' witches. You were raised not knowing anything about the powers you inherited from your mother or father. Most of you were adopted… some went through the foster care system. Do you know anything about your birth parents?"

"No," she replied. Her face was still nearly blank, probably through an extreme effort in self-control and nothing more. "The records were sealed."

There it was. Just the smallest tremor in her voice as she said those words, but Jeremy thought it might be enough. She didn't know anything about her biological parents…but she obviously wanted to. And while a lot of the time, it was nearly impossible to get into sealed records—depending on the state where a person was born—most people didn't have his kind of resources.

"I can get you that information," he told her, talking quickly. "That's my talent—working with computers and code, hacking things. I'll find out what you need to know, but only if you come back to Flagstaff with me."

Another of those long silences. Her eyes, which he knew from the security camera footage at the Twin Arrows casino were a dark gray-blue, looked nearly black in the dim lighting of the parking lot.

Then, "I'm going to drive myself."

"That's fine," he said at once. Actually, it would probably make the situation easier for all of them if she had her own wheels.

"And I need to go back to my hotel room and get my stuff."

Jeremy wasn't quite as sure about that. What if the guy who'd approached her in the parking lot of the Riverside Casino knew where she was staying?

"You can come with me," she added, as if guessing at his misgivings. Actually, she didn't need to guess, did she? All she had to do was look in his mind and see the truth. Otherwise, he doubted she would have agreed to come back to Flagstaff with him.

He had a feeling he still had better not push it. "Okay. I'll follow you."

"I'm staying at the Tropicana, in case you get lost."

And with those words, she went back to her Honda SUV and got inside. Jeremy also climbed into his truck and started it up, then followed her as she retraced their path, heading back over the river and into Laughlin proper.

Only then did he allow himself to let out a relieved breath.

Sloane knew she would never have allowed herself to keep listening to the stranger if he hadn't uttered the "w" word right at the beginning of their exchange.

Witch.

The same thing the guy at the Riverside Casino had called her. How he'd known she had a special talent, she couldn't begin to guess. His mind had been nearly opaque when they'd been playing at the same poker table together, and it was even worse when he confronted her like that in the parking lot. She hadn't been able to get a single glimpse at what he'd been thinking, what he intended to do to her.

Completely unlike Jeremy Wilcox.

She realized as she drove into the parking lot of the Tropicana that Jeremy had never actually given her his name. No, she'd pulled it from his mind, along with the truth of everything he'd been telling her. He really was a warlock—or at least someone with very special abilities —and he really was part of a big witch family that lived in Flagstaff.

At that realization, something inside her seemed to tear a little. Maybe if she hadn't been given up for adoption, she could have been part of a family like that, a family that accepted her for who she was because they were all just like her. A family where she wouldn't have to pretend to be something—someone—she wasn't.

Or maybe she was getting a little ahead of herself.

She parked the CR-V, and Jeremy found a spot a few spaces down and got out of his truck. The lot at the Tropicana was much better lit than the one at that empty Home Depot, and as she watched him climb out and come over to meet her, she noticed, as if for the first time, how good-looking he really was. That strong jaw covered in stubble, the eyebrows with a faintly ironic lift, that pouty mouth—oh, yeah, he was the kind of guy whose looks should have been screaming "trouble!" at her.

Except…they really weren't. Maybe it was because she could tell he really had no idea how gorgeous he was, not with his thick dark hair an untrimmed mess, as well as the sloppy clothes he wore: worn jeans, a faded Northern Pines University T-shirt, Adidas sneakers that looked like they probably should have been sent to Goodwill months earlier. Something about his complete disregard for his appearance helped to relax her. In her experience, guys who were obsessed with their grooming tended to be a complete pain in the ass.

Well, and being able to peek into his mind and see that he honestly was only concerned about getting her someplace where she would be safe also helped to settle her nerves, which still jangled after that encounter with the strange man in the parking lot of the Riverside casino. Honestly, she had no idea she'd be that quick on the attack when he reached out to grab her by the arm, but somehow she'd known the best thing to do was to follow up that blast of pepper spray with a quick jab to the groin. With any luck, the bastard would be walking bow-legged for a week.

As Jeremy got closer, she said, "My room's on the third floor. We can take the stairs."

He didn't comment, only nodded without asking why she wanted to use the stairs instead of an elevator. Just a habit of hers, doing her best to avoid notice. There was an entrance on the ground floor near the stairwell, and she could come and go that way without getting too close to the front desk.

They headed up to her room. When they got close to the door, she told him, "You can wait out here."

Looking resigned, he said, "Sure."

At least he hadn't forced the issue. Sloane went inside and quickly began packing her things. For a moment, she considered pulling off the wig, but she realized her hair underneath would be an utter disaster —which was part of the reason why she always wanted to laugh when she saw a movie or a TV show where a character removed a wig to reveal perfect bouncy hair underneath. It just didn't work that way in real life.

Instead, she settled for getting out of the form-fitting dress she wore and into a pair of jeans, a black T-shirt, and some flip-flops. The dress went in a suitcase with the rest of her clothes and other items, and in less than five minutes, she was back outside in the hallway. Jeremy was occupied with his phone—texting someone, it looked like—but he shoved it back in his jeans pocket as soon as she emerged in the hall and closed the door to the hotel room behind her.

"Let me give you the address of where we're going and my phone number, just in case we get separated," he said.

That sounded like a good plan. "Okay."

He gave her his number and then the address, and she entered it in the maps app on her iPhone.

"That your house?" she asked.

"No," he replied, to her relief. "It's a kind of safe house we've set up for any 'orphans' we find. You can crash there until we come up with something more permanent."

Sloane wasn't sure she liked the idea of "something permanent"—she'd done her best to make sure nothing in her life was that settled—but she pushed aside her concerns. Jeremy's thoughts had told her he didn't have anything nefarious planned, and so she figured she'd go along with the flow for the time being and see what happened.

Besides, while she was staying at the safe house, she wouldn't be paying for hotel rooms, and doing so would help stretch her funds that much further.

"Okay," she said, then paused for a second before asking, "Aren't you forgetting something?"

His brow furrowed in an expression of almost comical puzzlement. "Like what?"

"My name," she replied with a grin.

"Oh, right." He reached up to push a hand through his uneven hair. "I guess I kind of forgot to ask you that."

"Yes, you did. Well, it's Sloane. Sloane Kennedy."

"Nice to meet you, Sloane," he said, his expression almost comically serious. "I'm—"

"Jeremy Wilcox," she cut in, then tapped her temple before he could ask the inevitable question. "Mind reader, remember?"

"Right." He paused then, his brows drawing together. "Are you going to keep peeking in my mind?"

"No," she said. "That's rude. I just looked that one time to make sure you were telling me the truth."

His expression cleared. "Well, that's a relief." He looked down at the suitcases she'd set on the floor outside her hotel room. "Is that everything?"

It was. Gazing at her bags, she wasn't sure whether to be proud or sad that her entire life could fit into a couple of pieces of luggage. "It's everything," she said firmly. "Now, let's get going."

6

Jeremy still couldn't believe he'd managed to pull this off. In that moment when Sloane had thanked him for telling her she was a witch and then turned away, he was sure she was going to leave his life as mysteriously as she'd entered it. How he'd known to offer her the one thing she truly wanted and couldn't get for herself, he didn't know. Maybe fate had stepped in… or maybe his brain had finally figured out how to interact with a human being instead of a computer.

Whatever the reason, she followed him all the way back to Flagstaff—with a quick stop in Kingman for both of them to gas up—and let him give her the nickel tour of the little cottage down the street from Jake's house that served as a refuge for orphan witches. By that point, it was nearly one in the morning, so Jeremy simply told her to text him when she was up and ready to go the next day.

"There isn't much food in the place, but I can take you out for breakfast," he offered, and her mouth lifted slightly at one corner.

What she'd been thinking, he honestly didn't know, since he didn't have her mind-reading ability. Was she trying to see if he meant anything by the offer other than getting her something to eat? For all he knew, this was the first time a guy had offered to buy her breakfast without spending the night with her beforehand.

Luckily, Wilcox complexions didn't show blushes very well, or he might have inadvertently given away how much that particular thought sent his mind down exactly the wrong path.

Afterward, he'd hurried away and gone home, glad he hadn't done much else to reveal how out of his depth he was. No, it wasn't as though he'd never dated or been with a woman—even if none of his relationships had been ones for the ages—but something about Sloane Kennedy made him feel like an awkward thirteen-year-old with braces asking the popular girl if she wanted to dance.

He halfway wondered whether she would text him at all the next morning. It wasn't as though she didn't have her own car and couldn't go out to get her own damn breakfast. But no—a text came through a little after ten.

Ready when you are, was all it said...but that was enough.

Although he didn't want to look as if he was trying

too hard, he put on a newer pair of jeans and a T-shirt —this one from Lowell Observatory—that at least hadn't been through a hundred washes. There wasn't much he could do about his hair…he'd been meaning to get it cut for more than a month, but that particular detail kept slipping his mind…and so he wet-combed it as best he could and hoped Sloane wasn't too picky about that sort of thing.

Which was crazy, wasn't it? Since when did he care about what other people thought of his appearance?

Other people weren't Sloane Kennedy, though. Jeremy had texted Jake the night before while Sloane was packing her things, just to let him know that he'd succeeded in finding the elusive witch and that she was going to stay in the guest cottage. That way, Jake wouldn't be surprised to see them coming and going the next day, although Jeremy knew that sooner rather than later, he'd need to have Sloane meet the Trident HQ gang. What they'd do after that, he didn't know for sure. This wasn't like the situation with Addie, when it had turned out she was actually a Wilcox and belonged in Flagstaff. Presumably, Sloane had a clan of her own somewhere, even if they had no idea which clan that was.

They'd find out, though. As soon as she gave him as many details as she could about her birth and adoption, he'd get to work.

First things first, however. He drove over to the cottage, vaguely noting it was a pretty nice day. Most of the time, he didn't pay much attention to that sort of thing, unless it was snowing so hard that he didn't want to even venture outside. But he found himself glad the sky was blue overhead and the air mild and fresh. He hoped Sloane would appreciate it, would…

…would what? Want to stay here?

Getting way ahead of yourself, buddy, he thought, and parked the Ram at the curb in front of the cottage.

When Sloane answered the door in reply to his knock, he found himself standing there and staring like a complete idiot. This was the first time he'd seen her actual hair, which fell in lustrous waves past her shoulders, shiny and thick and a soft, warm brown that framed her face perfectly.

"Good morning," she said with a lift of her brows and that amused quirk back in the corner of her full lips.

Oh, hell. "Hi," he said. "I'm glad you got rid of the wig."

Her smile deepened. "Well, I don't really need it here, do I?"

"No, I guess not. Hungry?"

"Starved."

He took her to The Toasted Owl, partly because it was close enough they could walk, and partly because he knew they'd get a good breakfast at the restaurant no matter what they ordered. Since it was a Saturday morning, the place was packed, but a Wilcox cousin worked as a hostess there, and she slid them ahead of some of the others who were already waiting.

Getting seated before people who'd been waiting fifteen or twenty minutes earned him some serious side-eye, but Jeremy didn't much care. He rarely took advantage of his connections, but he figured he might as well show Sloane that there were advantages to hanging out with the Wilcoxes.

"It's good to be the king," she remarked with a grin as she picked up a menu. "Do you guys run this town or something?"

"No," he replied. "But my family's been here for generations. I guess that gets us to the front of the line sometimes."

She didn't reply, only shook her head slightly, then bent her head to study the breakfast offerings. A waitress came by and asked if they wanted coffee, and Sloane surprised him by requesting tea. Jeremy ordered a cup of coffee for himself, then tilted his head to regard his companion with some curiosity.

"What?" she said, then put down her menu. "Did you think I would be mainlining espresso or something?"

"I guess you just don't seem like a tea kind of person to me."

"I never developed a taste for coffee. I kind of came to it late."

"You did?" he asked, curious.

"Raised Mormon," she said briefly, then looked

relieved as the waitress came back with a mug of coffee for him and a little pot of hot water and a basket of assorted teas for Sloane.

Well, that was a revelation he hadn't expected. About a million questions bubbled to his lips, but he told himself he should back off. She didn't seem like the sort of person who would appreciate him prying into her past; he probably should have been glad that she'd volunteered even that much.

Still, her revelation felt as though it should elicit some sort of response, and so he said, "I guess you're not still practicing." That seemed like a safe enough guess, considering the teabag she'd selected from the basket she was provided was English Breakfast and not some caffeine-free herbal concoction.

Was that a hint of a dimple next to her mouth? "No, not really."

While he'd suspected as much, her answer relieved him. Not that he had anything against Mormons, but he'd gone to high school with a few of them, and it had always felt to him as though the Mormon kids had a sort of barrier between themselves and the rest of the student population. As a member of a witch clan that had to keep its existence hidden from the civilian world, Jeremy could relate. At the same time, though, he was glad he wouldn't have to worry about that sort of thing with Sloane.

Like it would even matter one way or another. He'd

help her figure out which clan she belonged to, and she'd go off to wherever they lived. End of story.

Before he could start to feel sorry for himself—which seemed like a pointless exercise at this stage of the game anyway—she spoke again.

"So…are you going to tell me more about you w—"

As soon as he watched her lush lips form the "w," Jeremy knew he had to interrupt. "We can talk about that someplace else," he said, giving the crowded restaurant a significant glance.

Sloane caught his meaning immediately. "Not for public consumption?"

"Not really. We can go to my house after this—" He stopped there, noting the flicker of alarm in her eyes. Obviously, she wasn't too keen on going back to his place. Could he blame her? She knew next to nothing about him, even if she had managed to take a look at his thoughts to reassure herself he wasn't a serial rapist or something. "Or better," he went on, "I can take you to where I work with my brother and my cousin. Then I can get started on the search for your birth parents right away."

Something about the set of her shoulders seemed to relax slightly. "Right. Because you're the computer genius."

"I don't know about 'genius,'" he said, "but I generally can find what I'm looking for."

"Okay. Where do you work?"

"Our office is just a few blocks from here. We can walk."

"Do you walk everywhere around here?"

He guessed such a concept might be foreign to someone who lived out of a suitcase and spent her life traveling from casino to casino. "I like to if I can. In the winter, the weather isn't always as cooperative."

To his relief, she chuckled. "I grew up in northern Utah. I know what that can be like."

Another detail he was surprised she'd revealed. Or maybe she'd decided that since she was going to have to give him a lot of personal information in order to aid him in his search for her birth mother, it really didn't matter if she allowed a few other bits and pieces to slip through.

Whatever the reason, their conversation after that was far more relaxed than he'd imagined it would be. He could see the questions in her eyes and knew she was fairly bursting with curiosity about the Wilcox clan and the witch world in general, but she only asked things about the town that any visitor might inquire about— his favorite restaurants, things to see and do, whether there was much of a nightlife. By the time they were done with breakfast, he found himself far more comfortable with her than he probably had any right to be. Yes, she was gorgeous, but she also had turned out to be surprisingly down to earth, considering what she'd been doing with her life.

They walked the few blocks over to Trident HQ,

and her expressive brows lifted slightly as she took in the modest two-story house with the green shutters and fresh cream-colored paint. "You work here?"

"Yeah—Jake bought the place, and I helped him renovate it. There are actually a lot of small businesses in the houses around here. I suppose it's because the neighborhood is zoned mixed-use, thanks to the park and the library being located here."

By that point, they were standing on the front porch. A normal person would have pulled out a key to unlock the door, but of course, a warlock didn't need to do anything so prosaic. No, Jeremy reached over and touched the doorknob, and the door swung inward. At once, he stepped forward and entered the code to the security system in the panel next to the entrance.

Sloane followed him, eyes full of questions. However, she waited until he'd closed the front door behind them before she spoke.

"Do you usually leave the place unlocked like that?"

"It was locked," he replied. "That's a power we witchy people have—we don't need keys to lock or unlock ordinary doors. It doesn't work on hotel room key cards or anything like that, but it still comes in handy."

She crossed her arms. The movement made her full breasts swell against the dark red knit top she wore, and Jeremy had to force his gaze upward. Damn, she was distracting.

"I've never been able to unlock a door like that," she

said, and her tone sounded faintly accusing, as if she wasn't sure whether he was telling her the truth.

"Because you didn't know that you could," he told her. "It's easy enough—I'll show you later. For now, let's get to work on those adoption records of yours."

He moved into what once had been the home's living room—or maybe the front parlor when it was first built around 1911—and sat down in front of one of the Mac Pro computers set up there. Sloane followed him, her gaze taking in all the details…and maybe mentally adding up the value of all those expensive computers and their accompanying cinema displays.

After a pause, she sat down in the office chair next to his workstation. "You work here with your brother and cousin?"

"Yes," he said. "I mean, they're not here today because it's Saturday, but usually, it's all three of us."

"Tracking down witches."

Her tone was almost too neutral. Was she still having a hard time believing that witches and warlocks actually existed? Jeremy supposed it was a lot to absorb. Then again, Sloane had been dealing with her own particular talent for more than a decade, so she had to know there was something unusual about her own background.

"That was the plan. Most of the time, we're born into our clans and that's the end of it. But Jake—my brother—started thinking about what it would be like if someone was born outside a witch family and had to deal with their powers all on their own. He enlisted my help, and that's how Trident Enterprises got started."

"Is he a computer genius, too?"

There was that word again. But hey, if Sloane wanted to think of him as a genius—

"No," Jeremy replied. "His power is telekinesis. It's pretty strong, too, but he can't use it on people, only on inanimate objects."

She was silent for a few seconds, apparently absorbing that bit of information. Was she imagining how things might have gone down the night before if Jeremy had been able to shove things around with his mind? Possibly, although, remembering the efficient way she'd deployed her pepper spray and then stomped her assailant, he got the impression that she was pretty good at handling those sorts of situations all on her own.

They hadn't brought up the topic at the restaurant, since discussing assault and battery in a public place probably wasn't a very good idea, but he had to ask. "Who was that guy last night, anyway?"

Her lips pursed. "I don't know. I played against him at the Aquarius casino earlier in the day, but he had a woman with him that I assumed was his girlfriend or wife. I'd never seen him before yesterday, though. He came after me in the parking lot and"—she paused for a second, as if deciding whether or not to go on, then took a breath—"and he called me 'witch.' Like he knew what I was. How is that possible?"

The story was disturbing on several levels, but

Jeremy figured he might as well answer her question before they really got into the weeds. "Because when witches and warlocks encounter one another for the first time, they always can tell. Maybe it's a twinge at the back of your neck, or maybe you get a ringing in your ears. Depends on the person. But if he sensed that from you, then that means he has to be a warlock, too."

Sloane's brows drew together, but then she gave a small nod, as if she'd gone over her own recollections of the incidents in question and put two and two together. "You didn't feel anything from him?"

"No," Jeremy replied. "But he was more than a yard away from me. I generally have to get closer than that to feel anything. You felt something, though, right?"

"I think so," she said. "I mean, I felt a tiny twinge when I went to sit down at the Texas Hold 'Em table at the Aquarius, but I didn't think much of it. Except...."

"'Except'?" Jeremy echoed.

"A while ago, I was in California at a casino outside Palm Springs. A man came up to me and told me I needed to leave, that I didn't have permission to be in 'their territory.'" Sloane tilted a sidelong glance at him. "He was a warlock, I guess. But how could he have known what I was if you have to get close to someone before you know for sure?"

"His *prima* probably felt your presence and sent him out to handle it."

The perplexed expression on Sloane's face might

have been comical…under different circumstances. "What's a *prima?*"

"The leader of a witch clan. They're almost always women, but the Wilcoxes have a *primus*—ours is a guy named Connor. Anyway, the *prima* of the Santiagos— they're the Southern California witch clan—would have sent someone local to let you know you were trespassing and that you needed to move on."

That explanation didn't seem to have the desired effect, because her frown only deepened. "But it's not like I left Southern California. I just went down the road to Temecula and spent a few days playing there before I left the state."

That bit of information made Jeremy think Marisol Vasquez's *prima* powers also weren't as powerful as some might have believed. Later on, he'd have to plot the distance from Pasadena, where Marisol lived, to Palm Springs in order to get an idea of the range of her stranger-sensing abilities. It would be a good piece of data to add to what he mentally referred to as his "witch files," a database filled with various bits and pieces of witch-related trivia.

However, he wasn't sure if it was the best idea in the world to tell Sloane that gifts could vary widely from *prima* to *prima,* and so he only shrugged and said, "Well, witch powers aren't what you could call an exact science. Anyway, were you able to see into that guy's mind and get an idea of why he was after you?"

"You mean besides me taking him for almost a thousand bucks in a card game?"

Her tone was so wry, Jeremy found himself smiling slightly despite the seriousness of the situation. "Yeah, besides that."

While her expression had been halfway amused, it sobered quickly enough. "No. I mean, I tried. Every once in a while, I run into someone whose thoughts are dark to me, and he was one of those people. Maybe that's why I didn't get much of a ping off him when I first saw him. I honestly don't know."

Her words were less than encouraging. Jeremy supposed it could just be a coincidence, and yet…. What if it hadn't been a random encounter? What if the guy was from a clan who'd somehow managed to figure out what Sloane was up to and wanted to recruit her for their own purposes? Her talent was a pretty valuable one, and somewhat rare. There weren't any true psychics in the Wilcox clan, and although Jeremy knew that Angela had a McAllister cousin who could read minds, her gift wasn't a very reliable one. From what he'd heard, Angela's cousin Jenny couldn't look into people's thoughts on command the way Sloane could. It was more like every once in a while, some barrier in Jenny's mind would lift, and she'd be able to see into the heads of everyone in a quarter-mile radius.

Anyway, he didn't like the idea that someone who could purposely shield his thoughts had been sent to go after Sloane.

And that's all it is—an idea, Jeremy told himself. *You don't know if any of this is what actually happened.*

He pushed all those concerns aside to be considered at a later date when Sloane wasn't sitting there next to him. After all, they'd come to Trident for an entirely different purpose.

"Well, you got away from him, and that's the important thing," he said, doing his best to keep his tone light. "So, why don't you tell me what you know about your adoption, and we'll go from there?"

If she'd been put off-balance by the abrupt change of subject, Sloane didn't show it. "There's not much to tell."

"Well, anything would help." He paused, then added, "I really need a date of birth and the hospital where you were born—if you know that much."

"January 9th, 1997," she said. "I was born at Logan Regional Hospital in Logan, Utah. And...that's pretty much it."

It was something, at least. "Do you know if it was a private adoption or through an agency?"

"An agency," she replied at once. "LDS Family Services."

Even better. An agency offered a lot more opportunity for some careful hacking. He cracked his fingers—a ritual he performed whenever he was about to get started on a new project—and noticed the way Sloane winced. "Sorry," he said, an automatic response.

"No biggie," she responded. "They're your knuckles,

not mine."

She was probably referring to the common misconception that cracking your knuckles somehow made them bigger, but Jeremy decided it was probably better not to correct her. He said, "I don't know how long this is going to take me. There's sodas and bottled water in the fridge in the kitchen, and we have some patio furniture out back if you want to hang there while I work."

This suggestion was met by a sideways look. "Will it bother you if I stay here?"

"No," he said. "But it might get kind of boring."

Just the faintest ghost of a smile. "I'll take my chances."

What was he supposed to say to that? Honestly, he never liked having an audience around while he was working...but then again, he'd never had an audience that looked like Sloane Kennedy, either.

"Okay," he said, figuring he'd leave it there. Besides, he needed to get started.

Even after living with his talent for almost fifteen years, Jeremy still couldn't explain exactly how it worked. It was almost as if some part of his brain came alive whenever he was confronted by a problem that needed to be solved, as though neurons he didn't require in his day-to-day life flared with activity as soon as he sat down at a computer and got to work. He'd aced every single computer class he'd ever taken, but he honestly couldn't say how. Friends had asked him to tutor them, and he'd always declined, knowing there was no way he could teach them something that was as instinctive to him as breathing.

In Sloane's case, he did a quick search and determined that the agency which had handled her adoption had stopped operating years earlier. Fewer women were giving up their children to be adopted, and so LDS Family Services' business model was no longer viable.

But they'd maintained their databases.

And for handling such sensitive information, the safeguards they had in place were subpar at best. Less than half an hour after he started testing their firewalls, he found a way in. From there, it was simple enough to enter the location and date of Sloane's birth. Immediately afterward, the documents he'd been searching for appeared on the screen.

"Got it," he said, and she looked up from her iPhone, where she'd been playing some version of *Bejeweled*—thankfully, with the sound turned off.

"Seriously?" she asked, expression startled. Clearly, even with her comments about his "genius," she hadn't expected him to come up with something so quickly.

"Yes. Here's your birth certificate."

Now appearing wary, as if she wasn't quite sure she wanted to know after all, she put her phone down on the computer table in front of her, then got up from her seat so she could lean in and get a closer look at the contents of his screen. Her eyes scanned the document, and she wetted her lips.

"That's my mother? Nora Cantrell?"

"I guess so." Why did that last name sound familiar to him? Jeremy didn't know anyone in Utah, which was a witch-free zone. Except....

"Hang on a minute," he said, and went over to another computer so Sloane could continue to inspect the birth certificate on the Mac Pro's display. A few keystrokes, and he was logged into his private server, the one that held all his own research and any other important documents. He pulled up the one he was looking for, then nodded, glad that his hunch had been borne out.

The name "Cantrell" sounded familiar to him because that was the last name of the witch clan in the western part of Montana. Why Nora Cantrell had gone all the way to Utah's Cache Valley to have a child in a small general hospital in a town two states away, Jeremy had no idea.

He came back to Sloane, who appeared still transfixed by the contents of the Mac Pro's screen. "She was only twenty when she had me," she said in a low voice. "I'm older than she was when I was born."

On the surface, it didn't sound so strange that Sloane's birth mother was young. If she'd been older and settled down, she probably wouldn't have seen any need to give up her child. Witch clans took after their own, even in the rare instances when a woman got pregnant outside marriage. It wasn't so much that people in the witching community were old-fashioned about such things, but more that witches and warlocks had a tendency to find their life partners early on, and therefore were married long before they decided to start their families.

Jeremy's gaze moved toward the computer screen and the electronic copy of the birth certificate it held. He noted at once that the space for the father's name was blank, but he'd been halfway expecting that.

"Nothing about my father, though," Sloane said, echoing Jeremy's thoughts.

"True, but at least now you know your mother's name," he replied. "And now that I know it, I can try to track her down."

No response except a faint nod. Maybe he'd been hoping for a little more enthusiasm—which he sort of wished would also reveal some admiration for his efforts —but at least she hadn't asked how he could do something like that. Obviously, his ease in producing the birth certificate had done a lot to soothe any worries on her part as to his hacking abilities.

The birth certificate also included Nora Cantrell's date of birth, and that, along with her full legal name and general geographic location, was pretty much all he needed. It wasn't as though members of the various witch clans tried to hide their very existence from the government—they all had Social Security numbers and driver's licenses, mortgages and bank accounts and pretty much the same paper trail that any regular citizen of the United States would.

In short order, he discovered that Sloane's mother

had been born in Missoula, Montana, and that she had gotten married in 2001 to a man named Thomas Archer. They had two children, a boy and a girl, and lived in Butte.

He related all this to Sloane, who looked slightly gobsmacked by the realization that she had a brother and sister out there in the world.

"I always wondered if I had any siblings. But...." The word trailed off as she seemed to wrestle with all this new knowledge. Then she shook her head. "I was going to ask why she gave me up if she went on to have a family, but I know that's an old story—she got pregnant at the wrong time and didn't want to be a single mother, so she placed that child with an adoption agency. Still...."

"No, it's unusual for someone in a witch clan," Jeremy said. Honestly, he wasn't sure if he'd ever come across the situation before. There were a couple of single mothers among the Wilcoxes, but not many, mostly because witches and warlocks tended to stay married. Adoption really wasn't a thing, since raising a nonmagical child in a clan full of people with special powers came with its own set of complications. Besides, most healers could manage any infertility issues that might crop up, thus negating the need for adoption in the first place.

Sloane stared at him, brows lifting. "Wait...you're saying my mother was a witch?"

Oh, hell. He realized he'd sort of forgotten to pass

that particular nugget of information along. "I think so," he said. "Her last name sounded familiar to me, so I looked it up. The Cantrells are the witch clan in the western part of Montana, just like we Wilcoxes are the clan up here in the northern section of Arizona. I can't really tell you anything more than that, since we've never had any interactions with them because they're so far away. We just know they exist."

For a long moment, Sloane didn't say anything, only stood there with her gaze fixed on the screen, almost as though she thought if she stared at it long enough, then it would give her the answers to questions she'd been asking for far too many years.

At last, she turned toward Jeremy. "Well," she said softly, "I guess I'll have to go ask this particular witch why she gave me away."

7

UP UNTIL THE MOMENT WHEN THOSE WORDS emerged from her mouth, Sloane honestly hadn't thought she knew what in the world to do with the information Jeremy had just given her. And so easily, too—he'd answered in less than half an hour the question that had been haunting her for most of her life.

My mother's name was Nora Cantrell. She was a witch, and she was twenty years old.

Of course, getting that information had only led to a flood of other questions. Who was her father? Was he a warlock, like Jeremy, or a regular guy? Did witches and warlocks even get intimate with regular mortals, or did they stay with their own kind?

And she realized that, while Jeremy could dig up all sorts of data for her, none of it would tell her who her father was and, more importantly, why her mother had seen fit to give her up when she'd gone on to get married only a few years after she gave birth to her first child.

Jeremy continued to stare up at her, frozen in his office chair. His mouth twisted for a second, and Sloane wondered if he was trying to come up with some sort of reason as to why she couldn't possibly go running off to Montana to grill her mother about the fateful decision she'd made nearly twenty-four years earlier.

Then he said, "That sort of thing isn't as simple for witch-kind as it is for regular people. You have to get permission to go to another clan's territory."

For a second, his flat statement took her off guard. She recalled all too well the man in the casino back in Southern California, the one who'd told her she wasn't supposed to be there. Obviously, getting permission to roam around in witch territories was a big deal. Why, she had no idea, except maybe it was a way to ensure that everyone stayed in their lane and didn't try to make a move in a region controlled by a rival clan.

But then she realized those rules didn't necessarily apply to her...at least, not in this particular case. "How can it be another clan's territory if I'm a Cantrell?"

Jeremy's eyes widened. She liked their warm, dark brown, even if she knew she probably shouldn't be paying attention to those sorts of details at that particular moment. "Um…." he said, obviously caught off guard by her question. Then he paused and added, "Well, I guess you have a point there. Except you'd have to travel through other clans' territories to get to Butte, Montana."

"Even if I flew?"

Again, he appeared taken aback. "Well, yes and no. It's not like you can fly direct from Flagstaff to Butte. You'd still have to take all kinds of connections...fly into Vegas, or Denver. I don't know for sure, since I've never actually flown anywhere."

Sloane didn't know why Jeremy's admission surprised her, especially in light of the obvious fact that witches and warlocks didn't seem to travel much. But she realized he had a point. She'd never done much flying, except for one time when her parents took her to visit relatives in the Bay Area when she was nine, and so she'd forgotten all about connecting flights.

"I could charter something," she said desperately, knowing even as she spoke that she was probably grasping at straws, and Jeremy grinned.

And wow, that was quite a smile he had, curving the sensual mouth and bringing out a glint in his dark eyes.

Stop it, Sloane. Seriously.

"You must have won big in Laughlin," he said. "Charter flights are expensive."

"How expensive?"

He turned back to the keyboard, his fingers flying. "You can charter a jet from Flagstaff-Pulliam to Helena Regional in Montana for around"—a pause as he typed something else in—"twelve thousand dollars."

She swallowed. "Oh, is that all?"

His left eyebrow tilted at an ironic angle. "One way."

Holy shit. She had no idea. Well, since she'd never had any reason to research exactly how much chartering a jet might cost, she supposed she could be forgiven for her ignorance. Still, there was no way she could afford something like that. Her current savings were just a little over seven grand, plenty to live on but definitely not adequate to the task of chartering a private jet.

"Well, what if I just drove really fast through another clan's territory?" she asked. "I mean, it's not like all these clans have people sitting at the border, waiting to give you a witch ticket or something, right?"

That question got her another smile. Sloane had a feeling Jeremy was chuckling at her inwardly, but she couldn't get too irritated with him, not when he looked like that.

"No, it doesn't work that way. But...." The word trailed off as he seemed to stop and consider something, one abstracted hand moving up to run through his already messy hair. Now it stuck up at odd angles, but she thought she kind of liked the effect. He opened another window in the browser he was using and did a couple of quick searches. "I might have a better solution."

"What?"

"My cousin Lucas owns a Piper Seneca. He could fly us both up there. I just wanted to check the distance in nautical miles to make sure it would be in range, because otherwise we'd have to land somewhere to refuel, and that could be a problem. Luckily, though, the numbers check out."

For a second, Sloane could only stare at him. Was this some sort of a joke? Had he really just offered one of his relatives as a pilot for this wild goose chase of hers?

When she didn't respond right away, Jeremy went on, "Of course, you'd have to bring me along for the ride...it might be kind of weird if it was just you and Lucas."

Oh, because it wouldn't be weird to go running off to Montana to look for her birth mother with a guy she barely knew?

Yes, it was weird. This whole thing was weird. But....

"Doesn't your cousin have anything better to do than fly some chick he's never met a thousand miles to Montana?" she inquired.

"It's not a thousand miles," Jeremy said reasonably. "Well, okay, if you're driving. But it's a little under eight hundred nautical miles."

Of course it was. Sloane resisted the impulse to run a hand through her own hair and mess it up as thoroughly as Jeremy's. "That's not what I asked."

He paused to consider her request for a moment. "My cousin Lucas is always up for an adventure. I know he'll do it."

"What about his work?" she asked next. But...did

warlocks even have to work? She realized Jeremy had never mentioned a job, had made it sort of sound as if his witch-finding gig was a full-time thing.

"It's the weekend," he pointed out. "But no, Lucas doesn't actually work. He manages the investments for the clan and a bunch of funds of his own. I guess you could call him independently wealthy."

Must be nice. But if Jeremy's independently wealthy warlock cousin wanted to fly her to Montana so she could meet the birth mother who'd given her up so many years ago, who was she to say no?

"Okay," she said, and steadily met Jeremy's eyes. "Give this cousin Lucas of yours a call."

By the time Jeremy got off the phone, Sloane was already being assailed by doubts. She'd jumped into this feet first, just like she usually did, but now she couldn't help wondering if she'd bitten off way more than she could chew. True, she'd held the hope in her heart for years that she might someday be able to track down her biological mother, even while admitting to herself that she probably would never be able to see that dream become a reality. All the same, now that it looked as though that particular reality would come to pass sooner rather than later, she wondered if maybe she should have stopped to think everything through first.

It didn't look as if she was going to have a chance to

back out, though. Jeremy set his phone down and said, "Well, Lucas is totally on board. He told me he's never had a real chance to put the Piper through its paces, since the farthest he's flown it is Tucson. So, this will be a big adventure for him. We can leave tomorrow morning—he wants to get everything prepped first. And he said he'd handle hotel rooms and a rental car for us once we get to Helena. It's about an hour drive from there to Butte."

"Great," Sloane replied, although even she could hear the lack of enthusiasm in her tone.

Jeremy frowned, his gaze sharpening as he appeared to study her face. "Having second thoughts?"

Damn, she really must be losing it if he could read her that easily. She pushed a lock of hair back off her shoulder and said, "No. That is…."

"What, then?"

She really hated being in a situation where she felt off balance. For the past three years, ever since she'd taken off on her own, she'd tried to make sure she was in control of every situation. Now, however, it seemed as though the world she'd constructed for herself stood on very shaky foundations. Hard enough that she'd learned about the existence of witches and warlocks— not to mention discovering she herself was one of them —but also that she finally had a name to give to the woman who'd abandoned her so long ago. Reality was crashing in on her, and she wasn't sure what to do about it.

"Nothing," she said. What an empty word. She used it as a barrier, nothing more.

And although Jeremy wasn't a friend or someone who knew more than the barest details about her, he seemed to guess right away that "nothing" was actually a whole bunch of something. "I suppose it would be hard to have all this information coming at you at once," he told her. "If you need more time to think about going to Montana, I can call Lucas back—"

"No," she cut in. She'd already committed to this, and she wasn't going to put Jeremy in a bad spot by suddenly changing her mind. "I want to do it. And I appreciate what your cousin is doing for me. I just—"

"Just what?"

Honestly, she wasn't even sure what she'd intended to say. She was used to keeping things to herself, and yet she'd already opened up to Jeremy Wilcox way more than she had to any other human being, even her friends from high school. On the surface, she'd seemed to have everything going for her, the pretty, popular girl on the cheerleading squad, the one who got good grades and seemed to be liked by just about everyone. In one way, her popularity in high school had stemmed from a need to be liked by as many people as possible, mostly because she never wanted to lose control of her "gift" enough to overhear any negative things the other kids at school might have been thinking about her.

She'd had to keep that part of herself hidden from everyone. No way did she want people to think she was crazy, even though she'd known she wasn't crazy. She was just…different.

Possibly, knowing she was different was what had compelled her to push so hard against the future her parents wanted for her. As the years passed, rebellion had begun to grow in her heart and her mind. She hadn't chosen any of the restrictions that were part of her daily life, but had them thrust upon her because of her adoptive parents' religion. Somehow, she'd known she was destined for something else, even if she couldn't have articulated what that destiny was supposed to be. When she left Logan a few months after her twentieth birthday, she knew she shocked a lot of people, because up until that point, she'd seemed like a model daughter.

But everyone had their breaking point, and she'd found hers when she realized her parents were angling for her to marry that creep, Rob Redfield. What else could she do except leave?

Apparently put off by her extended silence, Jeremy added, "You don't have to tell me if you don't want to. I mean, I'm not in the habit of telling my deepest, darkest secrets to near strangers, either."

"Are we 'near strangers'?" Sloane asked, an unwilling smile pulling at her mouth.

He shrugged. "Probably. I mean, we only met each other less than twenty-four hours ago. And I know you're getting hit with a bunch of stuff right now. Just learning about witches and warlocks probably would have been enough to shake your world, and now you've got this whole thing with your mother…."

From the way his eyes didn't quite meet hers, she had a feeling that he wasn't completely comfortable with the situation, either. She barely knew him, but something told her he was a lot more at ease when he was dealing with computers rather than people. Having a perfect stranger unload all the baggage of the past twenty-odd years on him had to be a little overwhelming.

"I can handle it," she said. "But maybe you should tell me more about this witch world of yours, just so I'm not walking into this whole thing blind."

That request made the set of his shoulders relax slightly, and Sloane knew she'd asked the right thing. She wasn't merely doing it to put Jeremy at ease, either; she really did want to know as much as she could, just so she'd have that bit of culture shock behind her before they headed out to Montana.

"Okay," he said. "Well, like I told you, most witches and warlocks live in clans that are scattered all over the world. Here in the United States, they're in pretty much every state except Utah and Wyoming."

No wonder she'd never encountered anyone who gave her that strange little twinge at the back of her neck. It wasn't too hard to figure out why the clans had never gotten a foothold in the state where she'd grown up—the Mormon population was already way too entrenched there, and trying to stay hidden would have been difficult, if not impossible.

"Why not Wyoming?"

"We don't know. That's just how it shook out."

From there, he went on to explain about *primas* and *primuses,* and how they bonded to their consorts. It all sounded, frankly, pretty medieval to her, but Sloane decided not to comment. This was her world now, after all.

Or…was it? She honestly didn't know what she should do next. Maybe there was no point in making any big decisions until she went to Montana. Would her mother be glad to see her, and tell her that she'd made a terrible mistake and that she wanted her daughter to stay there in Cantrell territory? Or would she try to pretend she didn't even know who Sloane was?

Either scenario seemed equally plausible.

"I don't know much about the Cantrells," Jeremy said next. "The witch clans tend to leave each other alone for the most part, although here in Arizona, the three clans have gotten a lot closer over the past eight years or so."

"Really?" Sloane asked, figuring she might as well try to concentrate on something other than her own personal drama. "What changed eight years ago?"

For the first time, he looked almost uncomfortable. "A lot of things," he said. "Our former *primus* died, and his brother Connor took over…and married the McAllister *prima.*"

"Does that sort of thing happen a lot?"

"No. It never happens. Anyway," he went on before she could ask anything else, "things opened up a lot after that, so in Arizona, you can pretty much travel all over the place without having to ask for permission or anything like that. But because the Cantrells are so far away from us here in Arizona, we haven't bothered to learn much about them. I can try to change that, though."

Sloane didn't bother to ask him how. Obviously, his magical gift with computers gave him access to information most people would never have a chance to see.

The thing was…did she want to know? On the one hand, it might be better to go into this trip to Montana armed with as much information as she could gather. At least that way, she wouldn't be flying blind. Then again, she wasn't sure if she liked the idea of digging into her biological mother's personal life any more than they already had. She deserved some privacy, after all. Besides, it was probably better to embark on this expedition without any preconceived notions.

But if Jeremy just got some basic facts on the clan and left Nora Cantrell and her husband and kids out of it—well, what could be the harm in that?

"Sure, go ahead," she said, and he gave her a rueful smile.

"Looking up information on a clan isn't exactly the same thing as targeting a single adoption record," he told her. "This will probably take a while."

From his tone, Sloane got the distinct impression that he didn't want her sitting there and watching him as he worked. Although a flicker of irritation went through her at the thought of being dismissed so he could concentrate, she reminded herself that he'd already done her an enormous favor by locating her mother and arranging for her to go to Montana. Insisting on sticking around just because he was the only person she knew in Flagstaff seemed pretty childish.

"No worries," she said. "I'll leave you to work. I saw some cute shops when we were downtown—I think I'll wander around there for a while."

His expression brightened. "That sounds like a good idea. And you can walk back to the cottage when you're done—and try letting yourself in using your witchy skills."

Right. She didn't have a key to the little house that the Wilcoxes used for their "orphans," but according to Jeremy, she didn't need one. Worst case scenario, if the door-unlocking talent she was supposed to possess failed her, she could just walk back over to Trident HQ and ask him for some help. By that point, he would probably have some information about the Cantrells to share with her anyway.

And in the meantime, she could take a little of her earnings from the gaming tables the day before to buy a couple of new outfits. Something that would be just right to meet the birth mother she'd never seen. Sloane realized that almost all of her clothes had been purchased to fit one of the personas she'd devised as her various disguises, and hardly anything that was truly her.

Shopping that day in Flagstaff might be a lot more fun than she'd imagined.

"I'll call you when I find something," he added, now looking slightly concerned. Had some of her previous annoyance shown up in her expression? "Give me your number."

"It's 555-592-1986."

He didn't bother to write it down. Sloane had a feeling he'd committed the digits to memory as soon as he heard them.

"Good luck," she told him, and he nodded, expression halfway distracted, as if he was already thinking of various ways to get the Cantrell clan to give up their secrets.

Right then, however, she had a feeling she was the one whose luck had changed...and definitely for the better.

8

He'd blown it, dismissing her like that, hadn't he?

Maybe. But he knew he would have been distracted by Sloane's presence, and the truth was, he worked better when he was alone.

Nothing he could do about it now, anyway. In the back of his mind, a little niggle of unease surfaced. Would she be safe wandering around downtown Flagstaff by herself?

Of course she will, Jeremy told himself. *Her biggest danger will probably be blowing too much money on new clothes.* He wondered then how much money she had on her, and whether it would be enough, and if she'd be offended if he offered her some. This was new territory to him; they'd given Addie money because she was a Wilcox and entitled to the clan stipend...plus much more as the daughter of a former *primus.* It seemed pretty obvious, though, that Sloane definitely had to be a Cantrell, and so it was really that clan's responsibility to make sure she was taken care of.

Then again, Trident Enterprises did have some petty cash in case of an emergency….

No, Sloane could take care of herself, in more ways than one.

He couldn't quite put himself at ease, though, no matter how much he tried. After all, there was the guy they'd left immobilized in the casino parking lot in Laughlin….

Who hadn't seen where they'd gone. Jeremy had constantly checked his rearview mirror the whole time they were in Nevada, and probably more often than was really safe on the drive to Flagstaff. During the trip, he hadn't caught a hint of anything that looked like a vehicle following them. And if someone had wanted to get to Sloane, they could have gone to the cottage while she was sleeping there alone. Yes, it had a security system, but an alarm wasn't always a deterrent when magic was involved.

Put together, all those bits of data were enough reassurance that Jeremy's mind was put somewhat at ease. He focused on the computer screen in front of him, hoping he'd be able to lose himself in his work the way he always did.

But he kept seeing Sloane's face, kept hearing her warm, throaty voice. Kept thinking of what it would be like to be walking next to her now, out there in the sunlight in Flagstaff's historic downtown. All right, they'd walked to breakfast and then back to Trident HQ afterward, so it wasn't as though he'd been deprived of that particular experience, but right then, those few moments spent with her didn't feel as if they'd been enough.

Oh, for God's sake.

He scrubbed a hand through his hair. All right, she was gorgeous. Better if he admitted it to himself now so he could put the acknowledgment aside, since it wasn't going to change anything. She hadn't shown the slightest sign of being at all interested in him. Why should she be? Someone as beautiful and smart and sophisticated as Sloane Kennedy could do a lot better than Jeremy Wilcox, the witching world's version of a computer geek.

Okay, then. He scowled and forced himself to get to work, doing a preliminary sweep of all data involving people with the Cantrell surname in Montana. From what he was able to tell, the clan appeared to be clustered in the central and western sections of the state. He pulled up his database of the various North American clans, and saw those findings lined up with the information he'd already compiled. A witch clan called the Walkers lived in the eastern half of the state, spilling over into North and South Dakota.

A bit more digging pulled up pretty much what he'd expected to find—that the Cantrells had been in the state for generations, and along the way had amassed a decent amount of property and investments. Nothing like the Wilcoxes…Jeremy was pretty sure he'd have to go far to find another clan with as much accumulated wealth as his own…but he could tell that the Cantrells weren't exactly hurting, either.

And although he'd gotten the impression from Sloane that she really didn't want him poking around in her biological mother's affairs too much, he couldn't help taking a closer look at Nora Cantrell, now Nora Archer. Her husband was a fairly prominent architect, and Jeremy guessed he was probably a civilian. At least, no other people connected to the Cantrell clan had the last name of Archer, and generally, even if someone didn't share the main surname of a clan, their family name still popped up frequently enough to show that they were related somehow, like the Garnetts in the Wilcox clan.

Nora and Thomas Archer lived in a renovated mansion that looked pretty swanky for Butte, and definitely wouldn't have been out of place in the historic neighborhood where Jake's house was located. Clearly, Thomas Archer was doing just fine for his family. As far as Jeremy could tell, Nora was a full-time mother and homemaker, although she was also active in local charities. Their kids were nineteen and sixteen; the boy was the older of the two and attending college at the university in Billings, while his sister was a junior at Butte High School.

On the surface, that all looked pretty normal. Then

again, witches and warlocks were very good at making themselves look like the regular family next door. Did Thomas Archer even know that his wife had given birth to a girl several years before they were married, a girl she'd given up for adoption?

That sort of information was a lot harder to dig up. Bank records and school information were one thing; the details buried in private conversations were an entirely different matter.

Jeremy hoped that Nora Cantrell had been honest with her husband. Otherwise, Sloane's arrival would be an even bigger bombshell than they thought.

Normally, he would have said it wasn't his problem. But he'd seen the hope in Sloane's eyes as she talked about her birth mother…just as he'd noted her hesitation about going forward. He might not have known her very well, but he knew one thing.

He didn't want to see her get hurt.

His phone buzzed then, and Jeremy dug it out of his pocket, hoping it was Sloane, even though she really didn't have any reason to be texting him. Well, unless she couldn't get into the cottage. But she probably hadn't been gone long enough to have finished shopping, and he realized as soon as he glanced down at his iPhone's screen that it was Jake contacting him.

How is Sloane doing?

Fine, he texted back. *We had breakfast, and I'm working now. She went shopping.*

You left her alone?

Funny how much condemnation could be packed into in four simple words. Jeremy scowled and sent back, *She wanted to go shopping. She's fine. No one followed us here.*

That you know of.

Well, that was true, but he'd already reassured himself on that front. *No one did. It's fine.*

Addie and I were thinking you could bring her over to our place tonight. We could barbecue and hang out.

Usually, Jeremy would be fine with such an arrangement. The more people around, the less he'd have to worry about holding up his end of a conversation. Not that he'd really had a problem talking to Sloane. For someone who could read your mind, she was kind of relaxing to be around.

However, the notion had popped up in his head to take her out to dinner that night. They'd eaten breakfast late enough that it had served as a sort of brunch, and so he wasn't too worried about skipping lunch. He'd need to get himself straightened up first—he vaguely thought that he had a clean button-up shirt somewhere at his house—but they both had to eat, right?

I was going to take her to dinner, he sent back.

You sure that's a good idea?

After what had happened between Jake and Addie, Jeremy thought his older brother was a fine person to lecture him about getting too personal with one of their "orphans." Bristling, he typed, *Nothing fancy. Just dinner. Anyway, we can't stay out too late tonight—Lucas is flying us to Montana tomorrow morning.*

He's what?

Damn. Jeremy realized belatedly that he hadn't told his brother anything about his and Sloane's plans. It had all happened so fast...and then he'd gotten busy researching the Cantrells....

I located Sloane's birth mother. She's a member of the Cantrell clan in Montana. I figured having Lucas fly us there would get around having to get permission to go through other clans' territories. He's totally down with it.

Jake's reply didn't come back right away. No big surprise there; he was probably figuring out the best way to chew his brother a new one for making such a command decision without consulting anyone else at Trident.

When the next text popped up, though, it wasn't nearly as biting as Jeremy had thought it would be.

Of course Lucas would be down w/something like that. It's risky, though.

Maybe, Jeremy allowed. *But isn't part of what we do finding people's clans and getting them reunited?*

He knew Jake couldn't really argue with him on that point, since it was no more than the truth. And all right, Jeremy knew he should probably admit to himself that he wasn't terribly eager for Sloane's reunion with her mother to be a lasting one. No, he'd much prefer for her to decide she'd rather hang around Flagstaff for the time being.

Not that he'd admit such a thing out loud, not when he'd barely known the woman for twenty-four hours. He'd keep his damn mouth shut and let her make her own decisions. Even so, he couldn't help thinking that she wouldn't be the only orphan to decide to settle in Wilcox territory. Ethan Sitko and Natalie Delacroix, both of whom had been rescued from the government's Daedalus Project, were now living off Fort Valley Road on the northern edge of Flagstaff, and even Randall Lenz, who'd been the project's director until he helped it go off the rails, was also living in town, although in a small cottage south of Route 66, a place less than half the size of the house he'd owned in Alexandria.

Ethan and Natalie had remained in Flagstaff because they wanted to stay together, and they didn't want any clan politics interrupting their relationship. Randall appeared to have settled in northern Arizona mainly because he didn't have anywhere else to go; both Connor and Jake had guessed that he was probably a Van Horn, since that clan lived in New York where he was born, but no one was quite ready to start asking questions of that extremely powerful family.

Anyway, the Wilcoxes had proven they were up to the task of taking in any stray witches or warlocks who needed sanctuary in their territory, so it wouldn't be all that strange if Sloane ended up there.

Or she could be welcomed in Montana with open arms, and that would be the end of it.

Okay, Jake sent back. *Addie and I would've liked to meet her, though.*

Those words sent a pang of guilt through him, which Jeremy guessed had probably been Jake's intention. Maybe it would be better to have an informal sort of get-together rather than anything that felt remotely like a date. At least that way, if Sloane decided to stay in Montana permanently, he wouldn't have invested too much in her emotionally.

No, it's okay, he texted. *We can come over. I hadn't even mentioned dinner to her. What time?*

The reply came back almost at once. *Great. 6:30 okay?*

See you then, Jeremy answered, trying to ignore the tug of disappointment within him.

Maybe it was better this way, but he still would have liked to take Sloane out to dinner.

Sloane stared at the doorknob to the cottage's front door. She felt like an idiot—had already paused twice to glance around and make sure no one on the quiet residential street was paying any attention to her—but she told herself to just open the damn thing. If it didn't work, well, then she'd call Jeremy and have him come to her rescue, or just walk back over to Trident like she'd originally planned, even though she'd bought enough stuff on her shopping expedition that she'd prefer to avoid hauling it all over town.

Since he hadn't really told her how this was supposed to work, about all she could do was put her hand on the knob and imagine it turning.

To her utter shock, that was exactly what it did.

In fact, she was so gobsmacked that she could only stand there on the porch for a moment, watching as the door swung inward a few inches and then stopped.

Damn. It worked.

Then she recovered herself, and bent and picked up the shopping bags she'd set down so she'd have both hands free to work her magic. Once inside, she closed the door and engaged the alarm, which helpfully had the code written on the side in fine black Sharpie. It wasn't that she didn't feel secure enough in the place—she'd just spent the greater part of two hours wandering around Flagstaff's adorable downtown district and happily shopping in the boutiques there without incident—but better safe than sorry.

The interior of the little house felt slightly stuffy, since she'd closed and locked all the windows before she left that morning. Now she went around and opened most of them, letting in the light, fresh breeze that had made her shopping trip even more enjoyable.

It was definitely one of the nicer places she'd stayed in recent memory. Only once in a great while had she allowed herself to stay at an Airbnb or vacation condo rather than a regular hotel room, and it felt better than she'd imagined to sit down on the overstuffed couch and lean back against the cushions, allowing herself to relax into the welcoming vibe of the little house.

She thought she could get used to this.

Which wasn't really an option. The next day, they'd be flying up to Montana, and the sort of reception she got would determine what she intended to do next with her life. Sloane couldn't really imagine herself living in Montana...mostly because she'd never been there...but she supposed she would have to get used to the idea of being a witch, being a member of the Cantrell clan.

It was still such a foreign concept. She couldn't really deny the truth of what Jeremy had told her about herself—or about his own family, his own powers—and yet it seemed utterly strange to believe that there were other people like her scattered across the country, across the world. How had the witch clans ever managed to keep such an enormous secret hidden from the rest of society?

Obviously, they had, or the news would have been full of accounts of people with strange gifts, supernatural powers.

And what would she ever tell her parents? Their relationship had been more than strained the past couple of years, but they'd always held out the hope that one day she'd come to her senses and return to Logan. Her mother had even, by way of an olive branch, told her the last time she'd called that she'd been able to talk the bishop out of excommunicating her.

At the time, Sloane hadn't known whether to be amused or offended. Not because she cared whether she was still a part of the church—that ship had sailed the second she packed her bags and hit the road—but because her mother obviously thought that the bishop's forbearance was something to be praised. Luckily, Sloane had managed to hold back all the biting comments she'd wanted to make, but she'd also realized she would never be able to make her parents understand why she could never go back to Logan.

And if they found out she'd hunted down her birth mother...well, she really didn't want to know what their reactions to that little tidbit might be. Most of the time, they liked to pretend that she'd been dropped off by a stork or something, rather than having a biological family out there in the world somewhere.

Her phone rang, and she got up from the couch to get her purse from the place where she'd set it on the rug next to her shopping bags. The number was unfamiliar, but it had a 928 area code, so she figured it must be Jeremy.

Her heart gave a happy little skip, even as she told herself not to be an idiot. Of course, he was calling; he'd told her he would.

"Hey," he said, sounding a little diffident and not quite like himself...or at least, what Sloane thought of as himself, even though she had to admit she didn't know him well enough to be sure. "My brother asked if you'd like to come to his place for a barbecue tonight. He and his girlfriend Addie—she's the first 'orphan' we found—would really like to meet you."

Interesting. So, obviously there was a precedent for a Wilcox to hook up with one of their foundlings.

Which didn't mean a damn thing. Sloane frowned at herself before answering, "Sure. That sounds like fun."

"Great. He actually lives two doors down from the cottage, so I'll come over to get you and then we can walk to his place."

Was it weird to have Jeremy's brother so close by? She supposed it didn't have to be; actually, she could see why it might make sense to have someone from Trident near, just in case anything weird happened. At the same time, she found herself wondering where Jeremy lived. He'd driven his big silver truck to the cottage that morning, which seemed to indicate he didn't live anywhere close.

Maybe that was a good thing.

"Okay," she replied. "What time?"

"Around six-thirty."

Which gave her a couple of hours. She planned to change into one of her new purchases, but even the most prolonged primping wouldn't take that much time. Well, she had her laptop with her and could find something to amuse herself, even while she privately thought she'd rather spend some of that time with Jeremy.

So she said, "I guess I'll see you then."

A pause. Then he spoke, sounding even more hesitant. "I actually found out some stuff about the Cantrells. Maybe I could come over a little earlier than that and tell you about what I found."

Perfect. She didn't want to give away too much of her inner enthusiasm, but she knew her voice warmed as she said, "I'd like that. So…five-ish?"

"I can do that. I'll see you in about a half hour, then."

He ended the call, and Sloane put her phone back in her purse. Only half an hour to get ready. Well, she could do that.

Since she'd put her face on that morning to have breakfast with Jeremy, she didn't need to do much except refresh her lip gloss and use a couple of blotting papers to get rid of some of the shine she'd picked up during her walk around downtown that afternoon. The day had been a breezy one, but her hair only needed to be brushed, since it always held a curl until the next time she washed it.

A backyard barbecue sounded fairly casual, so she didn't bother to change her jeans. A pretty embroidered top in a soft slate blue shade replaced the T-shirt she'd been wearing, and she slipped in a pair of dangly silver earrings she'd also bought that day. Once she was done, she surveyed her reflection in the mirror and gave it an approving nod. Put together but not dressy, and the cool blue of her new blouse reflected the hues of her eyes.

She was done not a moment too soon, because she'd just passed the brush through her hair one last time when the doorbell rang. A quick glance at the little old-fashioned clock on the master bedroom's dresser told her it was a couple of minutes before five.

Eager to see me? she thought with an inner smile.

Well, she couldn't give Jeremy too much grief over that. Lord knows she'd been looking forward to seeing him again, too, even though she knew she probably shouldn't allow herself to get emotionally invested. He was smart and good-looking and someone she definitely felt comfortable around, but that didn't mean they could have any kind of a future together.

As soon as that unwelcome thought crossed her mind, she shoved it aside. She didn't need to be thinking about the future right then. He'd come over to tell her what he'd found out about her mother's family, and she needed to focus on that.

When she opened the door, she saw right away that he'd taken a little effort for this meeting as well—he had on a clean T-shirt, a plain one in a deep burgundy shade that worked well with his dark eyes, and it looked as though he'd actually combed his hair.

"Hi," she said. "Come on in. Do you want a glass of water or something?"

That was about the only thing she could offer, since

the refrigerator at the cottage wasn't exactly stocked. The cupboards contained boxes of tea, both herbal and caffeinated, and there was coffee, too, but that didn't seem quite right if they were going to a barbecue immediately after their little meeting.

"Water would be great," Jeremy said, looking relieved that she'd broken the ice with such a prosaic offer.

"Give me a sec."

She went into the kitchen, got a couple of glasses, and filled them with ice and water from the refrigerator door. When she returned to the front room, Jeremy was already seated on the overstuffed couch, a big MacBook Pro open on the coffee table in front of him.

"This is your mother's house," he said, swiveling the laptop slightly so she could see the screen better.

Sloane handed him a glass of water and sat down on the couch, acutely aware of how close they were. All right, he actually sat a modest enough distance away, with no real danger of their knees bumping or anything like that, but it still felt far more intimate than the table they'd shared at lunch.

Her gaze traveled to the screen, which held an image of a large gray house, obviously old, but also meticulously maintained, with numerous windows and several chimneys. A broad green lawn bordered in flowerbeds stretched in front of the house, and a low hill covered with pine and fir trees rose behind the property.

Well, that answered one question. Her birth mother obviously had a lovely garden.

For some reason, though, she hadn't expected her to be living someplace quite so grand. It was definitely ten or fifteen steps up from the modest tract house where Sloane had spent her childhood in Logan.

"Nora Cantrell's husband's an architect," Jeremy said. Whether he was put off by her lack of response, Sloane couldn't tell for sure. "I guess his firm renovated the house—it's a local landmark. And your brother and sister—"

"I don't want to know," she cut in, and he lifted an eyebrow.

"What?"

"I mean," she said, knowing she needed to explain herself, "I'm supposedly going to meet my mother tomorrow, right? I think I want to hear about all that directly from her. Just tell me more about the Cantrells so I know what I'm going into."

For a second or two, he didn't respond. Had she offended him, cutting him off like that? It hadn't been her intention, but people didn't always react the way she expected them to. And she absolutely would not look into his mind to find out for sure.

Then he said, "Sure," and his tone sounded easy enough to her. She didn't quite relax, but she reached for her glass of ice water and took a sip, waiting to hear what he had to say.

"The Cantrells have been in western and central

Montana for about a hundred and thirty years, so they've been in the area just about as long as we Wilcoxes have been living in Flagstaff. I didn't dig much into why they ended up there, but I assume they came west for the same reason a lot of other people did—more opportunities, more room to spread out." He grinned then, and the smile did a lot to ease any lingering worries that she'd annoyed him in some way. "Things were getting pretty crowded back in New England where my clan originally came from."

"The Wilcoxes are from New England?"

"Yeah, Connecticut. But the first leader of the clan, Jeremiah, decided to strike out on his own, and here we are." Jeremy paused there to take a sip of his own water, then continued. "Anyway, the Cantrells seem to have made most of their money in ranching and mining. They're not a huge clan—there are probably about four hundred of them scattered throughout their territory. Most of them seem to live in Missoula or around there, but there's a smaller group in Butte, where your birth mother lives, and also a few in Helena."

"And no one knows they're a bunch of witches and warlocks?" Sloane was still having a hard time wrapping her head around that part.

"No. We're pretty good at covering our tracks. It makes life a lot easier."

She tapped her fingers against the tumbler she held. "That sort of defeats the purpose of having special powers, doesn't it? I mean, if you can't even use them."

Jeremy's dark eyes glinted. Sitting where they were, the afternoon light caught sparks of warm gold and umber within their depths, and Sloane had to force herself to look away, to pretend to be inspecting the image of her mother's house on his laptop's screen.

"Who says we don't use them?" he asked, then went on without waiting for her to comment. "It's all about not attracting attention. I use my powers all the time. Of course, mine are a little less flashy than some people's, but still—it's one thing to make sure you don't throw a fireball down Aspen Avenue and another to use your talents from the comfort of your own home."

"Can people do that?" she said, impressed. "Throw fireballs, I mean."

"I have a cousin who can. And my brother can move things with his mind, and his girlfriend Addie can control the weather. That doesn't mean she's sitting up on the roof, sending lightning strikes all over town. It's always a measure of degree."

Sloane absorbed those words, then nodded. What Jeremy had said made a lot of sense. In a way, she'd done much the same thing when using her own mind-reading gifts at the poker table. Yes, her talent had given her an incredible advantage, but at the same time, she'd made sure not to be too obvious about how she used it. No huge wins, no unbelievable strings of winning hands, just keeping enough ahead to make sufficient money to live on.

In other words, not being greedy.

Obviously, the witches and warlocks of the world appeared to live by that same principle. They understood that attracting too much attention was the last thing any of them wanted.

"And my birth mother's family?"

One eyebrow lifted as Jeremy gave her a sideways glance. "I thought you didn't want me to tell you about them."

"Not my brother and sister," Sloane said, realizing she'd slipped up there. "But the extended family. Does she have any siblings? Are my grandparents still alive?"

"Your mother was an only child," he replied, then added, "Witch families don't tend to be very big—one or two kids most of the time. Magical talents almost always breed true, so if people were doing much more than replacing themselves, you'd suddenly have a lot of witches and warlocks per capita. And the more there are of us—"

"—the more chances of being found out," she finished for him.

"Exactly. Your maternal grandparents are still alive, though. And obviously, we don't know anything about your father's side of the family."

So, she also had biological grandparents out there somewhere. That thought rocked her slightly, because she'd been so focused on discovering who her mother was that she really hadn't stopped to think about all the other relatives she might discover as well.

"Because I don't even know who my father is."

Sloane hoped her birth mother would be able to clear up that mystery. There had to be a reason why she hadn't listed his information on the birth certificate, especially since, if the records had been sealed, there would have been no way for anyone else to discover that information anyway.

Maybe she simply hadn't known who the father was. Not for sure, anyway. Sloane didn't know anything about how witches and warlocks felt about premarital sex, but she had a feeling they probably weren't as uptight about the whole thing as the Mormons were. The first time she'd had sex—with a guy she'd met in Las Vegas, more because she wanted to get rid of the unwanted burden of her virginity than because theirs was a love for the ages or anything—she'd been assailed by guilt the whole time. Never mind that it was perfectly natural, and as long as she took precautions, who cared? All the same, she had to experience several such encounters before she realized what she'd been missing out on and could enjoy herself wholeheartedly, knowing that she really wasn't doing anything wrong.

However, Sloane found herself hoping that there was some other reason her mother had left out her biological father's information. Not because she cared how many men Nora Cantrell might have slept with, but simply because if her mother didn't know, then she'd have no way of learning who he really was.

"Well, hopefully, your mother will tell you," Jeremy said, and left it at that. Although Sloane prided herself on her poker face, there was still a chance she'd allowed something of her inner turmoil to reveal itself in her expression.

"Hopefully," she echoed, and drank some more of her water. She glanced up at the clock on the wall opposite where they sat, and saw it was nearly six-thirty. "But I guess we should get going, right?"

If he was at all surprised by the change of subject, he didn't show it. A nod, and he set down his glass of water and closed the laptop. "Sure. Is it okay if I leave my laptop here? It'd be safer locked up in this house than in my truck."

"No problem," she responded, thinking, *Well, now I don't have to worry about manufacturing a reason to have him come inside after we're done at his brother's place.*

Then she wanted to shake her head at herself. For someone who'd just resolved to keep things casual and ignore her growing attraction to Jeremy Wilcox, she sure was doing a crappy job of it.

Well, she'd worry about that later...and with any luck, there wouldn't be anything to worry about.

9

JEREMY COULDN'T QUITE GET RID OF THE LITTLE knot of tension at the base of his neck, even as he told himself that none of this was a big deal. Addie and Jake wanted to meet Sloane because she was another orphan witch and nothing more. This was all casual, right?

Right.

Well, it was probably casual for his brother and his girlfriend. They greeted Sloane warmly, said it was great that she could make the time to come over during her brief stay in Flagstaff, and then guided both her and Jeremy out to the backyard. Over the summer, Jake had put up one of those canvas and wrought iron gazebos on the patio, and the table inside already had place settings laid out, with acrylic wine glasses for all of them.

"You okay with some rosé to start?" Jake asked,

fishing a bottle out of a metal wine cooler on an iron side table.

"Rosé would be great," Sloane responded. "This is a really nice setup you have here."

"Thanks," he said. "It was mostly Addie's idea."

Jake's girlfriend gave him a deprecating grin. "I like to think it was a joint decision. We had a lot of fun sitting on the patio, but the mosquitos were kind of a nightmare. Putting up the gazebo helped cut them down to a minor nuisance."

Sloane accepted the glass of rosé Jake handed her and said, "What…witches and warlocks can't get rid of bugs with a snap of the fingers?"

The rest of them smiled, and Jeremy replied, "That would be a handy talent, but no, we're stuck dealing with mosquitoes, same as civilians."

"'Civilians'?" Sloane repeated, brows drawing together slightly.

She really looked stunning in that blue blouse, which hugged her curves without being at all tight-fitting. He loved the way it echoed the color of her eyes and enhanced the warm tones of her hair. But then he blinked, realizing she'd asked a question. He really needed to get it together around her.

Addie beat him to the punch, saying, "Witches and warlocks call people without any magical gifts 'civilians.' Just kind of a shorthand, I guess."

Sloane gave a nod of comprehension. "That makes sense. Like Muggles."

"Exactly," Jeremy put in. "Although otherwise, we're not much like the wizards and witches in Harry Potter."

"No magic school?" she asked.

"No," Addie said, her expression sobering. Jeremy knew why; Addie could have definitely used some early training to rein in her enormous talent at controlling the weather. It wasn't until Jake found her and brought her to Wilcox territory to get some coaching from Joanna, the clan's weather-worker, that she finally got a handle on things.

Jake obviously decided it was time to add his two cents, because he said, "Usually, our families help us get comfortable with our magic. Sometimes it's our parents, and sometimes it's other people in the clan who have the same talent or something similar who mentor us."

"Gifts aren't inherited?" Sloane inquired.

"Well, being a witch or a warlock is definitely hereditary," Jeremy told her. "But individual talents…not so much. Jake has telekinesis, and I hack computers, but our parents don't have either of those gifts. Our mother has psychometry—that means she can pick up impressions and memories from inanimate objects. And our father has the ability to mold and shape and liquefy metal, which helps him in his work as an electrical engineer…although he's careful not to let any of his clients or his contractors see what he's doing."

Sloane nodded. "So, my birth mother could have any kind of talent?"

"Pretty much," he replied. "Some are more common

than others, though—almost every clan has a healer, and someone whose gift is working with growing things, and someone who can see the future."

She appeared to absorb that information, her expression thoughtful. Jake excused himself to go put the burgers on the grill, and the conversation after that moved to more mundane topics, with Addie asking Sloane how she liked Flagstaff, and Sloane waxing somewhat rhapsodic about her shopping experiences that afternoon in the city's historic downtown section.

It seemed obvious enough to Jeremy that she liked the town. And it was also obvious that all his fears earlier in the afternoon had been completely unfounded. She was perfectly safe here, as he should have known she would be.

Problem was, she didn't intend to stay.

She mentioned to Addie how Lucas was going to fly them to Helena the next morning, and Addie looked pleased at that revelation.

"Oh, well, if you have Lucas along, then you'll be in great hands."

"He's a really good pilot?"

Addie sipped some of her wine, then gave a deprecating little shrug. "Honestly, I don't know about that part, since I've never gone flying with him. No, it's that his talent is luck, and so nothing really seems to go wrong when he's around. Kind of makes it handy when you're heading into a dicey situation."

Those words were obviously a source of relief to

Sloane, because something in her posture seemed to relax a bit. She also swallowed some wine before saying, "Oh, that's good to know. And that sounds like an awesome talent."

"It's definitely come in useful a bunch of times," Jeremy remarked, and figured he might as well leave it at that. No point in telling Sloane that part of the reason the Wilcox investments had done exceptionally well over the past few decades was because of Lucas and his luck. She could probably tell that they were all doing just fine financially, but he didn't think it was necessary to go into detail when she was only passing through.

The thought hurt more than he expected it to. But he figured he might as well be blunt with himself now in order to be cool and blasé about the whole thing when Sloane walked out of his life.

"...ever flown in a private plane?" Addie was asking, and Jeremy forced himself to pay attention and stop borrowing trouble.

"No, it'll be a first for me," Sloane said. "I'm going to feel like a celebrity or something."

Well, she definitely looked like one, looked like someone who should be dining in five-star restaurants and attending club openings and whatever else it was that celebrities did. If asked, Jeremy would have said he didn't care about glitz and glam...and he didn't...but he also had to admit there was something almost mesmerizing about Sloane's perfection, as if she was a goddess who'd descended from some lofty heavenly plane to go slumming with mere mortals.

Not that there was anything "mere" about Addie Grant, either. Jeremy thought she was very pretty, and obviously, Jake just about worshipped the ground she walked on. But Sloane....

"I've only ever flown once," she went on. "But I have a feeling that flying on Southwest to go visit relatives in California probably isn't quite the same as being on a private jet."

"Probably not," Addie agreed. Was that just the teeniest glint of envy in her eyes? Maybe; Jeremy guessed that Addie had never flown anywhere, considering how poor she and her mother had been. Jake should get the hint and see if Lucas might be on board for flying them down to Tucson for a weekend away or something. Obviously, he didn't have a problem with chauffeuring clan members around.

"Food's ready!" Jake called out, and they all gathered up the melamine plates that had already been set on the table and went to load up. Burgers, of course—Jeremy shot a sideways look at Sloane, wondering if they should have asked whether she even ate red meat, but she took a burger without comment—and potato salad and corn on the cob that Jake had done on the grill as well. It had been a while since Jeremy had a feast like this, and he found himself glad for the invitation. Summer didn't last long in Flagstaff, and this was probably one of the last chances they'd have to sit outside like this, in shirtsleeves and no jackets, before autumn's cooler temperatures descended.

Over dinner, they talked more about living in Flag, and about Addie attending Northern Pines to finish her degree.

"Or partly have to start over," she said to Sloane, "since I decided to change my major to English lit. That's what I wanted to do from the start, but I was majoring in business administration because it seemed more practical."

"What're you going to do with an English degree?" Sloane asked, looking genuinely curious. "Teach?"

Addie spooned some more potato salad for herself as she shook her head. "No. I'm actually going to keep going and get a master's in library science. Then I can be a librarian and get paid for reading books."

Somehow, Jeremy doubted that was all librarians did, but he forbore from commenting. Addie was obviously a reader—she was always leaving paperbacks around Jake's place, claiming she wasn't that into ebooks —and she might as well do something she loved. As for being a librarian, well, there weren't a ton of job openings for that sort of thing in Flagstaff, but he had no doubt that she'd get the job she wanted when the time came. Things like that always seemed to work out when you were a Wilcox.

They ate, and chatted, and later on, Addie went in the house and returned with a platter of chocolate chip cookies, and they had cookies with the remainder of the red wine Jake had put out during the meal. By the time they were done, it was full dark, and although the day had been warm, the air took on a definite chill, reminding Jeremy that fall wasn't so far away.

Eventually, he and Sloane made their goodbyes and walked two doors down the street to the cottage. "My laptop," he said as they went up the steps to the front porch, and she turned toward him, smiling slightly.

"I didn't forget," she replied, then opened the door using her newfound witchy skills and went inside, waiting for him to enter as well so she could shut the door behind him.

Once there, he went straight to the MacBook Pro where he'd left it on the coffee table, figuring if he just picked it up and left, he wouldn't have to worry about a possibly awkward end to the evening. Or at least, no more awkward than it already felt.

"I had a nice time," she went on. "Tell Addie and Jake thanks for the invitation."

"It's no big deal," Jeremy said. "They wanted to meet you."

"It was fun meeting them." Sloane paused then, seeming to take in the way he'd picked up the laptop and now held it in front of him, almost like a shield. "Do you want some water?" she asked, her tone a little too casual. "We had a lot of wine."

That was only the truth, although he'd tried to back off toward the end of the evening so he wouldn't be in too bad shape to drive to his house. Having some water would definitely help…although he guessed he probably shouldn't analyze his desire to linger at the cottage too critically. All those inner admonitions to not get too close to Sloane didn't seem to be working very well.

"Sure," he said, and put down the laptop.

The glasses they'd used earlier in the afternoon still sat on the coffee table, so she scooped them up and disappeared into the kitchen. Jeremy remained where he was, standing awkwardly next to the sofa. Should he sit down? Would doing so be a signal that he planned to stick around for a while?

Damn it, he'd never felt this awkward around a girl before. Not that he had a huge amount of experience, but he'd gone out a little both in high school and college, although almost all of his dates had been civilians. The girls in the Wilcox clan had never interested him, even the ones from outside Flagstaff, from Winslow and Holbrook or Williams, the cousins whose connections with his immediate family were so distant, they might as well not be related to him at all. But the civilian girlfriends had never lasted, and they definitely had never made him feel like he had two left feet and couldn't figure out what the hell to do with his hands.

Sloane returned from the kitchen and extended one of the glasses of ice water to him. Well, at least that gave him something to do with one of his hands; he took it from her, murmured a thank-you, and sipped some water.

"Lucas texted me during dinner," he said then, glad

to have something neutral to broach as a topic of conversation. "He wants us to meet him at the airport at ten, so I'll come by and pick you up at about a quarter 'til."

"Okay," she responded, then took a swallow of ice water before setting the glass down on the coffee table. "I'll be ready. You said your cousin was getting us hotel rooms in Helena?"

"Yeah. We both figured that would be safer, since we didn't know how long you were going to be in Butte, and it's a four-hour flight one way."

He didn't add that also, none of them knew exactly how things were going to turn out in this meeting with Sloane's birth mother, and having the flexibility of hotel rooms in the area was probably a good idea. For all he knew, Nora Cantrell—Nora Archer, he corrected himself—would be so overjoyed to be reunited with her long-lost daughter that she'd want Sloane to stay with her. Not indefinitely, if for no other reason than Sloane would have to come back to Flagstaff to retrieve her car and anything else she might have left behind, but still, better to plan for the contingencies.

For a moment, she was quiet, her gaze fixed on his face as she looked up at him. He tried not to move, doing his best to look unconcerned, but something about her steady regard unnerved him.

At last, she said, "You don't sound very happy about any of it."

Well, he wasn't, but he knew better than to admit

such a thing to her. He shrugged as he set down his own glass, and she tilted her head, luxuriant hair sweeping against her slender shoulders.

"Is it because you're worried I'm going to stay in Montana?"

There it was. Of course he was worried—irrational as it sounded to him, he wanted her to stay here in Flagstaff, to adopt the Wilcox clan just as Ethan Sitko and Natalie Delacroix and Randall Lenz had—but he knew he'd be overstepping his bounds in a very big way if he were to say such a thing out loud. They'd barely known each other for twenty-four hours. How in the world could he already be imagining a future with her?

He needed to give her some kind of non-answer that would put her off the scent but also wouldn't give away anything of what he was feeling. Unfortunately, even though his brain went a mile a minute when he was cracking code and hacking firewalls, it seemed to have stuttered to a complete stop.

Her eyes seemed enormous under the extravagant sweep of her brows. "Would you rather I stayed here?"

"I—"

He didn't get any farther than that, because she stepped closer, so close he could now detect a faint hint of the perfume she wore, something warm and sultry, just like her. For the longest moment, they both stood there, staring into one another's faces, as the world seemed to skid to a halt.

No time to think. He bent, and touched his lips to hers.

Oh, God, she was so sweet. Or maybe that was just the chocolate chip cookies washed down with red wine they'd had a few minutes earlier. Whatever the reason, Jeremy thought he'd never tasted anything as good as Sloane Kennedy's mouth, never felt anything as luscious as the curves of her body pressed against his.

The world spun around them. Maybe it was just the intoxication of her nearness, the realization that he'd never known what a real kiss felt like until that moment.

She took a step back, her gaze still fixed on him. "I hope you didn't mind that."

Mind? How could she think he would mind a kiss that had blown the memory of every other kiss he'd ever had right out of the water?

Then again, this could be problematic for a whole host of reasons he wasn't sure he wanted to contemplate in that moment. "No," he said. "It was fine."

"Fine"? Seriously? Is that all you could come up with?

Her full lips—those kissable, kissable lips—lifted slightly at the corners. "I think it was a little more than fine."

"You're right," he said, and his voice now sounded hoarse, not completely his own. "But...I'm not sure what you want me to do with all this."

"Don't do anything," she replied. "I wanted to kiss

you, so I did. We don't have to make anything else out of it for now."

That sounded logical, like something he would have said. And since it seemed like good advice, he decided he should take it.

"Okay. But...I think I'll get going now. We have a lot going on tomorrow."

She didn't try to protest. Just a nod, still as she wore that ghost of a smile on her lovely mouth. Jeremy picked up his laptop and headed toward the door. Once there, he paused.

"I'll see you in the morning," he told her, and she nodded.

"Bring some tea and donuts."

Not even a "please," but he thought he understood. The request was a way to bridge from the moment they'd just shared to their plans for the next day.

"I'll come a little early," he promised, then let himself out. If he'd stayed...if he'd kept staring at those luscious lips of hers...he wasn't sure what might have happened.

It was safer to go.

Sloane knew she had a big day—probably a momentous day—coming up, and yet she couldn't quite bring herself to go right to sleep. She performed her usual nightly rituals of brushing and flossing and moisturizing, and pulled her hair back in a loose scrunchie so it wouldn't get tangled while she slept, but her mind was only partly attending to those tasks. The whole time, she couldn't help thinking about the pressure of Jeremy's lips against hers, the lean strength of his body as she leaned into the embrace.

No matter how you looked at it, that had been one hell of a kiss.

Even now, her skin seemed to tingle at the memory, and her need for him was a deep, throbbing heat in her very core. At the time, she'd wondered if she was crazy for initiating that kind of intimacy when there was a strong chance that would be the only kiss they'd ever share, but she had to know. She had to find out whether the attraction she felt for him was just some sort of misplaced gratitude for the way he'd found her and let her know who and what she actually was, or whether the desire that sparked along her nerve endings was something else, something far more visceral.

Well, now she knew. She wouldn't call herself the most experienced person in the world—she'd only been with four guys over the past several years—and yet she had a feeling that she could kiss a hundred men and not come close to the kiss she and Jeremy had shared earlier that evening.

Of course, now she really didn't know what to do with herself. It was silly to be imagining some kind of future with a guy she'd only met the day before, but damned if her brain hadn't already begun to travel in those directions, to explore scenarios where she stayed in Flagstaff and threw in her lot with the Wilcox clan. There were definitely worse possible futures in the world.

But she'd already agreed to go on this trip to Montana the next day, and she wasn't going to back out now. It was distinctly possible that nothing at all would come of it—Nora Cantrell wouldn't be at home, or she'd pretend she'd never had a daughter she'd given up for adoption. Both of those scenarios seemed more likely than having her reach out to embrace the child she'd abandoned so many years earlier.

Sloane didn't really want to think about what it would be like to face that kind of rejection after being rejected by her mother from the very moment when she was born.

So she wouldn't.

Instead, she did her best to focus on practicalities. If the trip was a bust, then at least she would have satisfied some part of her curiosity and could decide what her next step would be. Sloane honestly didn't know what that step might look like—ever since she'd left Utah, she hadn't really looked farther ahead than a few weeks or a month—but she supposed she'd figure it out.

If nothing else, the way Jeremy had kissed her seemed to be a pretty good indication that he'd be very happy if she stuck around. And she thought she might be perfectly happy with that outcome as well.

She sank down onto the extremely comfy queen-size

bed in the cottage's master bedroom and laid her head against the pillow. Just like the night before, she was struck by the stillness of the neighborhood around her. So much of her life over the past few years had been spent in hotels and motels, and there had always been the sounds of people coming and going—driving off in their cars in the middle of the night or having a knock-down, drag-out argument at three o'clock in the morning, or just the clunking sounds of someone going to get ice from the machine down the hall.

Here, though, it was so quiet, she could hear her heart beating. One hand stretched out to touch the empty space in the bed next to her. What would it have been like to have Jeremy sleeping next to her after they'd made love? Not that she really would have wanted things to progress quite so quickly; she'd fallen into bed a couple of times with men she'd just met, but she wasn't sure she wanted to do that with Jeremy. He meant too much to her.

Damn it.

How had she let him sneak up on her like that? She was usually so good at keeping her barriers firmly in place, and yet somehow, he'd managed to slip right past her defenses. It had been fun to see him with Jake and Addie, to get a feel for some of the dynamics in their family. The brothers were so relaxed around one another that she could tell they were close and didn't have many secrets. And even though she knew Jake hadn't been with Addie for very long, she also seemed completely comfortable with the two brothers, as if she'd been part of the family for years and years instead of barely two months.

Sloane wanted to know what that sort of belonging felt like. All while she was growing up, she couldn't shake the deep-seated belief that there was something very different about her, something that made her never seem to fit in, even as she was being raised in a culture that was all about fitting in. At the time, she'd thought that sensation of separation came from being adopted. Now, however, she knew it had been because she truly was different.

With the Wilcoxes, she wouldn't have to pretend she was anything but what she was.

It could be like that with the Cantrells, too, she argued inwardly. *And they're actually your family, unlike the Wilcoxes.*

That might be true…or it might not. Right then, she honestly couldn't say whether her birth mother would reject her or welcome her home.

Even odds, and there was really only one way to find out.

Sloane let out a breath, then rolled over on her side. An odd mixture of anticipation and dread knotted her stomach, and she wasn't sure whether she wanted this night to be over so she could skip ahead to meeting the woman who had given her birth, or whether she wished there were a way to hit the "pause" button while she tried to sort out her thoughts.

In the end, it didn't make any difference. Tomorrow would come on its own pace, and there wasn't anything she could do about it.

But at least she'd be going to that fateful meeting with Jeremy Wilcox at her side.

10

As promised, Jeremy showed up at the cottage at a little after nine, a bag of donuts in one hand and a coffee for him and a hot tea for Sloane balanced in a cardboard carrier in the other. He had to nudge the doorbell with an elbow since he didn't have any hands free. To his relief, she answered the door almost immediately, looking glowing and radiant in a pink wrap-style top and dark jeans.

"Come on in," she said, and stepped out of the way so he could go inside. He headed immediately for the round table in the cottage's small dining area, and put the bag of donuts and the drinks down on one of the woven-straw placemats she'd set out.

"I ordered black tea, since I didn't know what you wanted," he told her, glad he had something common-place to talk about. Just looking at her was enough to make all the memories of their kiss come rushing back in a flood. Not that those memories had been terribly distant to begin with, since he'd fallen asleep still thinking he could feel the touch of her mouth against his, and had woken up wondering if there might be an opportunity to have a repeat of their embrace sometime that morning before they went to meet Lucas at the airport. Intellectually, he knew that kissing her again probably wasn't such a great idea, but his brain and his body were on two entirely separate pages when it came to Sloane Kennedy.

"Black tea is perfect," she said. "I'm not too picky, although I can't stand Earl Grey. I think it's the bergamot."

Her tone was friendly, casual. To hear her, you wouldn't think anything significant had passed between the two of them the night before. But Jeremy gave her a quick glance, noting the way her gaze seemed to linger on his mouth as well, how the fresh color in her cheeks probably wasn't all makeup.

Good. He wanted to think he had an effect on her, even if now probably wasn't the time to get into an in-depth discussion about exactly what that kiss had meant to the two of them.

"No, the girl at the donut shop said it was Darjeeling. So I think you're safe."

"Perfect." Sloane extracted her cup of tea from the carrier, then popped the little cutout on the lid so she could take a sip. An approving nod, and she said, "It's great."

Okay, so he hadn't screwed up that part. He got out his coffee and swallowed some, glad of the caffeine. Usually, he would have had his first cup hours ago, but he'd decided to wait until he got their breakfast.

"And I got kind of an assortment of donuts," Jeremy went on. "I hope I didn't leave out your favorite."

"Is there a maple bar?"

"There is," he said with a grin.

"Then you did great."

She pulled out a chair and sat down, then reached inside the bag to retrieve the aforementioned maple bar and put it on the plate in front of her. Jeremy sat as well, and got out the bearclaw that was his personal favorite—although he would have sacrificed it for Sloane's sake if she'd informed him she wanted it. They ate in silence for a few moments, sipping their drinks in between bites.

After finishing her maple bar, she selected a cake donut with chocolate frosting and proceeded to make short work of that as well. Obviously, she wasn't the sort of girl who worried too much about what she ate—not that it seemed to matter. She was curvy but slender, with a narrow waist that the pink wrap top she wore only accentuated that much more.

"Well, that should do it for me," she announced as she wiped the crumbs off her hands with one of the paper napkins Jeremy had gotten with their food order. "I'm just going to brush my teeth and grab my suitcase, and then we can go."

She sounded breezy and unconcerned about the trip ahead of them, but he'd been watching her closely, and he noticed the way her mouth tightened for just a second or two, the slightest tremor of her hand as she reached up to brush her hair off her shoulder.

Well, he couldn't really blame her for being nervous. He knew he would have been on edge, too, if he was going off to meet the woman who'd given him up for adoption.

"Sure," he said, glancing at the clock on the wall across the room. Nine thirty-five, so they still had plenty of time, since the airport was only ten minutes away. "I'll put the leftover donuts in the breadbox."

"How did you know there was a breadbox?"

"Because Jake and I and our cousin Laurel all put this place together when we were getting Trident Enterprises set up. Laurel picked out most of the furniture, but I still helped get things in order."

This explanation seemed to make sense to Sloane, because she nodded before heading down the hall toward the bathroom. A moment later, the water started running, and Jeremy heard the hum of a battery-powered toothbrush.

The sound made him wish he had something to get rid of his coffee breath. Maybe a morning kiss wouldn't be such a good idea after all.

He released a half-annoyed sigh, then picked up the bag with its two remaining donuts and carried it into the kitchen. A stainless steel breadbox sat on the counter just where Laurel had placed it several months back, and he stuck the bag inside. A quick inspection of the pantry revealed a small package of mints among the various odds and ends inside, and he grabbed one and sucked on it for a minute before deciding he'd better save some time by chewing it to get rid of it faster.

By the time he was done, Sloane's footsteps echoed on the wood floor of the living room. He headed back out to meet her, and saw she had a small hard-sided suitcase with its wheels deployed sitting on the floor next to her feet.

"Ready?" Jeremy asked. Probably an unnecessary question, since she had the suitcase right there, but he figured he needed to say something.

"I think so." She pulled in a breath, then came over to him and laced her fingers through his, tilting her head up so their lips could meet.

Thank God for that mint. Jeremy kissed her back, tasting toothpaste and breathing in the warm scent of her perfume. His body stirred, and he forced the desire back as best he could. The last thing he wanted was to be all worked up when they went to meet his cousin Lucas.

Too late, probably, but he still needed to focus.

As gently as he could, he pulled away. Sloane didn't protest, but only offered him a quick smile. "I just wanted to make sure you didn't think I regretted last night or something."

Somehow, he managed to say, "Good. Neither did I."

She tilted her head, watching him for a second or two. "Well, now that we have that out of the way, we should probably get going."

Definitely a good idea. He nodded, and went to get her suitcase for her. It didn't feel particularly heavy, but why should it? This was going to be a quick trip, after all. Even if she decided to move to Montana permanently, she'd have to come back for the rest of her things.

They went outside to his truck, which he'd parked in the driveway behind her white CR-V. She gave the little SUV a considering look, as if wondering whether it was all right to leave it there, and he said, "Your car will be perfectly safe here. Jake and Addie will keep an eye on it for you, but this is a really quiet neighborhood."

"I can tell." She looked around at the houses on either side, at the neatly kept yards with the last of summer's flowers still blooming in everyone's yards. "No, I'm not worried about my car. I'm worried about…well, everything else, I suppose."

"It's going to be fine," he said stoutly, even as he wondered whether that was strictly the truth. But they'd decided to go ahead with this plan, so there wasn't much they could do.

Except get going to the airport.

He unlocked the truck, then stowed Sloane's suitcase on the extra-cab's back seat next to his own duffle bag. They climbed in, and he backed out of the driveway before pointing the truck south toward the airport.

For a minute or two, neither of them said anything. Then she spoke, sounding almost shy, which Jeremy guessed wasn't terribly in character for her.

"I don't want you to think I'm a tease or something," she said. "I kissed you again because I wanted to make sure what I felt last night wasn't just the wine talking or something."

How in the hell was he supposed to respond to that comment?

With the truth, he assumed. After all, he could tell she was doing her best to be honest with him.

"And was it?" he asked. "The wine talking, I mean."

Her fingers tightened on the brown leather of her purse, which she held on her lap. "No," she said simply. "I suppose that would have made things easier." For a second, she turned her head to look outside the window. Since they were currently traveling down Milton Avenue, Flagstaff's main drag, the view wasn't that picturesque; most of the real estate was taken up by gas stations and strip malls and restaurants. She looked back at him then, expression dead serious, with no trace of the half-smile she often seemed to wear.

While part of him was relieved to hear such an admission, Jeremy couldn't help wondering exactly where that left the two of them. "And so...?" He let the words trail off, since he honestly didn't know whether he wanted to dig that deep, not with the very real possibility of her disappearing from his life hanging over him.

"And so…." Sloane paused there. Although she'd let go of her purse strap, now she played with the gold and garnet ring she wore on her right hand, twisting the band back and forth as if she somehow thought doing so would help her straighten out her thoughts. "I kissed you last night because that was the first time in a really long while that I'd even wanted to kiss someone. And… well, it was amazing. So now I'm trying to figure out where I'm supposed to go from here. I mean, I've been with people, but I haven't been *with* them, if you know what I mean."

He thought he did. It seemed obvious to him that her existence wasn't exactly what you could call a settled one, not with the way she traveled from casino to casino, rarely staying anywhere longer than a few days. In the time since she'd left her parents' home in Utah, she'd probably hooked up with guys here and there, but none of those relationships could have been anything more than a temporary distraction.

Was she trying to tell him he was different, for whatever reason? Over and over, Jeremy had heard that when witches and warlocks met the person who was their soul mate—for lack of a better word—they tended to fall hard and fast, but that had certainly never been his experience. He'd seen his brother fall in love quickly and deeply, not once, but twice, but Jeremy had begun to think it wasn't going to happen to him, for whatever reason. Maybe the gift that made him able to communicate with computers and code in ways that no other witch or warlock could had somehow changed the wiring in his brain, had made it so he'd never experience that sort of connection with another human being.

Or at least, that was what he'd begun to believe… until he met Sloane Kennedy, which didn't seem to make a lot of sense. On the surface, they really had nothing in common. Sure, she was gorgeous, but in the end, looks shouldn't be the driving factor in a relationship. It was much more than that, though; he admired the toughness of her spirit, not to mention the way she seemed able to walk into any situation and have it instantly figured out. He knew he didn't have that sort of social ease, and he wondered whether she'd always been like that, or whether her particular brand of savvy was something she'd acquired during the years she'd spent on the road, using her magical gift to support herself.

"Where *do* you want to go from here?" he asked. A loaded question, he supposed, but he needed to know where he stood.

"Honestly? I'm not sure. I mean, if you had asked me a week ago what I wanted most in the world, I probably would have said it was a chance to talk to my birth mother and find out from her what really happened when I was born." Sloane stopped there and lifted her chin, her graceful profile silhouetted against the brightly lit morning outside. "Now, though…I guess now I'm feeling a little ambivalent."

"I'm glad you're ambivalent," he blurted out, and at last the smile returned to her glossy lips.

"You are?"

"Yeah." Jeremy's fingers tightened on the steering wheel, but once again, he reminded himself that if she was doing him the favor of being honest, then he needed to extend her the same courtesy. He'd never been one to talk about his feelings, and yet he knew he needed to now, if only so they'd have some of this hashed out before they even got on Lucas's plane. "That is, I totally understand why you need to do this—and I'm glad Lucas and I can help. But at the same time, I'll also be really glad if you decide you don't want to stay in Montana."

Sloane appeared to absorb those words, then nodded. "Okay. I guess I don't feel quite so guilty about thinking basically the same thing." She hesitated for a few seconds, then went on, "Is it crazy for us to be talking about this right now? We hardly know each other."

"It's probably better to be talking instead of ignoring what happened last night…or this morning," he told her, even as he turned left onto the road that crossed over I-17 and took them to Flagstaff's small airport. Lucas had told him which hangar to look for, and the best place to park, and so Jeremy pulled into the lot designated for overnight parking and went to the extreme southern edge, where he found an empty space. He slowed to a stop and put the truck in park before adding, "We don't have to figure out anything right now. I guess…just see what happens in Montana before you make any big decisions."

"I was trying to tell myself the same thing." She offered him a rueful smile. "But whatever happens…I'm really glad I met you, Jeremy Wilcox."

"Same here," he replied, although he wondered if that was actually the truth. Because if it turned out that Sloane would choose to stay with her mother's clan in Montana, maybe it would have been better if he'd never met her at all.

At least that way, it wouldn't hurt so much to not have her in his life.

Sloane wasn't sure exactly what she'd expected from Jeremy's cousin Lucas. Someone older and sort of staid, considering he handled the Wilcox clan's investments and played golf. And yes, she had to admit Lucas was probably old enough to be her father—if he'd started a family when he was the same age or younger than she was now, anyway—but he was also extremely handsome and kind of dashing, with the sort of smile that would make even much younger women sit up and take notice.

Considering how good-looking both Jeremy and Jake were, she had to wonder if all Wilcox men were that attractive. If that was the case, then maybe she was being extra foolish to even think about staying in Montana. Not that she thought she'd want to be with anyone except Jeremy, but she also had to admit it wouldn't exactly be a bad thing to have that much eye candy around on a daily basis.

"Hi, Sloane. Nice to meet you," Lucas said, extending a hand. Sloane shook it, feeling a little awkward. She wasn't used to shaking hands. Then again, it was probably better that Lucas wasn't the huggy type. An unexpected embrace would have been even more uncomfortable. "We're ready to go," he went on. If he'd noticed her awkwardness, he'd obviously decided to ignore it. "I've got clearance from the tower for a ten-fifteen takeoff, so you might as well get in the plane and get comfortable."

"Nice to meet you, Lucas," she responded. "Thanks so much for doing this."

He gave a negligent wave of one hand. "No big deal. Like I told Jeremy, I've been wanting to take this baby on a long-distance flight anyway. Come on inside."

Sloane needed to have Jeremy give her an assist to climb inside the cabin. Once there, she noted that the space wasn't overly large, but everything was sleek and comfortable. A peek into the cockpit revealed what looked like instrumentation complicated enough for a fighter jet, and she found herself hoping that Lucas knew what he was doing.

After stowing their luggage next to an expensive-looking black leather overnight bag and another bag stuffed full of golf clubs, Jeremy came and sat down next to her. "Don't worry," he said as Lucas went ahead and strapped himself into the pilot's seat. "Lucas has flown hundreds of hours. Maybe not as far as we're going, but this is a good time of year for this kind of thing—the weather is pretty calm."

"Maybe you should've asked Addie to make sure it stays that way," Sloane remarked, and Jeremy grinned.

"She's really powerful, but I don't think her talent does anything too long-range. It couldn't help us once we got more than fifteen or twenty miles beyond Flagstaff."

Good to know. Sloane reminded herself that Lucas's talent supposedly was luck, so it wasn't as if anything bad would happen as long as he was around. At least, that was the theory.

"All buckled up?" Lucas called over his shoulder.

"We're good," Jeremy said. His hand settled on Sloane's, stronger than she would have expected from a guy who was a self-proclaimed computer geek.

The comforting sensation of his warm skin against hers helped to settle some of the butterflies in her stomach. People flew in private planes every day, so there was no reason to think they'd have anything except an uneventful—if long—flight.

"We should be landing around three-thirty local time," Lucas told them. "Four-hour flight for us, though—Helena's on Mountain Time, while we're an hour behind in Arizona."

Right. That was a detail that had tripped Sloane up more than once during her travels—Arizona didn't observe Daylight Saving Time, and so half the year it was in sync with the west coast, while the other half of the year, it was on the same schedule as the rest of the states that observed Mountain Standard Time.

Four hours still felt like an awfully long time to be stuck in a small airplane cabin, no matter how comfortable it felt at the moment. Or maybe it was more that she knew she and Jeremy couldn't have any real heart-to-heart talks during the flight, not with Lucas only a few feet away up in the cockpit.

Well, they'd already settled a few things between them. Not everything, but at least she knew Jeremy wasn't exactly thrilled at the thought of her throwing in her lot with the Cantrell clan. They hadn't made any promises to one another—it was way too soon for that sort of thing—and yet hope had begun to blossom within her.

Crazy as it seemed, she might actually have a future with this guy.

If she allowed herself to.

11

LUCAS HAD THOUGHTFULLY BROUGHT ALONG A cooler with bottled water and sodas and sandwiches—actually, Jeremy had a feeling Lucas's wife Margot had put together the provisions—and so none of them had to worry about going hungry. However, as the flight stretched on, he had to admit that there was something to be said about flying commercial. At least jetliners had bathrooms.

Eventually, though, they reached their destination. Lucas brought the Seneca down so smoothly that Jeremy barely felt the wheels touch the tarmac, and they taxied down the runway to the location where the general aviation planes were parked. The airport wasn't huge, but it was much bigger than Flagstaff-Pulliam, and obviously had several large airlines flying in and out of there, since he spotted the American and United logos on the sides of several jets pulled up to the terminal.

It was great not to have to go through baggage claim, though. Jeremy excused himself and made a beeline for the restrooms almost as soon as they entered the terminal. Sloane shot him a knowing grin but didn't say anything as she followed Lucas over to the Enterprise rental car counter.

The bathroom was unoccupied, and Jeremy took care of business and went to find Sloane and his cousin in the Enterprise line—a line longer than he would have expected, considering that Helena, Montana, wasn't exactly a hub like New York or Los Angeles.

"I reserved two cars," Lucas said as Jeremy came and stood next to Sloane. "That way, you two can go together to find Sloane's mother, and I can stay here and amuse myself in the interim."

"Golf?" Jeremy said, trying not to sound too resigned. He should have known Lucas would find a way to slip off and get in a game as soon as he landed. It definitely was his cousin's ruling passion. Sometimes he wondered how Lucas managed to get through the long, golf-less Flagstaff winters without completely losing his mind...or driving his wife crazy.

"Exactly," Lucas replied. He appeared more amused by Jeremy's tone than anything else. "I'll swing by the plane and pick up my clubs once we have our cars—I figured it was probably better not to be hauling them through the terminal."

"Probably not," Jeremy agreed. "And I assume the hotel isn't too far from the golf course."

"Not too far."

Sloane also appeared amused by their exchange, but she remained silent as the line slowly inched its way forward until they reached the desk. Because Lucas had done most of the paperwork online already, all he and Jeremy had to do was produce their driver's licenses and proof of insurance, and that part of the procedure was taken care of more quickly than he'd thought it would.

Because it was Lucas, he'd secured higher-end cars for the trip—a Nissan Maxima for himself, and a Chevy Tahoe for Jeremy.

"We're staying at the Residence Inn," Lucas said. "You can program it into your nav while I go back to the plane to get my clubs."

"Sure," Jeremy responded. There was no point in going ahead without Lucas, since he'd made the reservations and everything was secured on his credit card. They'd just have to wait while he fetched his precious golf clubs.

Which didn't take that long. Still, by the time they got to the hotel and checked in, it was slipping past four-thirty, which was way too late to head down to Butte. He could tell that Sloane wasn't thrilled by the delay, even though they'd gotten the rooms for two nights to be on the safe side. Lucas had secured separate suites for all of them, which Jeremy appreciated. He supposed he and his cousin could have shared a room with two queen beds, but this felt a lot more convenient.

And of course it was far too soon for him to even contemplate sharing a room with Sloane.

Too bad.

"You two can go wander," Lucas told them as they headed to their various rooms—luckily, all located on the same floor. "There's still enough daylight left for me to get in nine holes, probably."

Sloane glanced over at Jeremy, brows lifted, and he shrugged. That was Lucas for you. The man had just flown a thousand miles, give or take, but he still had enough energy left for a round of golf...or at least, half a round.

"What about dinner?" Jeremy asked.

A knowing glint entered his cousin's eyes. "Oh, I think I'll just order something in. You two can figure out what you want—Yelp it, or whatever it is you do."

"You're sure?" Sloane looked slightly dubious, clearly not wanting to ditch the man who'd done her such a big favor, even if she might have preferred to have dinner alone with Jeremy.

"I'm sure."

Well, there didn't seem to be much point in arguing after that. Jeremy murmured to Sloane that he'd meet her at her room after he dropped off his bag, and she nodded. Lucas sauntered toward his suite like he hadn't a care in the world—which, to be fair, he probably didn't—and Jeremy headed to his own suite, which was two doors down from where Lucas was staying.

The place seemed like overkill to Jeremy, with its separate living area and an actual fireplace, but he wasn't going to argue when Lucas was footing the bill. His cousin always liked to do things in high style, no matter what. Besides, this was Helena, Montana—even the most expensive hotel rooms would be much cheaper than comparable rooms somewhere like New York.

When he went to fetch Sloane, she had her phone in one hand as she opened the door. "I was trying to do some research," she told him. "It looks like there's a street called Last Chance Gulch where there's a lot of shopping, kind of a historic district like downtown Flagstaff. I figured that would be a good place to check out."

She sounded upbeat, as though she was happy to go explore the local sights. Maybe making the best of a situation that wasn't so great—he knew she had to be champing at the bit to go look for her mother in Butte —but he figured he might as well go along for the ride.

And maybe they'd find a brewpub or a wine tasting room or something. Not that he had any plans to get wasted, but a drink might help to take the edge off.

"That sounds like a great idea," he said. Should he bring up the delay, or ignore it? A glance at Sloane's face told him it was probably a better move to just let it ride. She didn't look anything except excited to go out and do some exploring, but he got the impression that her current cheer was probably brittle at best. No point in mentioning something that might make her lose the tight rein she held on her emotions.

In the back of his mind, he wondered what would happen if they bumped into any Cantrells while they were out and about. True, his research seemed to indicate the branch of the clan who lived in Helena was fairly small, only about ten families, not even fifty people. The chances that he and Sloane would run into any of them were probably low.

And if they did cross paths with anyone from the local witch clan, well, he'd do his best to manufacture some kind of lie. What that lie would be, when there was absolutely no reason for a Wilcox to be in another clan's territory a thousand miles from his home base, Jeremy didn't know for sure. The one thing he did know was that he wouldn't reveal Sloane's identity. The first person to know who she really was should be her mother, and no one else.

"Well, I'm ready to go," she said. A pause, and she added, "Is it really okay for us to be bailing on your cousin like this? It feels a little weird."

While he understood her reservations, he knew what Lucas was up to. Yes, the man needed to get in his golf for the day. Beyond that, however, Jeremy hadn't missed the way his cousin had glanced from him to Sloane and had made a few mental calculations. Lucas might have seemed like the most easygoing guy in the world, but he didn't miss much. He'd probably caught the simmering attraction between Jeremy and the "orphan" he'd found, and had decided it was better to remove himself from the equation so he didn't interfere with anything that might be brewing.

"It's fine," Jeremy replied easily. "Lucas isn't about to pass up a chance to try a new golf course, and he's not really into going out on the town—he's got a six-year-old kid, after all."

Which was a bare-faced lie. All right, yes, Lucas and his wife Margot had a daughter who'd just started first grade, but having Mia around hadn't slowed down Lucas's socializing very much. From what Jeremy could tell, the couple went out for dinner at least once a week, and they regularly attended concerts and art gallery shows and special events at Flagstaff's Lowell Observatory. Homebodies, they definitely were not.

From the way Sloane was looking at him, one eyebrow lifted skeptically, Jeremy got the feeling that she knew he'd handed her a line of bull. Reading his mind? She had the ability, but she'd sworn she wouldn't do that again after her first peek into his thoughts.

No, it was probably more that she was good at reading people, and he'd never been what anyone could call an efficient liar. Probably, that was a good thing, but it did kind of get in the way when he was trying to tell a harmless fib.

Whatever was going through Sloane's mind, she didn't call him out on his lie. Apparently, she'd decided it wasn't worth getting into, because her shoulders lifted and she said, "Okay. Let me get my purse."

He waited while she disappeared back into her suite. A moment later, she emerged with the bag in question slung over her shoulder, then stepped out into the hallway and closed the door behind her.

It was too far to walk to their destination—more than a mile—so they headed to the parking lot and got in the Chevy Tahoe that Lucas had rented for them. Jeremy had already adjusted the seats and mirrors the way he liked them, luckily, which meant there wasn't any delay before he backed out of his parking space and headed toward downtown, with Sloane using the Yelp app on her phone to guide them rather than fussing with the Tahoe's navigation system.

They found a public parking lot close to their destination, so they left their rented SUV there and started exploring. As Sloane had found on her phone, there was a fun mixed-use area with shops and restaurants and bars along what had probably once been a public street but was now open only to foot traffic. On that particular late Sunday afternoon, some of the shops were closed, although there were still plenty of people out and about, walking or pushing strollers or simply window shopping.

The age of the buildings made Jeremy think of downtown Flagstaff, although this was on a smaller scale. Still, he was glad Sloane had found someplace interesting where they could go. The atmosphere between them didn't feel quite as charged when they were walking around and looking at their surroundings, rather than trying to figure out what in the world they were supposed to be doing with each other.

And there was a wine bar and bottle shop, with a very welcome "Open" sign glowing from one of the front windows. He'd been halfway worried they'd find someplace that looked interesting, only to discover it wasn't open for business on Sundays.

"Are you thinking what I'm thinking?" Sloane asked, pausing a few yards away from the wine bar's front patio, which seemed to offer outdoor seating inside some unobtrusive metal enclosures. On a warm summer day, that sort of seating would have been more inviting than it currently looked, since it was definitely chillier in Helena than it had been down in Flagstaff, and the wind was brisk.

"If what you're thinking is that you want to get a drink, then yeah," he replied.

She flashed him a smile and headed over to the door, Jeremy at her side. It felt good to have her next to him, although he told himself this wasn't a date or anything. They were just going for a drink.

Right.

The interior of the bottle shop was an interesting mixture of vintage and industrial, the fixtures and furniture sleek against a backdrop of old brick on the ceiling and warm wooden floors underfoot. There was bar seating in addition to several small round tables and a long table—obviously for large groups—in the center of the floor.

To his relief, Sloane headed for one of the round tables rather than going up to the bar. Not that Jeremy had anything against sitting at a bar, per se, but it was a lot easier to have a private conversation if you were seated at your own table.

They picked up the slender menus that had been left on the table. It looked like the wine bar also offered cheese plates, and he asked Sloane if she'd like split one.

"That's probably a good idea," she said. "I was starting to get the munchies, even though those sandwiches Lucas brought for us helped a lot."

Jeremy felt about the same way. While having one glass of wine on a not completely empty stomach wasn't the end of the world, he generally preferred to have something to eat when he was drinking.

And although he didn't know much about wines, he could tell that the wine bar had a lot of interesting offerings. He decided on a Monastrell from Spain, just because he'd never had one before, and it seemed that Sloane was feeling similarly adventurous, since she asked for a Cinsault from South Africa.

"I feel like a world traveler," she said with a chuckle as the woman who'd taken their orders headed back to the bar. "I don't even know what a Cinsault is."

"Well, it's red, right?" Jeremy asked, and Sloane grinned.

"It was in the 'reds' section of the menu, so I suppose so."

He was glad to see her looking so relaxed. Radiant, really, with the soft pink of her top bringing out a glow in her fine skin. As they'd entered the wine bar, he'd noticed the way several of the men sitting at the outdoor tables had swiveled their heads to watch her go by. She definitely attracted attention, that was for sure. No wonder she used so many different disguises while playing at the casinos—otherwise, she would have been far too memorable.

Their server returned with the wine and said she'd have their cheese board ready in a few minutes. Jeremy thanked her, then turned his attention to Sloane, who sat there with her glass slightly raised, as if she was waiting to make a toast.

He lifted his glass as well, if a bit clumsily, and a corner of her mouth twitched in amusement.

"I'm not sure what to toast to," she said. "But... here's to tomorrow, I guess."

That seemed as good a toast as any. And while they had Lucas along on this trip, Jeremy figured it couldn't hurt to try to invoke a bit more luck, just to be safe.

They clinked glasses and both took a sip. His wine was dark and rich, fruity without being overwhelmingly so. Since he didn't know all that much about wine, he didn't bother to analyze his selection further, was just glad it had turned out to be palatable.

The approving expression on Sloane's face seemed to

tell him that she was enjoying her wine as well. They exchanged a few comments on their drinks, both of them seeming to understand that there wasn't much point getting into any sensitive topics until their server had returned with the cheese plate.

Which she did a few minutes later. After giving a bit of information about the various different cheeses on the board, she went back to the bar, where another couple had just sat down. Glad that they wouldn't have to worry about being disturbed for a while, Jeremy returned his attention to his companion and asked the question that had been pricking at his mind ever since he realized exactly how Sloane had been making her living.

"So, what made you decide on poker?"

Her blue-gray eyes danced as she sipped from her glass of Cinsault. Then she set it down, picked up a cracker, and began to spread some Humboldt Fog cheese on it. "Well, what else was I supposed to do with this crazy talent of mine?"

"You could be a psychic or something."

She took a bite of cracker and washed it down with some wine. After wiping her fingers on the napkin in her lap, she said, "I would've been a crappy psychic. All I can do is see into people's minds—it's not like I can predict the future or anything."

Well, she had a point there. "You still could have probably made it work."

A shrug. "I really didn't want to be some kind of

supernatural shrink—I doubt that a couple of psych classes qualifies me for that sort of thing."

"So, you went straight into playing cards?"

"No." Sloane picked up her glass but didn't drink, and instead seemed more interested in the deep ruby glints the little oil lamp candle on their table awoke within the depths of the wine. "For a while, I was just doing bar bets. You know, betting people I couldn't guess where they were from, or which college they went to. Stuff like that."

Jeremy frowned, trying to do the math in his head. "How old were you when you left Logan?"

"Twenty," she said, another of those knowing smiles playing around her mouth. "So yes, I was underage, but since when did that stop anyone? I went to Reno first, got myself a fake I.D. It didn't even feel like that big of a lie—I was only about nine months out from my twenty-first birthday, not some high school sophomore trying to get a fake driver's license to buy beers for the football team or something. Or at least," she added, her smile fading, "I assume that's why high school kids got fake I.D.s. That sort of thing didn't happen too much at my high school…or if it did, I never heard about it."

No, probably not. The Mormon kids Jeremy had known at school were pretty straight-laced. He'd never even seen any of them drink a Coke. That didn't mean there weren't people who probably bent the rules, but he could see why Sloane's high school in Logan, Utah, hadn't exactly been a hotbed of underage drinking.

Had she been scared when she left? True, she was legally an adult—it wasn't as if her parents could have forced her to stay—but still, that was a pretty big deal, to strike out on your own without even knowing exactly how you were going to support yourself, where you were going to live, how you were going to survive.

The question was on the tip of his tongue, but he realized it was probably better not to ask. Obviously, Sloane had done pretty well for herself. Why make her dredge up those moments of worry and self-doubt when she'd clearly come out the other side just fine?

Even so, he hoped she would tell him one day…if only to show she trusted him with that information.

Of course, they might not even get a "one day" if everything went great with her birth mother.

"That was actually how I got my car," Sloane added. "Some jerk at a bar in Vegas. Spoiled college boy."

The contempt in her voice was so obvious that Jeremy had to prevent himself from smiling. It seemed clear to him she considered college kids a breed apart, even though she was basically that same age.

"He threw away his car in a bet?" he asked, not sure he wanted to believe someone could do something that stupid.

Another lift of her shoulders. "It was a present from his parents. He wanted a Camaro…they got him a CR-V. So, I don't think he cared what happened to it. Besides, he was drunk. And before you say anything about me taking advantage of a drunk guy—"

"I wasn't going to," Jeremy cut in, slightly offended that she'd think he was going to get all self-righteous on her. If someone did something spectacularly stupid while drunk—like losing their car in a bar bet—then that was on them.

"Oh." She took another bite of cheese and cracker, swallowed, then said, "Yeah, he'd been watching me beat other people for at least forty-five minutes before he decided he wanted to play, so he knew what he was getting into. And of course, I got an answer wrong here and there, because if you're too perfect, it's going to rouse people's suspicions, but still, the odds weren't on his side."

"What did he ask you to guess?"

"His middle name."

"That doesn't sound like it would be that hard, even without psychic powers," Jeremy remarked. And all right, there were thousands of names out there, but the law of averages dictated there really weren't too many that would be common among a certain age and ethnic group.

"Normally, no. But his middle name was St. John— a family name, I guess." Sloane sipped some of her wine, expression now amused once again. "I got it right, and he had to go out to his car and hand over the pink slip."

"I'm surprised he had the title with him." Honestly, that just wasn't smart. If someone broke into your car while you were driving around with the vehicle title, they could sign it over to themselves and make it look as if the car was legally theirs.

But then, Jeremy supposed that anyone who was willing to wager a new car on a bar bet—even if it wasn't the car they'd wanted—probably wasn't over-burdened with an abundance of functioning brain cells.

"He was going to register the car in Nevada or something. Anyway, I'd been using Uber to get around whenever I was in a city—and buses to get from Reno to Tahoe or whatever—so having my own wheels made life a lot easier."

"You're lucky he didn't report it stolen."

Her brows lifted. "You're a suspicious person, aren't you, Jeremy Wilcox?"

The ironic lilt to her voice told him that was teas-ing…mostly. "I don't know about 'suspicious,'" he replied as he lifted his glass to take another swallow of Monastrell. "I think it's more that I like to plan for contingencies so I don't get caught off guard."

"Fair enough." She moved on to the block of white cheddar on the cheese board, cutting herself a small piece. "I was a little worried about that, too, which is why I went to the motor vehicle department first thing the next morning and registered the car in my name. I never heard anything from him, though, so I guess either the guy or his parents realized there wasn't much they could do when he'd willingly signed over the pink slip."

"If bar bets worked so well for you, why switch to poker?"

For a moment, she didn't reply. Her full mouth pursed slightly as she appeared to consider the question. She popped the piece of white cheddar in her mouth and drank some more wine before saying, "I guess it felt more honest. I mean, even when I can see what other people's cards are, there's still some skill involved. I don't win all the time. I don't want to. It wouldn't be fair."

And it would attract way too much attention, a fact of which Jeremy guessed she was well aware. Still, he couldn't help but be glad that she knew her activities fell in a very gray area and did her best not to take too much advantage of people.

"What do you tell your parents you do?"

Her face went still. Right then, he wished he had just a little of her mind-reading abilities so he could get a glimpse of what she was thinking.

Voice almost too careless, she said, "I told them I'm in beauty-supply sales. It gives me a good reason for why I travel around so much. They're not happy, but…." The swallow of wine she took then was much larger than her previous ones.

She didn't finish the sentence, and Jeremy didn't try to prompt her. It seemed clear enough to him that, while she was willing to share some information, there was a host of topics she preferred to avoid. Maybe if they'd known each other a little better, she might have wanted to open up more, but he wouldn't push it.

"Enough about me," she said then, her tone shifting to something almost playful. "Tell me about you."

He wanted to say there wasn't much to tell, but he knew she wouldn't accept that sort of cop-out. Instead, he talked a little more about his work with Trident, about his utterly normal childhood in Flagstaff—well, as normal as any childhood in a witch clan could be— and about anything he could think of to make life with the Wilcoxes sound as appealing as possible. He didn't know whether he succeeded, because although Sloane seemed receptive, something about her expression had grown shuttered again, as if part of her mind was very far away.

Not that he could blame her…not with the meeting with her mother looming ever closer.

After they finished their wine and cheese, they wandered some more, going into the shops that were open. Normally, Jeremy would have been bored out of his mind by those sorts of activities—a shopper he was not—but he liked being with Sloane so much that he realized he was enjoying himself far more than he thought he would. Also, it was fun to watch her reactions to things, to see which piece of jewelry or which painting attracted her attention. He got a bit more of a feel for her tastes, which were actually on the conservative side, considering the way she'd been dressed when he first spied her at the Twin Arrows Casino—or when he'd rescued her from the parking lot of the Riverside casino in Laughlin. Maybe a bit more of her upbringing had rubbed off on her than she thought.

Eventually, they decided they wanted a real meal, and went into a pretty little Italian place on the ground floor of a local hotel. Because it was a Sunday night, the place wasn't too busy, and they were able to sit at a quiet table off in one corner. The food was excellent—a lot better than he'd been expecting from Helena, Montana—and Jeremy found himself wishing the evening wouldn't end.

Because rushing up all too fast was Sloane's meeting with her mother, and he didn't want to think what was going to happen after they saw each other face to face.

End it did, though, and he walked her down the hallway to her hotel room. They were all staying on the same floor, but his and Lucas's suites were at the other end of the hall from hers.

She paused at the doorway, clearly diffident. "I had a really nice time," she said.

"So did I," he responded. What a lackluster phrase to describe a magical few hours. That was what it felt like when he was with her—magic. Maybe magic shouldn't be a new concept to a warlock, but Jeremy realized it was…at least, the kind of magic he experienced with Sloane.

Her next words came out almost too quickly, as if she didn't know whether she should say them and so had pushed them out as fast as she could before she lost her nerve. "Do you want to come in?"

Was she asking what he thought she was asking? He gazed down into her face, at her slightly parted lips, at the flush in the smooth skin of her cheeks.

Yes, she was definitely asking that.

Holy crap.

His body knew how it wanted him to respond, but his brain just about skidded to a stop. As much as he wanted to be with her—ached to be with her, if he was completely honest with himself—he also didn't know if this was the right time. They hadn't known each other for very long, after all. And maybe he was being stupidly old-fashioned, but if they were going to be together like that, he wanted it to matter, not be some kind of throwaway because she wasn't sure whether she'd even see him again after the next day.

Voice steady, he said, "That's probably not a good idea."

Her heavy lashes swept over her eyes, and she stared down at the plastic card key in her hand. For a long moment, she was quiet. And at last, "You're probably right."

He bent and kissed her—a gentle kiss with no attempt to deepen it into something more. "Get some sleep, Sloane," he told her. "You have a big day tomorrow."

Before she could reply, he turned and made himself walk down the hall to his own room. The whole way, he couldn't help wondering if he hadn't just made the biggest mistake of his life.

12

THE NEXT MORNING, THEY DROVE OUT OF HELENA —Jeremy's cousin Lucas was nowhere in evidence, having disappeared to play golf before the two of them even went out to grab some breakfast—and headed south toward Butte. Sloane did her best to seem calm and cool, but inside, her stomach felt as though it was twisting itself into tighter and tighter knots.

It probably didn't help that she knew she was being horribly awkward around Jeremy. She had no idea what had possessed her to invite him into her room the night before, except possibly a compulsion to get as close as possible to him before he left her life altogether, but she honestly hadn't expected him to shoot her down like that. When she came to her senses, she realized it was probably for the best. Still, she didn't know quite what to do now that she'd put that odd extra strain on their relationship.

If it was even a relationship at all. They'd gotten to know each other a lot better the day before, but forty-eight hours in someone's company wasn't quite enough to be truly intimate...well, emotionally, anyway.

And she knew she was brooding over Jeremy because, fraught as it might be at the moment, thinking about him was still a lot easier to handle than the growing anxiousness in the pit of her stomach, a mixture of anticipation and downright fear at the upcoming meeting with her mother, now looming closer and closer.

The drive was a pretty one at least, winding its way through pine forests beneath clear blue skies dotted with a few pale, puffy clouds. When they got to Butte, Sloane found that it reminded her of a lot of Utah towns she'd seen—small but still sprawling, with large lots surrounding many of the houses and not much in the way of visible zoning. Hills ringed the settlement, giving the landscape a nice frame.

Nora Cantrell's place was difficult to find, even with the nav doing its best to guide them in. The house was off a private drive it shared with several other large homes that appeared to be around the same vintage, although none of them were quite as big and grand as hers. Jeremy parked at the edge of the property, as if he'd guessed that Sloane didn't want their approach to be too obvious.

She eyed the house. On Jeremy's laptop screen, the place had looked impressive enough. Now as she sat in the passenger seat of their rented Chevy Tahoe and stared at her birth mother's home, she wondered if she would even have the nerve to walk up and knock on the heavy dark oak front door. It looked like the sort of house that didn't want any unexpected guests, despite the cheerful flowerbeds that surrounded the lawn.

And she was so *horribly* unexpected....

"Do you want me to drive around a little more?" Jeremy asked her. "I mean, if you're not ready to get out yet."

A rush of gratitude filled her at his thoughtfulness. She wasn't used to people being like that—worrying about her, caring about what might be going on inside her head.

Actually, the warmth she was experiencing now was probably a bit more than gratitude, if she wanted to be completely honest with herself. Had any other guy ever made her feel this way?

Hell, no. She didn't even want to address the irony of Jeremy Wilcox entering her life right when she might be about to change it forever.

Put on your big girl panties, Sloane, she admonished herself. *You didn't come all this way just to back out at the last minute.*

"No, I'm okay," she said, and flashed him a smile. It even felt halfway genuine. "Let's go."

She pushed down on the door handle and let herself out, stepping with care because there wasn't a sidewalk and the ground below her feet was more than a little uneven. Good thing she'd dressed sensibly enough, in flats and jeans and a cute little embroidered jacket in a soft sage green shade that she'd found in one of the boutiques in Flagstaff.

Walking behind the SUV seemed a bit safer, and she navigated her way around to the driver's side of their rented Tahoe so she could meet up with Jeremy. The day was chilly, and he wore a plain long-sleeved T-shirt in the same burgundy shade she liked so much on him. It even looked like he'd done his best to subdue his unruly hair, but there wasn't much he could do to hide the obvious fact that it desperately needed cutting.

"Ready?" he asked.

She nodded, not sure whether she trusted herself to speak.

His hand stole into hers, warm, reassuring. How he'd known that she needed something to hold on to while she made the walk up to Nora Cantrell's front door, she had no idea, but she wrapped her fingers around his, willing herself to take some comfort from his touch.

Together, they walked along the neat flagstone path that cut its way through the expansive front lawn. It was carefully groomed, with not a dandelion to be seen—no mean feat when September winds would have been blowing the fluff all over the place.

Sloane knew she was distracting herself with silly details like that because she didn't want to think about what might happen after she knocked on the door. Her imagination had conjured literally thousands of different variations as to how this particular scenario might play out, but in all of them, she'd taken this walk to her birth mother's front door alone. Never in a million years had she ever thought she would trust someone enough to have them accompany her on such an important errand.

And yet, there was Jeremy Wilcox next to her, his fingers twined with hers, his mere presence giving her the strength she needed to propel her feet along the path. In what felt like no time at all, they were standing on the front porch, sheltered by the arched roof overhead, gazing at the four narrow windows cut into the door, windows so thin, they really didn't allow you to see much of the interior of the house.

By design, she assumed.

Should she ring the bell, or knock? In her mind, she'd somehow always imagined herself knocking, but the sound of the doorbell would probably carry farther.

Just do it. Does it really matter whether you knock or ring the doorbell?

No. She knew she was only stalling.

With a trembling hand, she reached out and pressed her index finger to the doorbell button mounted next to the front door.

It sounded inside, a distant *ding-dong,* no fussy Westminster chimes or anything like that. Despite the cool breeze that had greeted her as she got out of the Tahoe, a few drops of sweat trickled down her back under the camisole she wore beneath her embroidered jacket.

A few seconds passed as they waited. Sloane shifted her weight, wondering if she'd come all this way only to have everyone out for the day. That would be terrible, but what would be even worse was if her unknown half-sister or brother answered the door instead of her mother. She wasn't sure whether she was ready to face one of them without getting to meet Nora Cantrell first.

But no, that didn't make much sense. It was Monday morning, and they would have to be in school, wouldn't they?

Jeremy glanced down at her, his expression one of concern. "Maybe they aren't home."

"Maybe. Should I ring again?"

"I'd give it a minute," he replied. "She could have been on the phone or something."

Sloane noticed the way he avoided saying her mother's name out loud. Just being careful, or was he worried that uttering those syllables might increase her anxiety?

Honestly, she didn't even know if that was possible.

The door opened, and a small, rounded woman in her early forties looked out at them, obviously surprised to have two complete strangers turn up on her front porch. At once, Sloane got that strange little tingle at the back of her neck, the one that told her she was in the presence of a witch, a sensation the woman must have felt as well, because her blue-gray eyes—almost the same shade as Sloane's, except a bit lighter—widened in shock.

It was so hard not to stare. Sloane had spent years and years trying to guess what her birth mother looked like, doing her best to put aside the cliché of having a parent she closely resembled. Yes, that happened sometimes...and sometimes it didn't.

But she saw a few echoes of her own features in the woman before her, in the color and shape of her eyes, the curve of her mouth. Sloane's hair was darker—her mother was dark blonde, a surprise she hadn't been expecting—and her brows stronger, but the family resemblance was still there.

Nora Cantrell had obviously seen the similarities as well, because the color left her cheeks and she lifted a shaking hand to tuck a strand of hair behind one ear. However, her first words weren't exactly what Sloane had been expecting.

"Come inside, quickly," she urged them, stepping out of the way so Jeremy and Sloane could enter the foyer. He shot her a mystified look, and Sloane allowed herself the barest shrug in reply.

Maybe she was being melodramatic, but she could have sworn that was actual fear she'd seen in her birth mother's face.

Nora closed the door as soon as they were both inside. Sloane got a quick glimpse of walls painted a soft grayish blue, gleaming honey oak floors, an antique hall tree in that same warm oak shade. No time for more than that quick glance, however, because Nora was already leading them out of the foyer and into a large formal room with an enormous brick fireplace to one side.

"Did anyone see you?" she asked, and again Sloane and Jeremy exchanged a puzzled look.

"Um...I don't think so," Sloane said. This was definitely not going the way she'd imagined. Was her birth mother still so embarrassed by having a daughter out of wedlock that she wanted to make sure none of her neighbors had caught a glimpse of the girl in question?

Something in Nora's expression seemed to relax at that reply. In fact, she even gave them a small, rueful smile. "I'm so sorry," she said. "I know I must have sounded crazy. I kept thinking what I would do if you ever showed up, and...."

The words trailed off, and she made a helpless sort of gesture with her hands. A large diamond winked from her ring finger, and she wore an Apple watch with a fancy band. The house itself was enough of a clue to demonstrate that Nora Cantrell was doing pretty well for herself, but the expensive jewelry only reinforced the impression.

Her gaze fastened on Jeremy. "And you are...?"

"Jeremy Wilcox," he supplied, and at once her eyes narrowed. Then she looked back over at her daughter.

"So...you know."

Sloane didn't bother to ask what she was supposed to know. Clearly, Nora had been able to detect that they were both of witch-kind, and it seemed the name "Wilcox" hadn't been lost on her, either.

"That I'm a witch?" she said boldly.

Her mother blinked. "Yes, that."

"I just found out."

That news didn't appear terribly welcome; Nora's mouth thinned for a second or two, but once again, she looked more afraid than upset that the child she'd given up for adoption so many years earlier had found her way to her doorstep.

"Please, sit down," she said, indicating the two over-stuffed sofas that dominated the center of the room. "Do you want anything to drink? Lemonade, water… iced tea?"

That last option had been offered in a tentative tone, as if she wasn't quite sure whether Sloane even drank iced tea. Probably a logical enough concern, given Sloane's upbringing.

So…had Nora known that a Mormon couple would adopt her unwanted child? The odds of that happening had been pretty high, considering where Sloane was born, but still….

"Iced tea," she said boldly, and Jeremy nodded.

"Same for me, please."

Nora managed another fluttery smile and left the room, presumably to go fetch iced tea for her unexpected guests. Since Sloane's legs were feeling a bit shaky, she went ahead and sat down on a couch, with Jeremy settling himself next to her.

"Well, that was weird," he said in an undertone.

"No kidding," she responded. She still couldn't figure out what was going on. If her birth mother wanted nothing to do with her, why would she be offering refreshments instead of telling them to go away before she called the cops?

There wasn't time for anything more than that brief exchange, however, because Nora returned with a silver tray carrying three glasses and a pitcher of iced tea. A matched set, too, of pink-hued pressed glass designed to mimic the styles of a hundred years earlier.

"Well, then," she said as she set down the tray and poured tea for everyone. "How did you manage to find me?"

Her tone was just a little too bright and chirpy, as if she was doing her best to compensate for the worried, urgent way she'd greeted them just a couple of minutes earlier. However, Sloane could still detect an underlying edge to her birth mother's voice, telling her that Nora Cantrell wasn't very happy to be found.

It would be so easy to look into her thoughts....

No. Sloane had told herself over and over again that she wouldn't use her gift to pull the truth from her birth mother's mind. Either she'd hear it straight, or she wouldn't hear it at all.

To her surprise, Jeremy said, "Oh, that was my fault. The information wasn't that hard to dig up."

Nora's brows pulled together. Sloane was finding it hard not to stare at the woman, not to analyze her every shift in expression and wonder if her own face looked that way when she was frowning, or worried. Yes, there were plenty of differences in their appearance, but still….

"And how do you know Sloane?" she asked.

I never told her my name, Sloane thought then. *So, did she name me?*

That seemed the most plausible explanation. Her adoptive mother had always been kind of evasive as to where the name had come from. It wasn't like the Kennedys were the type to be huge fans of Ferris Bueller or something.

"Our paths crossed recently," Jeremy said. "My gift is with computers, so I can dig up stuff that a lot of people can't."

"Ah," said Nora. Something in her posture seemed to relax suddenly, as if she'd realized upon hearing Jeremy's reply that the only reason her long-lost daughter had been able to find her was because she'd had help from a gifted warlock. She reached for her glass of iced tea and took a sip, then smiled. "That's an interesting talent. I haven't heard of it before."

He shrugged. "I don't know of anyone else with it, either. But I suppose there might be a few more people like me in the world."

Listening to that remark, Sloane wasn't so sure. As far as she was concerned, Jeremy Wilcox was one of a kind…and she liked it that way.

"Well, Jeremy," Nora said. "I appreciate you helping

Sloane and coming here with her to lend emotional support. But I hope you don't mind if you let me talk to her in private for a few minutes."

Considering the circumstances, it wasn't that odd a request. Even so, Sloane tensed, wondering what it was that her birth mother wanted to say to her that couldn't be said in front of Jeremy Wilcox.

He didn't protest, only responded, "Sure, no problem," and got up from the sofa.

"There's a porch swing out back," Nora told him. "You can take your iced tea with you and wait out there."

Her voice was friendly, no-nonsense. The voice of a mother, Sloane realized, since she'd heard that same tone from her adoptive mother on plenty of occasions. She didn't know why it should surprise her to hear Nora speak that way; maybe somewhere in the back of her mind, she'd continued to think of her as the young, scared single mother she once had been, and not the woman she'd become over the intervening years.

"Sounds good," Jeremy said. His gaze shifted toward Sloane, faintly questioning, and she nodded. Obviously, Nora didn't feel comfortable speaking in front of an audience, and since Sloane desperately needed to hear what she had to say, Jeremy needed to give them some space.

Apparently satisfied with her response, he picked up his glass of iced tea and headed toward the back of the house. A moment later, there came the faint thud of what must have been a door closing, seeming to indicate that the two women were now alone.

Nora turned back toward Sloane. Something in her expression softened, and she said quietly, "You've grown up to be a beautiful young woman. I knew you would."

Since Nora Cantrell was a very attractive woman, Sloane didn't think that had been an unreasonable expectation. Still, she really didn't care about her looks, or what her birth mother thought of them.

She wanted answers.

"Why?" she asked simply, and Nora's fingers tightened on the pressed-glass tumbler she held.

"You can't look for yourself and find out?"

For a long moment, Sloane could only stare at the woman who'd turned out to be her biological mother. How could she have possibly known that her daughter's gift was reading minds? From what Jeremy had said, witchy talents were completely random, and no one knew what sort of powers their children might have until they got old enough for their gifts to manifest. Sloane had been given up when she was only a few hours old; there was no way in the world Nora could have known which power her tiny daughter would one day possess.

Unless....

"Do you read minds, too?" she demanded, and suddenly her mother looked pinched and tired.

"'Too,'" she echoed. She paused to sip some tea, and

Sloane could see the way her hand shook as she raised the glass to her lips. "So, you are psychic."

"Yes," Sloane replied. No point in denying it, not when they were all witches here. "Aren't you?"

A shake of the head. "No…but they were sure you would turn out to be."

That comment didn't make any sense. "'They' who?"

"You're not reading my mind?"

"No," Sloane said, her voice flat. "It's rude to do that to people. But I've come a very long way, and I want to know the truth about why you gave me up. About who my father was."

Again that flash of fear in her mother's blue-gray eyes, so like her own. Nora swallowed some more iced tea before setting her glass down on a coaster on the oak coffee table before them. "You're sure no one followed you here?"

Sloane didn't bother to keep the impatience out of her tone. "Yes, I'm sure. And we didn't bump into any other witches or warlocks in Helena, either. What are you so afraid of?"

Nora's hands clenched on the knees of her jeans. New ones, dark blue, unfaded. They were crisp and perfect, just like the house, just like her birth mother's perfect façade of suburban prosperity. But her eyes were shadowed with worry.

"I didn't know who he was," she said. "What I mean is, I didn't know anything beyond what he told me. I thought he was one of the Bradshaws—they're the clan over in Idaho. The Cantrells are friendly with them, and there's some intermarriage, just to keep our respective gene pools from getting too shallow."

That made sense. Sloane had wondered how the witch clans kept themselves from getting hopelessly inbred, but if they sometimes married people from other clans or those who weren't magic at all—"civilians"—then that would probably add enough variety.

"He wasn't a Bradshaw?" Sloane asked. "Who was he?"

A deep breath. Nora eyed her iced tea with the expression of a woman who wished it was something just a bit stronger. "He was—is—from the Walker clan. They're based in eastern Montana and part of the Dakotas. They're…." She stopped there, jaw tight, then said in a low murmur, "I really hoped I would never have to tell you any of this."

"No, you just wanted me to stay in Utah, oblivious," Sloane shot back, a little surprised at herself. Over and over, she'd vowed that she wouldn't get confrontational if or when she ever met her birth mother, that she would do her best to listen to her story and try not to judge. But all the evasions and oblique comments were starting to roil up the deep well of anger she'd carried inside her for years.

"Because you would have been safe there," Nora said. "I knew there wasn't anything I could do to prevent your powers from waking up, but I hoped you'd still have a normal life, that you'd be someplace well away from any witch clans."

"So…that's why you went to Utah to have me?"

A nod. Once again, Nora reached for her iced tea and sipped from the glass. "The Walkers are…dangerous."

The anxious feeling that had been building all morning seemed to intensify tenfold. Trying to sound calm, Sloane asked, "Dangerous how?"

"They're…." The syllable dragged itself out, breaking off into the stillness of the big house. Suddenly, the ticking of the clock on the mantel seemed very loud. "They've spent generations figuring out which combinations of magical gifts will produce the powers they desire the most. So they…breed for them."

Sloane's eyes widened. "You mean people in their clan can't choose who they want to be with?"

"No. The *prima* decides who will be with whom, based on their talents and their bloodlines."

Jesus Christ. Sloane took a gulp of her iced tea and also wished it was something much higher-octane. Maybe straight whiskey. "But if my father was a Walker…." She trailed off there, not sure what she'd meant to say. "I guess I don't see what that has to do with you, since you're not even part of that clan. I'll admit I'm new to all this, but it seems to me as if mostly the witch clans leave each other alone."

"That's the theory," Nora said. Now her voice sounded tight, brittle enough to shatter like a fragile piece of crystal. "Oh, there'd been rumors that the Walkers sometimes helped themselves to witches whose gifts they coveted, but those were always more like urban legends to us Cantrell girls. There certainly hadn't been an incident in any of our lifetimes." She stopped there and pulled in a ragged little breath. "Until me."

The question escaped her lips before Sloane could make herself stop to consider whether she really needed to be digging up such an obviously painful past. "What happened?"

"At first, I didn't even know he was a warlock," Nora replied. She wore a sad little smile, as if she somehow mocked her youthful innocence. "Some of them have a gift like that—they can hide who they are, so you can't tell they're of witch-kind. I thought he was a good-looking civilian, someone who was spending a few weeks in the area before moving on to his next destination. We had a fling, and he eventually told me he was a member of the Bradshaw clan, which shouldn't have been a problem, except that he wasn't supposed to be in Cantrell territory and so he couldn't stick around."

"And then you got pregnant."

"Yes. We were supposedly being careful, but he must have sabotaged his condoms. Not that hard to do."

No, not at all. There didn't even have to be any magic involved; a couple of deliberate pinholes would do the trick just fine.

"What's your talent?" Sloane asked abruptly. It had

to be something valuable, or a Walker warlock probably wouldn't have taken such a risk. Even if no one had been able to sniff out his witchy nature, she thought that spending days or weeks in enemy territory must have been problematic at best.

"This," Nora replied, and abruptly, her appearance shifted to that of a popular actress who had just won an Academy Award the year before. A gasp escaped Sloane's lips before she could hold it back, but then the woman sitting across from her shifted and became Nora Cantrell once more. "It's an illusion, but a very powerful one. I can shift to look like people who are much taller or heavier than I am, and I can hold it for hours." She spoke simply, without any boasting in her tone. Stating facts, nothing more. "And that's how I was able to hide my pregnancy from everyone."

And what an effort that must have taken, to conceal her changing shape for months and months, to hide the morning sickness and all the other alterations of her health and body. "You never saw a doctor?"

She sighed. "A few times. I went to Planned Parenthood, went someplace where no one would know me. I didn't know what else to do. I kept thinking I should tell someone—it's not the end of the world to have a child out of wedlock when you're in a witch clan, even if the father happens to be a member of a different clan. But…."

"But?" Sloane prompted.

"But he came back to see me. Your father. Garrett Walker."

"He knew you were pregnant?"

"He guessed. He found me, and came up and put his hands on my belly." Nora stopped there, one hand touching her flat stomach as if she could still feel it rounded with pregnancy. "You see, since it's an illusion, I still feel the same underneath. I had to start coming up with all sorts of excuses for not hugging people…my parents…as I got bigger and bigger. But anyway, he knew at once I was carrying his child…and that was when he told me who he really was, and that I needed to come away with him to his ranch in South Dakota. That the combination of our gifts would make a powerfully psychic child, and we should raise that child together."

Although obviously, she hadn't been there—except as a rapidly growing fetus in her mother's belly—Sloane couldn't quite hold back a sympathetic shiver. What must it have been like to discover that your child's father was a member of a feared witch clan and not the innocuous warlock you thought he was?

Scary as hell, she imagined.

"What did you do?"

Nora crossed her arms and settled herself against the back of the couch. It was a protective stance, as if she was worried that she still had something to fear from Garrett Walker, even after all those years.

"I told him okay, that I'd been worried about how I

could keep hiding the baby from everyone and I knew it would be much better to go with him. I said I needed to go pack my things, but I'd meet him at the hotel where he was staying."

A meeting that obviously never happened. "But instead, you ran."

"Exactly. I did pack a few things, but only enough to get me away from Montana. Utah seemed safest. I didn't know what else to do—clearly, the Walker *prima* thought your powers would be valuable enough to risk making a Cantrell witch have Garrett's child, and so I figured the best thing to do would be to have the baby in Utah, give it up for adoption…and then come back to my clan's territory and pretend none of it had ever happened."

That was a whole lot to unpack, and Sloane wasn't sure which question to ask first. However, Nora's story had filled in some blanks, so Sloane figured she might as well jump ahead a bit. "And you never told anyone?"

"I told Thomas—my husband," she added, as if she wasn't sure whether Sloane would know who Thomas was. "He's a civilian, but of course, he knows about the Cantrells, knows about that part of my world. But I never said anything to Andrew or Taylor…your half-brother and sister. And I certainly never told my parents. I couldn't risk the story getting out to the rest of the clan."

"Why not?" Sloane asked frankly. "It's not as if you did anything so terribly wrong. You were tricked."

Nora's mouth tightened, and she glanced toward the rear of the house, as if she was worried that Jeremy might decide to come ambling back into the living room at exactly the wrong moment. "This kind of thing means war between clans. I couldn't risk that happening —the Walkers are far more powerful than the Cantrells, and the consequences could have been...dire. It was better to just let it go."

Let go that she'd had a child, had been seduced under false pretenses by a member of a rival clan. That her daughter had been allowed to grow up not knowing who or what she was.

Then again, after what Sloane had just learned about her biological father, she thought that was a piece of information she would have been happy to avoid.

"But now, you need to go," Nora went on, her expression darkening. "You took a huge risk coming here. The Walkers have spies in our territory—we know it and can't do much about it, because they have powers of stealth that we don't possess. Go back with Jeremy to Wilcox territory. You'll be safe there."

"I will?" Sloane asked. Maybe that was a stupid question, but her head reeled a bit at the way she was being summarily dismissed.

Being abandoned once again.

Nora didn't seem to notice that her first-born child was still trying to process everything she'd just been told. "Yes. The Wilcoxes are strong. Even the Walkers wouldn't want to cross them, not after what their *primus* and his wife did to Joaquin Escobar."

Sloane blinked. "Who's Joaquin Escobar?"

"An evil warlock, probably the strongest the world has seen for decades." Nora made an impatient gesture. "It doesn't matter. What matters is that news of his death traveled, and now most everyone knows that the Wilcoxes are a clan you shouldn't cross. You'll be safe with them."

"But—"

Her mother's expression softened. She rose from the sofa where she sat and came over to Sloane, then bent and gave her a quick, fierce hug.

"I wish I could do more for you," she said in near-whisper. "But I can't. Just go with Jeremy, and get out of Montana."

For a second, Sloane didn't move. She'd done her best to imagine what it would be like when her birth mother hugged her for the first time, but she'd never thought it would be anything like this. No welcome here, only an admonition to get the hell out...and not come back.

"All right," she said, then stood up as well. "I'll go." A deep breath, and she added, "Have a nice life."

Nora looked stricken, but she didn't say anything, only watched as Sloane made her way out of the living room. The house had a central hallway, so it was easy enough to follow it to the kitchen and then head out the back door, where Jeremy sat on the porch in a two-seated rocker, his head bowed down toward the phone he held in his hand.

At her approach, he glanced up, surprise clear on his features. Obviously, he'd been expecting her meeting with Nora Cantrell to last a bit longer.

"Let's go," Sloane told him.

"What—?"

She cut him off. This wasn't the place to discuss what had happened. Anger burned within her, but Sloane told herself they needed to honor Nora's wishes and get out of there. "We can talk in the car."

All sorts of questions seemed to spring up in his eyes, but he didn't protest, only stood and shoved the phone back in his pocket. Sloane followed him back to their rented SUV and got in, eyes burning. She wouldn't cry, though. Not now. Not ever.

And as Jeremy pulled out into the street and pointed the Tahoe toward the highway, she thought there was one silver lining to all this mess.

At least now she knew that staying in Flagstaff with the Wilcoxes was exactly the right thing to do.

13

Jeremy knew from Sloane's white face and the hard, almost glassy look in her eyes that something terrible must have happened while she was in there talking to Nora Cantrell. However, he also knew that he'd probably get zapped if he tried to ask any questions before Sloane was willing to talk, so he made himself guide the Tahoe through Butte's quiet streets and back onto I-15 heading north without saying anything.

They'd probably been on the highway a full fifteen minutes before she spoke.

"Have you ever heard of the Walker clan?" she asked.

That question felt as though it had come out of left field. Unless....

"Is your father one of the Walkers?"

Her full lips pressed together. "Apparently."

And apparently, she wasn't too thrilled by that discovery.

Damn. While he completely understood why Nora Cantrell would want to talk to Sloane in private, he really wished he could have been a fly on the wall during that conversation.

"I've heard of them," he said carefully. "But I don't know anything about them, except that they exist. I've got a database of all the various U.S. witch clans and where they live, but that's the only information I have on most of them. We all stay out of each other's ways... especially when it comes to clans that are several states away from us."

Her fingers tightened on the brown leather purse she held in her lap. And while her gaze was fixed on the wooded landscape just beyond the highway, Jeremy had a feeling she wasn't seeing any of it.

"They sound like really lovely people," Sloane said in an ironic tone that seemed to indicate she meant the exact opposite of her remark. "I guess they have kids with each other based on what kind of talents their offspring will have."

Good God. "That's what Nora told you?"

"Yes. And she slept with my biological father because at first she thought he was a civilian...only he wasn't. Later he supposedly confessed, but he still lied and told her that he was a member of the Bradshaw clan over in Idaho. She said the Walker clan has a lot of people like that—witches and warlocks who can hide their magic from others."

This was just getting better and better. Jeremy realized he was gripping the steering wheel so tightly that it had begun to bite into his fingers. He relaxed his hold a bit and said, as delicately as he could, "And he was with your mother because…?"

"Because the combination of his talent and hers would supposedly produce a strong psychic. Me," Sloane added with a humorless smile, just in case he didn't get the implications of her words. "So, she ran away and left me in Utah to be adopted because she thought it was the only place I'd be safe."

Which made a lot of sense, actually, but still….

"I guess it's a good thing that I never traveled this way before," she went on. "Otherwise, they probably would've grabbed me at some point."

"In Cantrell territory?" Jeremy asked, then wondered why he should be so surprised that they'd pull a maneuver like that on another witch family's lands. After all, his Wilcox forebears had gotten up to some pretty shady stuff in the clan's distant past.

Or not so distant, actually, when you stopped to think about some of the crap Damon Wilcox, Connor's late brother, had pulled.

"The Walkers control part of Montana," Sloane reminded him. "I just never came this way because I didn't see the point. It's too spread out, with not enough people to make traveling here worthwhile. Staying in

Nevada and California and Arizona worked better for me."

Which made sense, considering the way she traveled from casino to casino. Jeremy knew next to nothing about the *prima* of the Ludlows, the clan that held sway in northern California, but maybe her ability to detect interloping witches and warlocks wasn't all that strong, either. He knew the Ludlows' home base was in the Bay Area, so if Sloane had stuck mostly to Lake Tahoe and environs when she was in that part of the state, there was a good chance she'd been far enough away that her presence would have slipped under the radar.

"And so…." he said, letting the words trail off so he could give her the chance to tell him what she wanted to do next.

"And so, we need to get on your cousin's plane and get the hell out of here," Sloane said. "Nora was very clear about that. She said it wasn't safe to stay. Is it going to be a problem, flying out of Montana as soon as we get back to Helena?"

Except for cutting his cousin's golf game short, probably not. It was still early in the day—not yet noon —and so Jeremy knew they had plenty of time to retrieve their luggage from the hotel, get to the airport, and fly back to Flagstaff before night fell.

"No, it'll be fine," he said. "Actually, let me send a text to Lucas so he knows what's going on. That way, we can meet him directly at the airport. We have to return our rental cars anyway."

Sloane's expression was one of mingled relief and worry. "Should you text him, though? You're driving."

"I'll dictate the text."

She nodded, and relaxed against the back of her seat as he dug his phone out of his pocket and composed a quick text. Not too much detail, just enough to let Lucas know he needed to pack it in and meet them at the airport.

We can be at your plane around 1, Jeremy finished, then sent the message.

Once he'd dropped the phone into one of the cupholders, he glanced back over at Sloane. She was still watching the landscape flash by, her face quiet and somehow forlorn.

"I'm sorry," he said, knowing those words were completely inadequate.

A corner of her mouth lifted. "It's all right. I mean, I suppose I should have guessed that my mother left all the information about my biological father off my birth certificate for a very good reason. It's not like either of my birth parents were in my life before, so I can't really say I'm going to miss them. You can't miss what you never had."

On the surface, Jeremy supposed she was right. But what she had lost was the dream of having her biological parents in her life. He might not have been there to hear her conversation with her mother, but it seemed obvious enough to him that Nora Cantrell wanted her daughter out of Montana as quickly as possible.

Hearing that had to have hurt, even if Sloane understood the very real danger she was in.

He had to hope that Nora had maybe exaggerated
things just a little in order to add some urgency to their
departure. After all, he and Sloane had wandered
around Helena's historic downtown for several hours the
day before and hadn't come across anyone who looked
even remotely shifty. And although he hated to admit
such a thing to himself, Jeremy knew that if a couple of
Walker warlocks had tried to get the jump on them,
there probably wasn't much he could have done about
it. His talent wasn't exactly the sort of thing that would
be of much help in a back-alley brawl.

So, as far as he could tell, they'd escaped detection,
and soon enough, they'd be gone. The Walkers could sit
and stew in that.

"Still, I'm sorry," he said. "I know you were hoping
for something more from this trip."

Her shoulders lifted ever so slightly. "It is what it is."
She went silent for a few seconds, then said in a hesitant
voice that didn't sound much like hers, "Is it—is it
going to be okay for me to come back with you to
Flagstaff?"

"Of course it is," he replied, the vehemence in his
tone surprising even himself. "Why would you even ask
that?"

"Well, it just seems like everyone in the witch world
is so fixated on clans, and I don't really have one—at
least, not one I'd want to be a part of."

Jeremy hated the helplessness in her voice. If asked even a few hours ago, he would have said that Sloane Kennedy didn't have a helpless bone in her body. He knew it was only the shock of learning the truth about her origins, of realizing that the family she'd hoped to find really didn't exist. Still, he needed to do what he could to reassure her that she wasn't going to be an outcast.

"We have people living in Flagstaff who aren't part of the Wilcox clan," he told her. "People we...found...a few months ago." He decided he really didn't want to go into all the details of how they'd rescued a large group of witches and warlocks from a government testing facility in Virginia. It would take too long, and besides, most of them had already been united with the clans they'd been born to. But Natalie and Ethan had stayed, and Randall Lenz as well. "They didn't have anywhere else to go, so we wanted to make sure they knew they'd always have a home in Flagstaff if they wanted it."

Sloane appeared to absorb that information without question, giving a small nod, but her demeanor didn't seem noticeably cheerier. "And you...you're okay with it?"

Way more than okay. Actually, he was sort of ashamed of himself for feeling as relieved as he did. While he was doing his best to understand her disappointment, at the same time, he would also allow himself some measure of cautious joy. She would be staying in Flagstaff, and that meant there would be plenty of opportunities to get to know her better.

Much better.

"Yes," he said. "I don't know whether you'd noticed or not, but I wasn't exactly thrilled about the idea of you staying here in Montana."

That remark actually made her chuckle. She pushed a gleaming lock of chestnut-brown hair over one shoulder and said, her tone arch, "I might have noticed something."

He shook his head, glad that her mood seemed to be lightening somewhat. Also encouraging was the road sign they'd just passed, the one that said Helena was now only twenty-five miles away. Neither of them had all that much to pack, so it really did look as though they'd be wheels up a little after one o'clock.

And good riddance. Montana was beautiful, but he couldn't wait to get out of there and back to the safety of Wilcox territory.

Then Sloane asked a question that made a sudden chill work its way down his spine.

"Who was Joaquin Escobar?"

Jeremy risked a sideways glance at her, but her expression was more one of curiosity than any kind of fear.

"Did Nora tell you about him?"

A nod. "She mentioned him. She said he was a powerful dark warlock and your clan had beaten him, and that's why I'd be safe with you...no other clans want to tangle with the Wilcoxes, apparently."

Well, that was something. He had to admit it was sort of odd to think that the story of Escobar's defeat had traveled all the way to Cantrell territory in western Montana, but he supposed if the clans adjacent to the Ludlows had heard something of the incident, and it kept moving outward from there, then eventually the tale would have filtered through the western half of the United States...if not even farther than that.

Since Joaquin Escobar was dead and gone and couldn't be a danger to anyone ever again, Jeremy figured it was safe enough to talk about him. "It's a long story. But basically, his son caused a bunch of havoc among the Arizona witch clans, and Connor and Angela ended up taking the son's powers away."

"They could do that?" Sloane asked. Her tone was frankly skeptical.

"They can do all sorts of things when they're working together," Jeremy said. "But that got Joaquin all riled up, I guess, and he went to Southern California and basically took over the clan there, and the Arizona clans worked with the Castillo clan in New Mexico to take him down."

"All those people, just to get rid of one warlock?"

"Well, it was mostly Connor and Angela and the *prima* of the Castillos. But yeah. Joaquin Escobar had all sorts of magical talents—he could basically control people's minds and bend them to his will and do a bunch of other stuff. On top of that, he was a null."

Sloane tilted her head to one side, clearly confused by the term. Not that Jeremy could blame her; he'd never heard of a null, either, until Joaquin Escobar came along.

"A null is a witch or warlock who can nullify the powers of anyone around them," he explained. "So, fighting him was really hard, because he could pretty much neutralize any witch or warlock who went up against him. In the end, it took Connor and Angela and Isabel Castillo fighting together to beat him…and Isabel died."

No response for a moment, although some of the fresh color left Sloane's cheeks and it seemed clear enough that she'd been rattled by his comment. "Wow, you guys play for keeps, don't you?"

"If we have to," Jeremy said. He figured it was probably better not to list the trail of dead bodies Joaquin Escobar had left in his wake. Not just Isabel Castillo, but Luz Trujillo, the *prima* of the de la Paz clan, several of Luz's relatives…innocent civilian bystanders…even two of the men who'd been Escobar's son's accomplices. The final tally was a bit frightening when you stopped to count everyone the Escobar warlock had murdered, or at least caused to be killed. "But if word has gotten out among the other clans that it's better not to mess with the Wilcoxes, then that makes life easier for us… and for you."

"I had no idea I'd fallen in with a bunch of badasses," Sloane remarked, and he couldn't help grinning.

"Some probably more than others," he replied. "Mostly, we just try to live our lives without too many complications. But we also don't like it much when someone tries to impinge on our territory or our clan members, and we definitely don't like it when people try to throw their weight around where they shouldn't. Anyway, I guess what I'm trying to say is that I doubt you'll have anything to worry about from the Walkers, even if they somehow manage to figure out where you've ended up."

"They haven't found me so far," she said then, looking a bit more cheerful, and Jeremy nodded.

"Exactly. If you've been traveling around the western U.S. for the past, what, three years"—he paused to get confirmation on that, and she nodded—"and they never found you in all that time when you were on your own, then I doubt they're going to figure it out now. But even if they do, like Nora said, they're not going to want to go up against the Wilcoxes. It's going to be fine."

Sloane was silent for moment, then reached over and pressed her hand against his where it held the steering wheel. Just a brief touch and not much more, but even that light brush of her fingers against his skin was enough to send a rush of heat through his body. Damn, he wished they were someplace where he could pull her close and hold her, and let her know that even though he wasn't some kind of warrior warlock, he'd do his best to make sure she was safe.

"Thanks, Jeremy," she said simply, and settled back against her seat.

They were quiet after that as he drove the last leg of their journey into Helena. When they got to the hotel, Jeremy didn't see any sign of Lucas's rented Nissan Maxima. Since Lucas had responded to the text Jeremy had sent with a brief, *Will do,* he at least knew his cousin was on board with the plan. Most likely, since all Lucas had to do was drive over from the golf course and get his things together, he'd already come and gone, and was now waiting for them at the hangar where he'd left the plane.

Jeremy and Sloane went their separate ways to pack their belongings. Within five minutes, they were back in the Tahoe and driving it over to the Enterprise agency at the airport. To his eyes, she already looked more relaxed, as though the distance they'd put between themselves and Butte had helped her to get some much-needed mental space. He'd encourage her to talk more about her meeting with her mother if that was what Sloane wanted, but he'd also allow her to come to terms with the disappointment in her own way if she was the kind of person who preferred to thrash those sorts of things out alone.

Either way, he was just looking forward to being there for her, in whatever form that support might take.

Which he had to admit was not his usual style.

With the women he'd dated previously, he'd tried to listen to their concerns with some measure of sympathy, but he definitely was not the kind of guy who immediately offered a shoulder to cry on. Not that Sloane looked as though she was in imminent danger of breaking down—she'd held it together a lot better than he'd anticipated—but still, the very fact that he'd be okay with holding her and comforting her while she had a meltdown seemed to be a signal that she'd affected him more than any other woman he'd ever known.

Once upon a time, that realization might have only made him want to put some distance between them. His single state had never bothered him; he'd never cared one way or another whether he had someone to share his life, since he had so much to occupy him anyway.

Now, though…now he thought he cared very much.

He could deal with those new and unexpected feelings later, though. The important thing to do now was to get on Lucas's plane and leave Montana in the rearview mirror.

Dropping off the Tahoe was easy enough, since Lucas had prepaid everything and they had unlimited miles within the state. Jeremy slung his duffle bag over his shoulder and offered to carry Sloane's one small suitcase, but she only shook her head.

"It's fine," she told him. "There's not much in there. Plus, wheels."

And she deployed the wheels and started towing it along behind her.

So much for chivalry. Still, he had to admit she had a point, so he didn't see any reason to argue with her. Anyway, it wasn't as if she hadn't been hauling her stuff around from casino to casino for the past three years.

They headed out of the terminal and toward the hangar where Lucas was waiting for them. The wind had picked up, and tugged at the shining waves of Sloane's hair. Jeremy loved the way it looked shimmering in the sun, with glints of gold reflecting from within its warm depths. Right then, he wondered what it would feel like to have those heavy masses of hair running through his fingers…brushing against his face as she straddled him and bent to offer a kiss.

Oh, damn. He really needed to banish those thoughts—for the time being, anyway. Since Sloane had tried to invite him into her hotel room the night before, he knew she was open to taking the next step in their relationship, but even so, he really didn't want to be all horny and flustered right before climbing into a plane where he'd be spending the next four hours in close proximity to his cousin.

As they approached the hangar where Lucas had parked his plane, however, Jeremy frowned. Yes, there was the gleaming white Piper Seneca, ready to go, and there was Lucas standing next to it.

Only…he wasn't alone.

Two men flanked him, one of them probably

around Lucas's age, maybe a little older, the other at least twenty years younger. They both had brown hair—although the older of the two had some gray at his temples—and wore jeans and cowboy boots, and probably shouldn't have looked all that threatening.

Except that they each grasped one of Lucas's arms, clearly holding him in place.

What the hell?

"Hi, there," the older of the two strangers called out. "It's Jeremy, right?"

Now they were only a yard or so away. The ringing in his left ear told him the men were warlocks—or rather, the one who'd spoken obviously was. Jeremy couldn't get a read off the younger one.

"Oh, my God," Sloane murmured.

He sent a quick, worried glance down at her but managed to respond to the man, "Yeah, I'm Jeremy Wilcox. Who're you?"

The man smiled. "I'm Garrett Walker."

14

It was like being in a slow-motion car crash. Sloane wanted to grab Jeremy by the arm and run...but how could they run with the man who was supposedly her father gripping Jeremy's cousin Lucas in a way that seemed to indicate he didn't have a problem with causing the other warlock bodily injury if they didn't cooperate?

Even worse, though....

The other man, the one who stood on Lucas's other side...she knew him. No, she didn't know his name, but he was the man she'd first seen gambling at the Aquarius casino in Laughlin, the one who'd confronted her in the parking lot of the Riverside casino later that night and called her "witch."

He'd known who she was. How long had he been tracking her?

"Let go of him," she said distinctly, and Garrett Walker—her father—lifted an eyebrow. His brows were thick and dark, making his blue eyes that much bluer in contrast.

Well, at least now she knew where her eyebrows had come from.

"Sure thing," he replied. "You just have to come with Trey and me."

Jeremy made a sound of muffled anger in his throat, and Lucas said, "Hey—hey, everyone. I'm sure we can talk about this calmly, like adults."

If he was worried, he sure didn't show it. He might have been gathered with a group of his golf buddies, discussing where they wanted to go for a drink after they were done with a round of eighteen holes.

Then again, maybe he didn't need to worry. His gift was luck, supposedly. Maybe he knew that, whatever happened, he'd skate out of this none the worse for wear.

Of course, his gift didn't necessarily protect anyone else, and a shiver thrilled along Sloane's spine as she wondered exactly what Garrett Walker would do to her, or Jeremy. Clearly, he didn't seem deterred by much.

"No problem," Garrett said. "That girl there is my daughter. You Wilcoxes don't have any business with her."

"She's under our clan's protection," Jeremy shot back, but Garrett only shook his head, while Trey grinned derisively.

"That doesn't count, and you know it," Garrett said. "What connection is she to you? None. You two need to get in your plane and go back where you came from. No point in causing a ruckus over something that's got nothing to do with you."

He sounded calm, reasonable. Sloane couldn't figure out why he seemed so sure of himself—after all, the odds seemed pretty even, two against two, even if she stayed out of the fight—but the unease roiling in her gut told her something else was going on here.

"I'll cause a 'ruckus' if I want to," Jeremy growled. "She's a grown woman and can make her own decisions. She—"

The word cut off abruptly there as he pulled in a gasping breath, then sank to his knees on the tarmac, doubled over in pain.

"What are you doing?" Sloane cried out, fury and desperation surging through her. Then she went to kneel by Jeremy's side and put a hand on his arm, even though she had a feeling her touch couldn't do much to help him. His face was distorted into a grimace of agony, sweat standing out on his brow.

"Just a little demonstration," Garrett said. "Now, we don't want any trouble. You come with Trey and me, Sloane, and these Wilcoxes can go back where they came from. They should know better than to meddle in another clan's business."

"N-no!" Jeremy gasped, cords standing out on his neck as he forced out the word.

But Sloane remembered all too well what Nora Cantrell had told her. The Walkers were ruthless, without mercy. If she didn't agree to go with them, they might very well kill Jeremy and Lucas…and they'd take her with them anyway. It wasn't as though either she or Lucas had the sort of magic that could prevent them from doing pretty much anything they wanted.

"All right," she said. "Just stop it."

"Come over here," Garrett told her.

Face twisted in agony, Jeremy shook his head. But she couldn't do as he asked—she needed to make sure he got out of Helena safely, no matter what.

She pulled in a breath and got to her feet, then grasped the handle of her suitcase and trundled it over to where Garrett and Trey stood, although she went closer to Trey, since she wanted to avoid standing too close to the man who was her biological father. At once, Trey took the suitcase from her, as if trying to demonstrate that they wouldn't allow her to back out.

Not that she would. She couldn't let herself think about what might have happened between her and Jeremy if they'd been able to return to Flagstaff together, but she did allow herself to acknowledge in some tiny corner of her soul that she cared about him, might have even let herself love him if they'd been given enough time.

As soon as she was safely next to Trey, Garrett let go of Lucas. At the same time, Jeremy released a hoarse gasp and stood, face pale and damp with sweat.

"You bastard—" he growled.

Garrett held up a hand, bright blue eyes narrowing even as he wore a falsely friendly smile on his wide mouth. "I'd watch what you say, boy. You and your cousin get in that plane and leave our territory. No harm done, since you didn't know what you were stepping into, but I'll thank you kindly to stay out of this part of the country in the future."

Sloane had a feeling that Lucas rarely showed any anger, but right then, a frown pulled his dark brows together, and the hard line of his mouth spoke of words he wanted to say and was holding back through sheer force of will. He went over to Jeremy, extending a hand, but Jeremy only shook his head, his eyes meeting Sloane's as a desperate plea burst from his lips.

"You can't go with them!"

"I don't want to get you in any trouble," she said, doing her best to sound calm, even though her heart was beating about a thousand times a minute and her feet and hands felt like they'd been encased in ice. "You've already helped me more than you can know."

A single despairing syllable escaped his lips. "Sloane!"

Apparently, Garrett Walker had had enough, because he came over and grasped her by the arm, then said, "We're going."

She walked with him away from Lucas's plane, away from the wild, despairing expression in Jeremy's dark eyes. Maybe if she'd struggled, she could have turned and gotten one last look at the man who'd managed to steal into her heart over the past few days, but what would have been the point?

It was over.

From behind her came the sound of the two Wilcox warlocks, voices raised. Lucas trying to keep Jeremy from running after them, she guessed. She had to hope that reason would prevail. There was nothing either of them could do except get the hell out of there.

Parked not too far away from the hangar was a big black Ford truck. Garrett got behind the wheel, while Trey pushed her and her suitcase into the rear seat in the extra cab before climbing into the passenger seat. Almost at once, the engine roared to life, and they were pulling away, leaving the two Wilcoxes behind.

Sloane made herself buckle her seatbelt. For a moment, she considered dipping into Garrett's mind, just to see what he had planned for her. There was no point in trying to look at Trey's thoughts; she'd already discovered at the Aquarius casino that he was one of those who were completely opaque to her.

A trait they'd bred for? Maybe.

But she decided that sometimes it was better not to know. She wasn't sure she wanted to go walking around in the mind of a man who had no problem lying to a woman in order to get her pregnant with the super-psychic baby his clan wanted.

"You're quiet back there," he said as he guided the truck onto the southbound 287.

"What am I supposed to say?" she retorted.

His shoulders in their jean jacket lifted, although he had his face fixed forward and she couldn't see his expression. "I don't know…maybe, 'hi, Dad, it's nice to meet you'? That's why you came to Montana, isn't it? To find your birth parents?"

There was no real way to respond to that question, mostly because it was exactly why she'd made the trip in the first place. Of course, she never could have imagined the current scenario, couldn't have realized that her biological father was a monster.

She ignored his query and asked instead, "How did you know where to find me?"

"Because of Trey here," Garrett replied. "He's your cousin, by the way. Well, distant cousin. Second cousin once removed, right, Trey?"

He nodded, and shifted in his seat just enough so he could look into the back seat and meet Sloane's eyes. Something in his gaze made another one of those uncomfortable shivers crawl across her skin, although she forced herself to gaze back at him as if she couldn't care less what he was thinking.

"Yeah, that's it," Trey said. "Tracking's my power— or one of them. You might have figured out what the other one is."

"Blocking psychics?" she asked, and he grinned. Back at the Aquarius, she'd registered him as fairly attractive and then dismissed him, because he was there with a date and she was working. Looking at him now, however, she wondered how she could have ever thought he was good-looking.

"Something like that. And hiding my warlock nature, just like your father here can…when he feels like it. That's something a lot of us Walkers can do."

Apparently. Inside, Sloane bristled at the way Trey had referred to Garrett as her "father," but she knew better than to call him on it. She had a feeling he'd done it on purpose just to see if he could get a rise out of her.

Ignoring him, she directed her next words toward Garrett. "Where are we going?"

"To my place. It's just outside Spearfish—that's in South Dakota."

Sloane had never heard of Spearfish, but she supposed that wasn't so strange. Not once had she ever contemplated visiting South Dakota, and so she'd never bothered to learn much about it.

Well, now it looked as though she was going there, whether she liked it or not.

"It's a long drive," he went on, apparently undeterred by her lack of response. "We'll stop in Billings for an early dinner and press on from there."

Great. As if being forcibly kidnapped by her biological father wasn't bad enough, now she was going to be stuck in the back seat of his truck for an extended road trip. She thought of the phone in her purse and wondered if she'd have a chance to text Jeremy when they paused in Billings. There was no way she could use the phone while she was in the truck with Garrett and Trey—she hadn't missed the way both of them kept flickering their gaze toward the rearview mirror to keep an eye on her—but maybe if she excused herself to go to the bathroom....

"Got it," she said, and settled against the seat back, trying her best to look unconcerned. Yes, her legs felt rubbery and the beginnings of a headache had begun to throb behind her temples, but she wanted to act as though none of this was a big deal.

However, it seemed as though Garrett wasn't quite ready to let her sit quietly in the back seat and go along for the ride. Once again, he glanced up at the rearview mirror, obviously trying to get a good look at her expression. "I'll bet your mother told you all sorts of tales about me."

"Not really," Sloane said coldly. "She said you knocked her up on false pretenses, but that was about it."

He chuckled. "Well, I suppose that is mostly what happened. But I never meant to walk out on her—I wanted her to come to South Dakota with me, raise our child together. Or did she leave out that part?"

No, she hadn't. Or at least, she'd told Sloane that Garrett had done his best to cajole her into leaving her clan to be with him. As much as she'd hated to hear the story, she had to admit that Nora Cantrell had been almost brutally truthful about the whole situation.

"She might have mentioned something about it," Sloane said. "But you can't really blame her for not wanting to spend her life with someone who lied about who he was and poked holes in his condoms to make sure they wouldn't be having safe sex."

"No, I suppose not," Garrett agreed. From what she could see of his expression in the reflection from the rearview mirror, he didn't look at all bothered to have his misdeeds called out to his face. A happy sinner, her biological father. "It's just that I knew she wouldn't have been with me if she'd known I was one of the Walkers. And I wanted to be with her. Beautiful girl, your mother. Is she still pretty?"

"Yes," Sloane said, but didn't bother to elaborate. Nora Cantrell had probably put on a few pounds over the years, but she was a very attractive woman. "She's also very married, from what I could tell."

That comment made him laugh outright. "Oh, I don't have any designs on her, if that's what you're worried about. I was just wondering."

"I'm surprised you didn't have Trey sneak a snapshot for you or something," she remarked. "I mean, I assume he was skulking around somewhere while Jeremy and I were in her house."

Even in the rearview mirror, she could see the way Trey scowled. "I wasn't anywhere near you. That's not how my talent works."

"How does it work?" she asked, genuinely interested. After all, he must have known who she was when she encountered him at the Aquarius, but how had he known to find her there in the first place? If she was really that easy to locate, shouldn't he have been able to track her down much earlier in her travels?

"You don't need to know that," he said, his tone sour, and once again, Garrett chuckled.

"You two kids need to play nice. I don't want you squabbling all the way to Billings."

Sloane wanted to retort that they weren't squabbling, but she realized doing so would only make her sound like the quarrelsome child he clearly thought she was. So she settled for a shrug and pretended to be watching the landscape pass by outside the truck's windows. At that point in their journey, there really wasn't that much to see, just flat, dun-colored terrain occasionally broken up by the odd tree or green field. Still, it was better to stare outside than have to respond to the man who'd contributed to half her genetic makeup. She really didn't want to admit to herself that she'd seen something of herself in him, in the strongly marked brows and the stubborn chin.

Like it or not, she was pretty sure he really was her father, even if she hated the very idea.

Trey had shifted once again and was now facing forward, jaw set. Sloane began to wonder who'd pissed in his Wheaties, but then reminded herself that he didn't have much reason to be kindly disposed toward her. After all, she had given him a face full of pepper spray and then kicked him in the balls. If the situation had been reversed, she probably would have been cranky, too.

The miles spooled away under the wheels of Garrett Walker's big black truck, and Sloane did her best to sit in the back seat and not think about very much of anything. She had no reason to believe either of the two men up front could read her thoughts, but better safe than sorry. It was a talent she'd honed over years of zoning out during the interminable church services she'd been dragged to throughout her childhood, so the time passed more quickly than she'd expected it would.

At a little past five-thirty, they pulled into the parking lot of a Texas Roadhouse just off I-90 in Billings. By that point, Sloane was more than happy to get out of the truck. While she was used to spending long stretches on the road, she normally would be driving, not cooped up in the back seat of someone's extra-cab truck, and she hated knowing that they were only a little more than halfway through their journey.

Doing her best to look meek, she followed Garrett and Trey inside. Since it was still a little early for the dinner crowd, they were seated at a booth right away, one in the center of the restaurant near the bar. In a way, she supposed that was a good thing; she doubted either of her companions would misbehave too much in a spot where so many people could see and hear what they were doing.

"Um, I need to go to the bathroom," she said, and began to slide out of the booth.

Garrett eyed the purse she had slung over her shoulder. "Leave your bag here."

Damn it. "I need to take it with me," she lied. "I'm on my period."

As she'd expected, Trey and Garrett traded an uneasy glance.

"Then give me your phone," Garrett commanded. "You think I don't know you'd try to call someone for help?"

She muttered an inner curse but did as he asked, extracting her iPhone and handing it over to him. "Be careful with that," she said. "I only bought it three months ago, and it was expensive."

That admonition earned her a lazy grin. "Sweetheart, you're with the Walkers now. You really don't have to worry about money."

Are all witch clans rich? she wondered, thinking about all those expensive computers at Jeremy's "Trident Enterprises," his brother's fancy house…the late-model vehicles they all seemed to drive. However, she knew she shouldn't waste time speculating on such a topic, and so she pushed the thought aside.

"Whatever," she replied, and finished sliding out of the booth so she could head over to the women's restroom.

Both men were smiling as she left, and she gritted

her teeth. Did they really think she had only one weapon in her arsenal?

She honestly did need to go to the bathroom, though, so she went in and took care of business, then washed her hands and lingered at the basin, staring at her reflection in the mirror. The lighting in there was crap, but she still didn't look too great—pale and strained, with most of her lip gloss gone. She fished out the little cosmetics bag she always carried in her purse and did a quick touch-up, more to improve her mental state than because she gave a rat's ass what either Trey or Garrett Walker thought of her appearance.

Well, and also because she was stalling, praying that someone might come in and lend her a hand.

Maybe the universe hadn't entirely abandoned her, because just as she was putting the tube of gloss back in her cosmetics bag, the door to the restroom opened and a cheerful-looking, stout woman in her late forties or early fifties came in. She sent a friendly smile at Sloane and began to head toward one of the stalls.

Now or never.

"Excuse me," Sloane said, using her sweetest Mormon-girl voice.

At once, the woman glanced over at her, now looking a little concerned. "Yes?"

"Um…I know this is going to sound like an imposition, but I was wondering…could I borrow your cell phone for just a sec? It's just that mine died, and I'm driving cross-country from Missoula to Chicago, and if

I don't check in with my mom and send her regular texts, she's going to think something awful has happened to me."

To Sloane's relief, the woman smiled. "Oh, sure, honey. That's quite a distance for a girl to be driving on her own."

"I know. The farthest I've ever gone by myself is Helena, so this is a big stretch. And of course my phone had to crap out on me."

The woman accepted this pack of lies without a blink. Well, Sloane had been pretty much playacting her entire existence for the past three years, so a few more fabrications weren't that big a deal.

A bit of fishing around in the oversized purse she had slung over her shoulder, and the woman produced an Android phone and unlocked it, then handed it over to Sloane. "Here you go."

Thank God Jeremy had given her his number, and she'd made sure to memorize it. Why doing so had seemed so important at the time, she couldn't really say, since of course, she'd also put his information in her contacts list.

At any rate, it was easy enough to go to the messaging app, enter his number, and then quickly type, *They're taking me to Spearfish,* and hit "send." There really wasn't much more information she could provide, since she didn't know exactly where in Spearfish they were headed. Still, it didn't sound like that big a place. Jeremy, with his amazing hacking skills, should be able to track her down without too much trouble.

What he'd do after that, she had no idea. As Garrett had said, this really wasn't any of his affair, since the Wilcoxes had no business meddling in the Walker clan's matters. However, while she couldn't pretend to know Jeremy all that well, she had a feeling he wasn't going to let this lie. He'd come up with some kind of plan.

At least, she really hoped he would.

The message fired off into the ether, but she didn't have any indication that it had been received. Crap.

Well, of course he wouldn't have gotten it, she told herself. *He's probably thousands of feet up in the air, flying back to Flagstaff. It'll go through once they land.*

Either way, she couldn't stand there and wait for a response. Instead, she deleted the message, and then handed the phone back to the woman and smiled.

"Thanks so much. Now my mom will know everything is okay."

"Good luck with your drive," the woman responded, tucking the phone back into her purse. Then she turned toward the farthest stall and went in.

That was Sloane's cue to leave. She headed back to the booth where Garrett and Trey sat, both of them now with glasses of soda in front of them.

"Took you long enough," Garrett grumbled, but she only shrugged and climbed back into the booth.

"Wrong time of the month, remember?" she said sweetly, then picked up a menu. She knew being snarky wasn't too much of a problem, because she'd already shown him that she wasn't easily cowed. Underneath, though, she was shaking.

She'd played her cards. Now all she could do was wait and hope that Jeremy could figure out what to do with the hand they'd been dealt.

15

"I'M REALLY SORRY," LUCAS SAID AS HE SETTLED himself into the pilot's seat in his Piper Seneca. "I was just putting my stuff in the plane when those two goons showed up and jumped me."

"It's all right," Jeremy replied, even though he knew everything was just about the exact opposite of all right. Inwardly, he was berating himself. He should have set it up so they all met at the hotel and then went to the airport together. It might have been a bit more of a hassle when it came to returning their rental cars, but at least Lucas wouldn't have been left on his own to face those Walker bastards. "We couldn't have known."

Only…they sort of had known. Nora Cantrell had tried to warn them. She'd told Sloane that the Walkers were dangerous, but Jeremy had thought it would be enough just to get out of Montana as quickly as possible.

He'd really blown it.

"You need to strap yourself in," Lucas said next, his tone almost too gentle. "We've got clearance from the tower to take off."

Crap. He wanted to protest, wanted to tell Lucas that they weren't going anywhere, but he knew his objections wouldn't change anything. The situation stank to high hell, but at the core of it was the understanding that witch-kind stayed the hell out of the affairs of other clans.

Gritting his teeth, Jeremy sat down in the passenger compartment and grimly fastened his safety belt. He'd figure some way out of this…or Sloane would. She was smart and resourceful, and obviously knew how to land on her feet.

In the real world, he thought glumly. *She's totally new to this world. She barely knows anything about how clans operate…and the Walkers sound like real winners.*

What he didn't want to admit to himself was that a lot of witches and warlocks would have said the same thing about the Wilcoxes only a few years earlier. Maybe he wasn't getting the whole picture.

Except he didn't want to get the whole picture. If the Walkers wanted to breed their people like prize pigs at the county fair, well, have at it. He found the whole concept repellent, but if Sloane hadn't been involved, he would have told himself to stay out of it and then gone on with his life.

But she *was* involved. That greaseball who'd been with Garrett Walker was the same bastard who'd attacked her in the parking lot of the Aquarius. Had he been tracking her? That seemed the most likely explanation. Either way, Jeremy definitely didn't like the way the man had been looking at Sloane. And as much as he wished he could tell himself the guy was her brother, and that was why her biological father had dragged him along, he didn't think that was the real story. That other Walker warlock hadn't looked anything like Sloane, except for maybe a superficial similarity in coloring.

No, he had to get her out of there. Too bad he had absolutely no idea where "there" even was.

Maybe when he got back to Flagstaff he could reach out to Nora Cantrell, let her know what had happened. Surely she should know something about the Walkers, could possibly give him a few ideas as to where he could start looking for Sloane.

The little plane began to taxi down the runway, and Jeremy scowled. He hated the thought of leaving Montana, even though he knew he couldn't do any good there, not without some actionable information to work with.

Crap.

Soon enough, they were in the air, flying south to Arizona. Jeremy unfastened his seatbelt but didn't get up; Lucas needed to focus on getting them safely back to Flagstaff and probably didn't want to be interrupted. Or rather, he didn't want to be distracted by Jeremy telling him all the reasons why he should turn the plane around.

To his surprise, Lucas spoke then, although he kept his attention fixed forward on the array of instrumentation before him. "What're you going to tell Connor?"

"The truth," Jeremy said. God, he was tired. Out of nowhere, his limbs suddenly felt as though they were made out of lead. "I mean, he needs to know about the Walkers. They're far enough away that they're probably not a huge threat to us, but still...."

Right then, he reflected that it wasn't always a good thing to return an orphan witch to her clan. Sloane would have been much better off if she'd stayed in Flagstaff, had never even heard of the Walker family. Now, she was probably getting a crash course in a clan she hadn't even known existed until earlier that day...a very dangerous clan. Even though her father had stopped his attack as soon as Sloane had showed she was capitulating, Jeremy could still feel the stabbing pains in his head. That was one hell of a scary talent.

Worry gripped his gut as he wondered what was happening to her right then. Garrett Walker and his companion had frog-marched her out of there and around a corner of the hangar, so Jeremy hadn't been able to see where they were headed. Had they also taken a private plane to their destination, or were they driving? Sloane had said that the Walkers supposedly controlled the eastern part of Montana and the western regions of North and South Dakota, and that was a hell of a lot of territory to cover, almost all of it sparsely populated, probably with plenty of places to go to ground.

And sure, once he got back to Flagstaff, he could try tracking her by her cell phone…if she even still had it. If he'd been in Garrett's shoes, he would have confiscated the phone right away. Then again, all he'd really have to do would be to put it in airplane mode so it wasn't being tracked by any local cell towers, and it would be pretty much untraceable after that.

"I suppose that's a silver lining," Lucas said. He shifted in his seat then; they'd reached cruising altitude, and apparently he thought it was okay to look away from his instruments for a moment or two. "Still, I'm really sorry. I'm also trying to figure out why my talent let those two get the jump on me like that. It doesn't make much sense."

No, it didn't. You'd think that Lucas's luck would have made sure he didn't suffer any harm, would have done something to deflect those two bastards and keep them far away.

Unfortunately, that wasn't what had happened. Maybe his gift had thought it was doing fine by making sure he got out of Montana without suffering any ill effects from the ambush. After all, it was Jeremy they'd attacked, not him.

Or had they?

"Did Garrett put the whammy on you, too?" he asked.

Lucas didn't bother to inquire what Jeremy meant by that question. "He gave me a little taste, enough to let me know what I was in for if I didn't cooperate." His mouth turned down, and he shook his head. "That's a hell of a talent. I've never heard of it before—at least, I've never heard of any Wilcox being able to do something like that."

Neither had Jeremy. Family legend held that the clan's patriarch, Jeremiah Wilcox, had a whole stable of magical gifts at his command, but no one had ever claimed that he was able to inflict excruciating pain simply by looking at a person. It definitely didn't sound like the sort of talent a McAllister or a de la Paz would have, either.

He wouldn't be surprised to learn Joaquin Escobar had that sort of gift, but if he did, no one had mentioned it. Since the man was dead, it probably didn't matter one way or another.

The Walkers were a much bigger problem.

"Well, I guess that's what you get when you breed your clan members for the gifts you want," he commented, and Lucas stared at him, brows lifted in shock.

"They do that?"

"According to Sloane's biological mother, they do." Jeremy ran a distracted hand through his hair. "But I'm not going to worry about that now. I need to focus on getting her out of there."

Lucas's usually sunny expression now looked downright funereal. "You know what Connor is going to say about that."

Unfortunately, Jeremy did. It wasn't that the *primus* wouldn't care about what happened to Sloane Kennedy, but he had to worry about the Wilcox clan's welfare first. Open interference would only cause a clan war, and none of them could afford for that to happen.

But he also couldn't allow Sloane to stay with those people. He didn't care that Garrett was her biological father—she clearly didn't belong with them. No, she belonged with the Wilcoxes in Flagstaff. She'd already agreed to come back there with him, had all but said she was interested in some sort of shared future.

And Garrett Walker had blown that all to hell.

Jeremy didn't know how he was going to get her back…but he also knew he wouldn't rest until he did.

At nearly nine o'clock that night, Garrett guided the big black truck down a small private lane that cut off from a two-lane road outside Spearfish. Sloane couldn't tell much more than that, since it was pitch-black out there, with zero street lights and only those little reflector things by the roadway to guide them in. She had an impression of tall trees almost meeting overhead, hiding their progress.

Not that there were probably any nearby onlookers, not out in the boonies like that. Eventually, the lane they traversed curved around and came to a stop in front of a large detached garage with what appeared to be six bays.

Garrett didn't pull into any of them, however. Instead, he shut off the truck's engine and got out, and Sloane wearily followed suit. Before she could reach for her suitcase, however, Trey came around and grabbed it instead.

"I'll take that," he said, and hefted it out of the back seat.

What, was he expecting her to thank him? If he wanted to play bellboy, fine. She was tired and cranky, and frankly, just wanted to go to sleep and put this day behind her. Maybe she would wake up in the morning with a fresh outlook...and possibly a few ideas on how to escape.

For the moment, though, she allowed herself to trudge after the two men, following them to an enormous gray stone house a few dozen yards away from the garage. The night was dark, with no moon, and the only illumination appeared to be the two iron and glass fixtures to either side of the double front door, but even so, she got the impression that the house looked like something you'd find in a ritzy suburb of Los Angeles or San Francisco or whatever, not stuck out in the middle of Nowhere, South Dakota.

It looked like Garrett hadn't been joking when he'd said she didn't need to worry about money.

What she saw of the interior was equally impressive

—vaulted ceilings, floors of stone or wood, neutral, expensive furniture, original art on the walls.

"Nice place," she remarked. "You live here by yourself?"

"No," came a new voice, a woman's voice. "It's actually my house."

She advanced into the room, keen blue eyes locked on Sloane. The woman was much older than Garrett, probably in her late sixties, her hair almost pure white and coiled back in a neat French twist. She wore a black shirt and jeans, with turquoise at her throat and on the belt buckle at her waist.

"I'm Liz Walker," the woman went on. "The *prima* of this clan…and your grandmother."

Sloane's eyes widened. No wonder the house was so ritzy—the *prima* ruled the clan, didn't she? At least, that's what she thought Jeremy had told her. The Wilcoxes were an exception, because Jeremy's cousin Connor was in charge, and not a woman.

Right then, she felt an irrational spurt of anger at Nora Cantrell. Might have been nice if her birth mother had let her know her grandmother just happened to be the Walkers' head honcho.

But maybe she hadn't known. It hadn't sounded as if Garrett had told her very much, only that he was a member of the Walker clan. He'd probably figured they'd have plenty of time later for those sorts of revelations.

"Hi," Sloane said. "You'll forgive me if I don't give you a hug."

The woman's mouth thinned, and she shot a sideways glance at Garrett. "Obviously, her Cantrell blood is showing."

"No, that's just me," Sloane replied, crossing her arms. "I'd never even heard of the Cantrells before this week, so don't blame it on them."

Garrett stepped forward, his expression almost apologetic. "Don't mind her. She's had a long day, and a long drive."

"Making excuses for her already, I see." Liz Walker made a noise that sounded suspiciously like a sniff. "But I'll allow that it's getting late. You can see her settled in, and we can get all this worked out in the morning."

That sounded like a great idea. Or at least, the part about getting settled in. Sloane wasn't sure whether she would approve of anything the Walker *prima* had "worked out," but she also had to admit that her options were somewhat limited at the moment.

"Come along," Garrett said, sounding almost sheepish. "I'll show you where you'll be staying."

He went over and took Sloane's suitcase from Trey, who had stood silently off to one side during the previous exchange. Liz Walker went to him and patted him on the arm before murmuring something that Sloane couldn't quite hear.

Whatever it was, he headed back outside, and she

allowed herself an inner sigh of relief. With any luck, he wasn't staying at the house, and had only ridden along with Garrett to make sure she made it safely to her destination.

"Have a good night," Liz said. It was impossible to think of the woman as her grandmother, and so Sloane didn't even bother to try. "Breakfast is at nine. Make sure you're prompt—I won't abide tardiness."

She swept out of the room after delivering that shot. Before that moment, Sloane wouldn't have believed that someone wearing jeans would be able to "sweep" anywhere, but Liz Walker somehow managed it.

Since Garrett was already at the foot of the stairs, waiting for her, Sloane walked over to him and followed him up the sweeping, curved staircase. Down a long upstairs hall, and then he opened a door at the end, saying, "This will be your room."

Well, if she had to be spirited away and forced to stay with this terrible newfound family of hers, she had to admit she could have done worse. The bedroom was huge, nearly the size of the entire cottage where Jeremy had put her up in Flagstaff, with a little sitting area and an *en suite* bathroom and a large bay window that probably provided an amazing view during the daylight hours. Now the shutters were closed, hiding the night.

"Thanks," she said, a careless syllable with very little meaning in it. No, she wasn't actually thankful at all, but she figured she might as well offer that small courtesy.

He set her suitcase down on the floor near the love

seat in the sitting area. "Are you thirsty? I could go get you some water—"

"I'm fine," she cut in. She didn't want him pretending to be nice to her. She just wanted him gone so she could shut the door and give herself a little breathing room. "Breakfast at nine, right?"

His lips compressed slightly. In that moment, he resembled his mother a good deal, with that pinched look to his nose. However, he only said, "Right. I'll be along to get you and take you downstairs in the morning, just so you don't get lost."

"The house is that big?"

"It's large," he said, which didn't really answer her question. "See you tomorrow."

He let himself out, and Sloane went to the door and locked it. Probably not all that helpful, what with the way witches and warlocks could ignore locks with impunity, but she figured she might as well make the gesture.

Unpacking felt like surrender. On the other hand, she really didn't want to face Liz Walker the next morning in a wrinkled shirt.

Frowning, Sloane went ahead and pulled out the few pieces of clothing her suitcase contained and put them away, then took her toiletries into the bathroom. It was as luxurious as the rest of the house, with a sunken tub and expensive stone tile, the shower enclosed in glass blocks to let the light through but still afford some privacy.

How much had this place cost? She'd never imagined herself in the market for real estate and so only had a hazy idea of relative housing prices, but she guessed it had to have been at least a million, even out in the middle of nowhere like this.

On an impulse, she went to the window and unlatched the shutters, then swung them out of the way. A quick tug to raise the sash, and cool night air flooded the room.

Actually, it wasn't just cool, but downright cold. However, she hadn't opened the window because she wanted some fresh air. No, she wanted to get more a sense of where she was, even if she couldn't see anything.

And maybe see if she had any chance of escape.

The night was very still, with only a rustle of leaves now and then to tell her that a small wind moved about the place. From somewhere off in the distance came a low murmuring sound that might have been a creek. Then, mournful against the soft background noises, an owl cried out as it swept through the dark air. Sloane thought she might have even seen it, a pale blur against a backdrop of black trees, but she couldn't be absolutely sure.

And at last, a crunch of tires and a flash of headlights moving down the lane that led to the main road. Her eyes strained against the darkness as the vehicle came to a stop next to Garrett's and a man got out. He looked vaguely familiar, and then she realized it was

Trey. It didn't seem as though he'd been gone long enough to run any sort of errand, but maybe they weren't as far away from Spearfish itself as she thought.

He went around the back of his truck—she thought it might be similar to the one Garrett had been driving but couldn't be completely sure—and got out what looked like a duffle bag. Holding it in one hand, he approached the front door. Because of the angle, Sloane couldn't exactly see what happened after that, but she assumed he'd come back inside.

Maybe if she cracked the door to her room and listened down the hallway, she'd be able to hear what he was doing. But no, that didn't sound like a very good idea. What if Garrett or Liz were lurking in the upstairs hall, just waiting to pounce if she should so much as stick her head outside?

Holding back a sigh, Sloane went ahead and got ready for bed, mostly because she couldn't think of what else to do. She wondered what Jeremy was doing…if he'd gotten her message, if he and Lucas had gotten back to Flagstaff safely. The drive to Spearfish had taken almost twice as long as their flight to northern Arizona would have, so he'd probably been home for hours and hours.

Find me, Jeremy, she thought, doing her best to send that prayer winging outward into the darkness, focusing all her intent on that single thought.

Get me the hell out of here.

16

Jeremy's phone buzzed almost as soon as they began their final approach to Flagstaff Pulliam Airport. He drew the iPhone out of his pocket and looked down at the screen. The number was completely unfamiliar—he didn't even recognize the area code—but he went ahead and opened his messaging app just in case it wasn't some kind of spam.

Just five words, but they were enough.

They're taking me to Spearfish.

God bless Sloane's resourcefulness. Clearly, she'd managed to borrow someone else's phone to get the message out, probably because Garrett had confiscated hers.

Where the hell was Spearfish?

He went to his browser and did a quick search. Okay—northwest South Dakota, not far from Deadwood. Definitely in Walker territory, and sort of out in the middle of nowhere. Spearfish was a real town, but it wasn't too big, only around ten thousand people. Most likely, the local residents had no idea there were a bunch of witches and warlocks living amongst them.

Lucas guided the Piper down to a picture-perfect landing, the wheels making hardly a bump as the plane came in contact with the tarmac. A few minutes later, they were taxiing to the hangar where he stored the plane.

As soon as he emerged from the cockpit, he arched an inquiring eyebrow at Jeremy. "You're looking pretty cheerful for someone whose girlfriend was just kidnapped by a bunch of eugenics-happy warlocks."

No point in telling Lucas that Sloane wasn't his girlfriend. She was special to him, true, but Jeremy knew their relationship wasn't nearly so formal.

He just hoped that one day it would be.

"She got a message out to me," Jeremy said. "I know where she is."

That declaration didn't appear to cheer up his cousin. If anything, he only looked more worried. "You need to stay out of it, Jeremy."

Fat chance of that happening. However, he didn't want to get into an argument with Lucas, mostly because he knew if he acted too vehement, word would get back to Connor even more quickly, and he'd prefer to keep the *primus* out of this for as long as possible. Connor wasn't the type to lay down the law, but he might in this case if that was what it took to avoid a messy inter-clan confrontation.

"Hey, I'm just glad to know she's okay," Jeremy said easily.

Lucas didn't appear exactly convinced by this about-face, but he didn't comment on it, only said, "Well, that's good news. You probably want to get home—I'll go ahead and get the plane sorted out."

That was a dismissal if he'd ever heard one. Which was fine; Jeremy definitely did want to get home, just so he could start taking a whack at the Walker problem and let himself know what he was up against.

"Thanks, Lucas," he said. "Have a good night."

And he hurried off before he could say anything that might give away what he was planning. No doubt Lucas wanted to get home as quickly as possible to his wife and daughter, so there was no reason to prolong the conversation.

Jeremy's truck was waiting for him in the long-term parking lot, a little dusty but otherwise fine. He got in and headed toward his townhouse, which was located about five minutes away.

Silence greeted him as he entered the place, but that was to be expected. He didn't have a dog like his brother Jake and lived alone. In the past, the quiet of his house had always been appreciated, something that allowed him to focus on his work, but right then, Jeremy could only think about how much he wished Sloane were there with him. He realized he'd never even shown her the place, since they'd met at the cottage and had only gone to Trident HQ and Jake's house together.

Well, he'd be sure to have her over just as soon as he got her back.

Which meant he needed to get to work.

He got a glass of water and went into the ground-floor bedroom he used as his office. Although he'd taken one of his laptops with him on the trip to Montana, his preferred machine for serious hacking was the custom-built desktop PC he kept at home. Insanely fast, it was loaded with everything he needed to tunnel into secure websites and take a poke around without having to worry about anyone detecting his presence.

First things first, though. He figured he might as well take a general survey of the Walkers, just as he had with the Cantrells, to figure out who they were and how many of them he was dealing with. They lived in a part of the country that wasn't exactly known for its population density, but the size of their territory made him think there had to be more of them than the Cantrell clan.

It didn't help that they had a very common last name. Luckily, Jeremy had algorithms in place that allowed him to separate the wheat from the chaff, to use a combination of land purchases and bank accounts to figure out who was with a clan that had been steadily accumulating power and wealth over the past hundred-plus years, and who was simply a civilian with the bad luck to share the same surname as the local witch family.

About an hour later, he thought he'd gotten the facts of the matter nailed down enough to paint a portrait of the situation in a few broad strokes. Yes, the Walker clan was scattered throughout the eastern part of Montana and the western regions of North Dakota and South Dakota, but there was a heavy concentration of them in the Spearfish area, and another large group way over in Billings, Montana. As far as he could tell, the Walkers had settled in the area in the late 1870s, drawn there by the gold rush in the nearby Black Hills. They were heavily connected to local mining interests and also had invested a great deal in land, and, like most witch clans he'd studied, had prospered over the years, spreading north and west into North Dakota and Montana.

Best guess, the current *prima* of the clan was Elizabeth Walker, age sixty-eight. She owned what appeared to be the most expensive house in the area, a huge chateau-style place that had been built in the early 2000s after the earlier mansion on the property was torn down. Jeremy couldn't find any documentation as to why she'd decided to demolish the older house, but he assumed she simply wasn't as bound up in tradition as the McAllisters or the de la Pazes or the Castillos, clans that had made it a point of pride to have a house that was passed down from *prima* to *prima* for generations.

What caught his attention, though, was the name of her only son.

Garrett Walker. He supposed there could be more than one Garrett in the clan, but Jeremy kind of doubted that, especially since the man in question was the correct age—forty-six—to be Sloane's biological father.

No wonder they'd worked so hard to get her. She wasn't just the daughter of a Walker warlock; she was the granddaughter of the clan's *prima*.

This could be…interesting.

Jeremy's stomach growled, and he frowned as he glanced at the time stamp on his computer screen. Six forty-six, and he hadn't eaten anything since the breakfast he'd shared that morning with Sloane—a breakfast that might as well have been consumed a lifetime ago, considering everything that had happened in the intervening hours. While he hated to waste valuable time eating, he also knew he wasn't going to be of much use if he was so hungry he couldn't concentrate.

So, he got out his phone and used the Door Dash app to order some food from his favorite Greek restaurant, then leaned back in his office chair and stared at the computer for a moment, considering his options. It seemed obvious enough to him that they'd taken Sloane to Spearfish because her grandmother wanted to see her. For what purpose, Jeremy had no idea. He doubted it was simple familial curiosity, though. There was no need to threaten bodily injury to people if your only reason was a desire to see your long-lost granddaughter.

He decided to shelve that topic for the moment and see what he could dig up on Garrett Walker. The man also lived in Spearfish, in a house that was a little less grand than his mother's but still fairly showy, a five-bedroom chalet-style place on fifteen acres, with stables and an indoor swimming pool. According to local property tax records, he owned a good deal of other property in town, including two restaurants, a western wear store, and the local Ford dealership.

Oddly, he'd never married and didn't seem to have any children except for Sloane—unless, of course, he'd knocked up some other unsuspecting witch from a different clan. Jeremy didn't think that scenario was particularly likely, but he also couldn't dismiss it out of hand. He was Elizabeth Walker's only child, which made Jeremy wonder who the Walker *prima* had designated as her *prima*-in-waiting, or heir.

That was the sort of thing he couldn't really decipher from public records. It wasn't as though witch clans spread their private internal business where it could be easily discovered on the internet. Still, he wondered why Garrett had never married. Although inheritance didn't always go directly from mother to daughter—and obviously the Walkers were ruled by a *prima* and not a *primus*—you'd still think that Elizabeth Walker would want her only son married and possibly providing a candidate to be a future *prima*-in-waiting.

Unless that was why they wanted Sloane.

Jeremy frowned, not liking the sound of that prospect very much. It was one thing to try to pry her away when she was only a long-lost grandchild who needed to be welcomed back into the clan. If Elizabeth Walker wanted Sloane as her *prima*-in-waiting, then getting them to give her up was going to be difficult, if not downright impossible.

The doorbell rang and Jeremy jumped, then reminded himself that he'd ordered Door Dash and that his food must have arrived.

He pushed himself away from the computer and went to answer the door, fumbling for his wallet so he could tip the driver in cash.

To his utter shock, it was Randall Lenz standing on the doorstep, a bag from Taverna in one hand. "You're driving for Door Dash?" Jeremy blurted out, too startled to remind himself that maybe he should have kept his astonishment to himself.

Lenz didn't look surprised at all to see him…probably because Jeremy's name had been on the order, and so of course he'd known whose house he was going to. "I don't want to be an utter leech on the Wilcox clan's largesse," he said coolly, then handed over the bag.

Jeremy took it, mentally debating with himself whether it would be too weird to give the guy a tip or whether he should go ahead and offer Lenz the money. But if the guy was working as a Door Dash delivery driver, then he must need the cash. Or not. He'd heard through the grapevine that the former federal agent had made a killing when he sold his house in Alexandria, so maybe he was doing the gig thing just to keep himself busy. Besides, Connor had made sure that Lenz received the Wilcox monthly stipend as a way of saying thank-you for his assistance in getting all those witches and warlocks safely away from the facility where they'd been kept, so he couldn't have been hurting that badly for money.

Oh, hell. Jeremy extended the ten-dollar bill with his free hand, and Lenz shook his head.

"Not necessary. You have a good evening."

He turned and began to walk away. A sudden idea popped into Jeremy's head, and he called out, "Wait!"

Lenz swiveled back toward Jeremy, a faint frown deepening the lines around his eyes. "Is there something wrong with your order?"

Since he hadn't even looked inside the bag, Jeremy couldn't really answer that question one way or another. "No, it's not that. It's just…a situation has come up, and I could use some advice."

"You want *my* advice?" Lenz asked, now looking almost amused.

Most likely, that wasn't a request the man had been expecting. Jeremy hadn't paid much attention to what Lenz had been doing since he'd moved to Flagstaff a couple of months earlier—mostly because he figured it wasn't any of his business—but he'd gotten the impression that Lenz kept to himself and didn't have many interactions with the clan that had given him shelter.

"Yeah, I do," Jeremy said. "Could you come in?"

Maybe the faintest shrug. The guy was dressed casually, in jeans and running shoes and a blue polo shirt, but he still held himself like he was wearing a suit with a shoulder holster hidden under the jacket. "All right," he said. "But if I get a call, I'll need to leave."

"This won't take long."

At least, he hoped it wouldn't.

They went inside. Jeremy headed into the kitchen and deposited the bag of takeout on the counter, figuring he'd nuke it if necessary after Randall Lenz left. "Want a glass of water?"

"I'm fine," Lenz replied.

All right, then. Jeremy shoved his hands in his jeans pockets and said, "I've come up against kind of a situation."

Maybe the faintest lift of an eyebrow. "What kind of a situation?"

As briefly as he could, Jeremy described meeting Sloane and what had happened when he helped her track down her birth mother. A few details about the Walkers, and he concluded by saying, "I need to get her out of there, but I'm just a computer guy. It's not like I can go storming the castle to rescue her or something."

His remark made Lenz smile thinly. "Are you asking

me to stage a commando raid? That's not really my field of expertise, either."

No, probably not. Jeremy supposed he should have realized that a Homeland Security field agent wasn't necessarily the same thing as someone who had specialized military training. "Well, I'm not going to give up."

"I didn't say you should." Lenz paused for a moment, eyes narrowing as he appeared to contemplate the problem. "I think what you really need is some leverage."

"'Leverage'?" Jeremy repeated. "Like what?"

"You're the computer guy," the other man said. "Think about it. You need to hit them where it hurts. Sounds like they're prosperous. What if they suddenly…weren't?"

For a second or two, Jeremy could only stare at Lenz blankly. Then realization set in, and he nodded. He'd never done that sort of hacking before…but that didn't mean he couldn't.

"I think you've got it," Lenz went on. "I won't keep you from your dinner. Have a nice night."

Without waiting for Jeremy to reply, he headed for the foyer. A few seconds later, the front door closed with a soft thud.

Hit them where it hurts, Jeremy thought with a grin.

He grabbed the bag of takeout, and hurried back to his office.

~

Sloane wished she could have a moment or two of blissful ignorance so she could forget where she was. Unfortunately, as soon as she opened her eyes and took in the elegant, unfamiliar room where she lay, she knew exactly whose house this was.

Her grandmother. Liz Walker.

If she could have one wish—just one—it would be that she could roll back time to the day before yesterday, when she hadn't known who her biological father was. Or maybe roll it even further back, to the time before that moment when Jeremy had offered to track down her birth mother. After all, ignorance was bliss.

But if that had happened, she might not have gone with him to Flagstaff. He'd coaxed her along with the promise to locate the woman who'd given her up for adoption. Otherwise, Sloane was pretty sure she would have walked away, despite his revelations about witches and warlocks and her own powers.

Despite how gorgeous she thought he was.

She ached for him then in a way she'd never ached for a man before. It wasn't even physical desire, exactly, only a need for him to wrap his arms around her and comfort her with his very presence. And that was kind of crazy, because on the surface, Jeremy Wilcox really didn't seem like the world's most reassuring person. But there was something about the way he made her feel when she was around him, like he was just fine with who she was and didn't expect her to be anything different.

Unfortunately, he was a thousand miles away, and while she had to hope he was doing his best to figure out how to get her out of the Walkers' clutches, she also knew she couldn't sit around and wait for that eventuality. No, she needed to do what she could to rescue her own damn self.

The clock on the nightstand told her it was a little past seven-thirty. Plenty of time to get ready, even though blow-drying and styling her hair always took at least a half hour on its own.

Since she'd only packed three days' worth of clothing for the trip, she didn't have a lot of choices when it came to getting dressed. Luckily, when she peeked out past the shutters and saw what promised to be a gorgeous sunny day, she decided that the button-up shirt she'd hung in the closet the night before should do just fine. It was a muted shade of teal that went well with her warm brown hair, and a little conservative in style, which she figured could only help. If she looked demure and well-behaved, then they might not expect her to fight back.

Well, except Trey. He already had firsthand experience of her fighting skills.

She showered and got dressed, then brushed her teeth and applied makeup and got to work on drying and curling her hair. At least she had all her toiletries and styling tools with her, even if she didn't have a very big wardrobe to work with. If they planned to keep her here for a while, then Liz Walker would have to do something about getting her some more clothes.

That's not going to happen, she told herself as she finger-combed the soft waves she'd just set and gave her reflection a final critical inspection. *One way or another, you're not sticking around.*

Her inner voice sounded confident. She hoped it was right.

Back to the nightstand to put on the gold and garnet ring her parents had given her for her eighteenth birthday, and the small gold hoops she'd bought for herself when she was still in college and working part-time at a restaurant. Done with five minutes to spare.

Which gave her time to make the bed and go back to the window so she could open the shutters and let in the bright morning. It really was a gorgeous day, the sky a perfect sapphire blue with just a cloud every once in a while to break it up, the hills still mostly green, although she caught a glimpse here and there of an early leaf turning gold or glorious scarlet.

No wonder the Walkers had settled here. Sloane hadn't known anything about Spearfish before she'd heard of it the day before, but she could tell it was beautiful.

A knock came at the door, and she pulled in a breath and went to answer it. Outside in the hall was Garrett Walker, brown hair slicked back from his face and well-worn cowboy boots on his feet. In the morning light, she noticed the gray at his temples, the deeply graven laugh lines around his eyes, but he still had an oddly youthful energy for all that.

"Morning," he said, looking far too cheerful for the current situation…at least, as far as Sloane was concerned.

Then again, why shouldn't he be cheerful? she thought sourly. *He got the better of a couple of Wilcoxes and was able to scoop up his daughter and bring her home to Mommy.*

"Morning," she responded. That was about all she could manage right then, although she tried to keep her tone as neutral as possible. No point in starting a fight so early in the day.

His blue eyes twinkled, as if he'd easily picked up on her sulkiness. To her relief, however, he didn't say anything beyond, "Let's go down to breakfast."

Sloane followed him to the stairs and down to the ground floor. Now that the house was more brightly lit, she was able to see more of the art on the walls, the sculptures in their niches in the downstairs hallway. The place was beautiful, like something you'd see on TV or in the movies, but nothing about it felt at all welcoming. That could have been her own mood coloring her perception of her surroundings, but she wasn't sure. Everything felt as though it had been chosen because it was a good investment and because it coordinated with the other pieces in the collection, and not because the person selecting each piece had felt any joy in its intrinsic attributes.

They passed door after door, and she began to see why Garrett had said he'd guide her to the place where they'd have breakfast. She probably would have gotten lost on her own. Eventually, though, they entered a large room with a long table in the center and a series of tall windows that looked out over an open field with a creek meandering along its border.

Well, that explained the sound of rushing water Sloane had heard the night before.

Already sitting at the table were Liz and Trey Walker. Or at least, Sloane assumed he had the same last name, but maybe not. Just because people were related didn't mean they shared the same surname.

To her surprise, Trey rose as she entered the room, although Liz remained seated. Was he trying to impress her with his manners or something?

Like that was going to work.

"Good morning, Sloane," Liz said from her place at the head of the table. She wore a crisp white shirt that morning, with a magnificent sterling and turquoise squash blossom necklace on top. Sloane was no expert in Native American jewelry, but she'd seen enough pieces in gift shops from Nevada to New Mexico to know that thing had to have cost at least a couple grand. "You may come and sit by me."

The words might have been phrased as a request, but she knew better than to refuse. Not looking at Trey, who was watching her with a studiously neutral expression on his guy-next-door features, she made her way to the place at Liz's right that the *prima* had indicated, then sat down and put the fabric napkin in her lap.

"Coffee?" Liz asked. "Or tea?"

"Tea, please."

Sloane was surprised again when Trey got up from the table at a nod from the family matriarch and went out a door on the other side of the room. She cast a sideways glance at her grandmother.

"Do you always make him fetch and carry?"

The older woman's lips curved in an indulgent smile. "Trey likes to make himself useful."

As they were speaking, Garrett came around the table and sat down in the spot to his mother's left. "We can't have civilian servants, obviously," he said. "So, we need our own to help out."

"I could have gotten my own tea," Sloane protested. No, she wasn't about to let herself feel sorry for Trey, but....

"It's fine," Liz said in quelling tones.

In the next moment, Trey reappeared, a coffeepot in one hand and a teapot in the other. He set the teapot down in front of Sloane and the coffee directly in front of Liz.

"And go ahead and bring in the sweet rolls," she said.

He vanished again, coming back a little more quickly this time with a basket covered in a red napkin that matched the one in Sloane's lap. "Anything else?" he asked, his tone as neutral as his expression.

"No, that should hold us for a while. Go ahead and sit down."

As Sloane tipped some fragrant tea into her cup—the aroma told her it was probably English Breakfast—Trey resumed his seat and waited for the others to pour themselves some coffee before he reached for the pot. A moment or so passed as they all busied themselves with doctoring their beverages with their add-ons of choice. Then Liz pulled her cup of coffee toward her, although she didn't appear ready to take a sip.

"I know this must all seem very strange to you, Sloane," she said. "And if I could have come up with a more…graceful…way of approaching you, I would. But I knew that once you spoke with Nora Cantrell, she would have done her best to poison your mind against your father's side of the family, and there simply was no other way."

Right. Like they'd even tried to do anything halfway civilized. No, they'd just threatened Lucas Wilcox, had hurt Jeremy. Liz Walker could try all she wanted to rewrite history, but Sloane had been there.

"I would have come and talked to you," she said. "There was no need to hurt my friends."

"Oh, Garrett didn't *really* hurt them," Liz replied. "Just gave them a little poke, so to speak. His powers can't physically hurt you—they just feel that way."

Good to know. Still, Sloane recalled the agony on

Jeremy's face and thought it had all looked pretty real to her. She picked up her tea and took a very small sip; the milk she'd added had cooled it down a bit, but it was definitely plenty hot. Ignoring the other woman's comment, she said, "Why don't you tell me why I'm here, then?"

A long pause. Liz glanced at her son, then looked over at Trey, gaze resting on him for an uncomfortable few seconds. Then she lifted her cup of coffee and sipped from it.

"It's not enough to want to see the granddaughter I didn't know I had?"

For someone else, it might be. For you...I doubt it. However, Sloane only shrugged and took another sip of her tea.

Something in Liz Walker's expression hardened, the false friendliness she'd worn a moment earlier gone as if it had never existed in the first place. "You're a very direct young woman, Sloane. I appreciate that. I think we can work with one another."

She definitely didn't like the sound of that comment, but she made herself meet her grandmother's gaze as she said, "Work with one another on what?"

"I suppose Nora Cantrell told you something of how we Walkers ensure that the most useful magical gifts survive from generation to generation."

Breeding people like horses, or show dogs. Once again, though, Sloane kept her thoughts to herself and only replied, "She said something about that."

"Nothing good, I'm sure." Manner brisk, Liz went on, "It's the best way to ensure the success of this clan. You know for yourself how strong your psychic talents are. The reason for your amazing gifts is the blending of your father's powers with the power your mother possessed. I was not lucky enough to have a daughter to be *prima* after me, but that doesn't matter now that we've found you. Your talents guarantee that this clan will have a strong leader after I'm gone."

Holy crap. Of all the scenarios she might have imagined after being brought to Walker territory, being told she was going to be their next *prima* was definitely way down on the list.

"You don't even know me," she said, her tone flat. "How do you know I would even make a good *prima?*"

"Instinct, my girl. Besides, Trey has told me how… resourceful…you are. This clan needs someone like that as its leader. And if you don't believe me, go ahead and look into my mind."

As she issued that challenge, Liz fixed Sloane with a hard, blue-eyed stare. Sloane could only gaze back at her, thoughts churning. Although peeking into her grandmother's mind might provide answers to a variety of questions, she honestly wasn't sure whether she wanted to take that look. Who knew what she would find?

"You mean…you mean you're not 'opaque' like Trey?"

A chuckle. "No. Many of us Walkers have that

talent, but I'm not one of them. Mine lie in different areas." Her eyes narrowed, the lines around them deepening. They must have been caused by squinting at the sun, because Sloane had a feeling her grandmother definitely hadn't laughed that much in her life.

Nothing for it. She took a larger swallow of tea this time and almost instantly regretted it. Not because the liquid was too hot, but because it seemed to churn acidly in her empty stomach, eating her from the inside.

Her fingers clenched in the napkin in her lap, and she made herself stare back at her grandmother. That odd little mental flip she always performed to unlock a person's thoughts, and then she was in.

A pretty girl, although she could be taller. Takes after her mother there, I suppose. It won't matter in the end—Trey is tall, and their children should take after him. And the combination of their gifts will bring the child this clan needs...a null.

Stomach churning even worse than before, Sloane backed out of Liz Walker's mind. The dregs of tea on her tongue now seemed bitter as gall. She should have known that her grandmother's notion to install her as *prima*-in-waiting was only part of the plan. No, she wanted Trey to be her consort, to create a child with the horrible power Jeremy had described, the power to take away the magic in everyone around them.

A *prima* with that talent could make the people in her clan do anything she wanted.

Sloane stood up with such force that her chair

screeched backward across the polished oak floor. And then she fled, bolting through the door Trey had used just a few minutes earlier.

Yes, that was the kitchen, and there was another door, one that opened to a back stoop and the field she'd seen through the dining room's windows. That seemed as good a place as any.

She ran, and didn't look behind her.

17

HE PROBABLY WOULD HAVE COME UP WITH THIS plan on his own, given time, but Randall Lenz's suggestion had sent Jeremy's brain into overdrive. Fingers clacking away on the keyboard, he allowed his gift to take hold and to blossom, to create algorithms and subroutines that would hunt down every single bank and brokerage account Liz and Garrett Walker owned. If that strategy proved ineffective, then he'd branch out to other members of the Walker clan—including Trey, the man who'd been with Garrett at the Helena airport, although his last name had turned out to be Mitchell— and see what damage he could do there. Eventually, they'd have to realize it wasn't worth it to them to hang on to Sloane, even if Liz Walker might want to make her the clan's next *prima*.

Their wealth, once he'd gathered all the data, was pretty impressive. Maybe the Walkers weren't quite as rich as the Wilcoxes, but still, they definitely had enough family money that none of them would ever have to worry about earning a living. As far as he could tell, they all got a stipend from a central fund, just like the Wilcoxes did. It would have been easy enough to hack that account and drain it of every last penny, but Jeremy considered that his nuclear option. After all, he doubted every single member of the clan was in on the plan to kidnap Sloane, and he would prefer to avoid punishing innocent people unless he had no other choice.

Liz and Garrett Walker, on the other hand, were about to suffer a world of hurt.

It was pretty easy to make money disappear, when you got right down to it. Yes, those funds were backed by actual cash somewhere, but all bank accounts were really just data, a sequence of ones and zeroes, numbers that could be made to flow anywhere you wanted. In this case, he made all that money make its way into accounts he set up for himself, untraceable, unhackable files where he could sit on the funds until Liz Walker let Sloane go.

Jeremy didn't take all of it, of course. No, he left about a grand in what appeared to be the Walker *prima's* main household account, just so she wouldn't be completely cut off if she needed to buy groceries or pay her electric bill or whatever. He left a little less in Garrett Walker's primary checking account, again, for operating expenses. But while both of them had fairly substantial wealth, they also had a number of outstanding claims on that money, including the payroll at Garrett's car dealership and restaurants and clothing store. The employees who worked at those businesses might have been Walker witches and warlocks, and they might have had their stipends to fall back on, but they still probably wouldn't be over-joyed to discover they weren't getting their next paycheck if this little face-off lasted for any amount of time.

The most pressing concern, however, turned out to be a real estate deal that Liz Walker was in the process of closing—she had plans to buy a large parcel of undevel-oped land on the southern end of town, and a meeting with the sellers had been scheduled for the next day. As far as Jeremy could tell from poking around in her calendar, she was supposed to present them with a cashier's check for nearly a quarter million dollars at that meeting.

All fine and good, but when she asked her bank to cut the check, she was going to find out she was just a wee bit overdrawn.

Jeremy took a bite of his lukewarm gyro and washed it down with a swallow of brown ale, wishing he could see Liz Walker's face when she realized all the money she depended on to maintain her lifestyle had vanished without a trace.

Don't fuck with the Wilcoxes, he thought with some satisfaction.

His phone rang, and he shot it an irritated look. He hated being interrupted when he was working.

But the number displayed on the iPhone's home screen was his brother's, and Jeremy had a feeling that Jake would just keep calling—or worse, come over to the house—if he didn't answer.

He put down the beer bottle and picked up the phone. "Hey," he said.

"'Hey' yourself," Jake returned, clearly annoyed. "I thought you said you were going to check in when you got back into town."

Had he? Jeremy had a vague recollection of possibly making such a promise to his brother, but he couldn't remember for sure. "I got busy."

"Well, Lucas called me and told me what happened. I'm sorry, man."

That sounded like genuine sympathy in Jake's voice, and Jeremy pushed aside his irritation as best he could. Ever since Jake had hooked up with Addie, he'd been dropping hints about Jeremy possibly doing something to remedy his single state, although he hadn't been too pushy about it. Still, he'd probably picked up on some of the vibe between Sloane and his younger brother, and had been hoping something would come of it.

"It's all right," he said. "I'm working on it."

"Working on what?" Jake asked, his tone sharpening. "This sounds like something we need to stay out of."

"I'm not going to tell you," Jeremy said. "And I'm

not going to tell Connor, either. That way, you all have plausible deniability."

"Jeremy—"

"I don't need another lecture on how this is the Walker clan's business and I need to stay out of it. Sloane doesn't deserve to be forced into something she doesn't want."

A pause. Then Jake said, "You don't know that's what's happening—"

"Oh, I have a pretty good idea that she has absolutely no desire to stay with the Walker clan. Before they ambushed us at the airport in Helena, she was talking about coming back to Flagstaff with me. Doesn't she get a say in any of this?"

Once again, Jake was silent. Jeremy guessed his brother was chewing over what he'd just told him and trying to figure out a way to have a good outcome for everyone involved without causing grief for any of the interested parties. Problem was, Jeremy didn't think such a scenario existed.

Which was fine. He didn't give a rat's ass if he inconvenienced the Walkers, since they were completely out of line. Being *prima* didn't give you the right to stomp all over someone else's future.

At last, Jake said, "Well, whatever you're doing, try not to start World War 3, okay? The last thing any of us need right now is more drama."

Jeremy thought it was probably a little late for that, although he understood where his brother was coming from. After all the mess in tracking down Addie and busting her and the other witches and warlocks out of the SED facility in Alexandria, the Wilcox clan had earned a little peace and quiet.

But if it took World War 3 to get Sloane free from the Walker *prima's* clutches, so be it.

"I'll be careful," he promised, and left it there. Jake could probably read between the lines and realize such a promise didn't necessarily guarantee that everything wouldn't blow up into an enormous mess, but at least Jeremy could say that he'd tried. And it also sounded as if his brother was going to stay out of things and not drag Connor into the mess, which was something Jeremy wanted to avoid if at all possible.

"All right," Jake said. "Hey, Addie and I were going to hike up around Lockett Meadow tomorrow afternoon since she doesn't have any classes. You interested?"

While Jeremy appreciated the olive branch—and the change of subject—he knew he wasn't going to allow himself to get distracted by something like going on a hike when he had so much on his plate. Solving Sloane's predicament came first.

"Thanks, but I don't think I'll be free," he replied. "I've got some stuff at Trident that I need to get handled."

Which wasn't exactly a lie. He still had those new algorithms to debug, even if they'd been sent to the bottom of his priority list. However, he also knew that saying he was going to be working at Trident was probably the best way to get Jake off his back. Jake was almost as crazy about his pet project as he was about Addie.

When he spoke, Jake sounded a little disappointed, but at least he didn't keep pushing. "All right. Maybe next time."

"Sure," Jeremy said, figuring he should throw his brother a bone. And who knows—if this all turned out okay, maybe he and Sloane and Jake and Addie could all go hiking together. If Sloane even hiked. He had to admit that she didn't really seem the type.

They ended the call there, and Jeremy turned back to his neglected sandwich and took another bite. Really, his work was pretty much done. Now all he had to do was sit back and wait for the Walkers to discover the price for messing with the Wilcoxes.

Sloane didn't even know where she was running to. All she knew was that she needed to get out of that house, away from Liz Walker. Oh, sure, she guessed her father also had to be in on the plan to hook her up with Trey, but it seemed clear enough to her that the Walker *prima* was the main motivating force behind this particular scheme.

Her steps slowed as Sloane approached the creek, which was more substantial than she'd thought, at least two yards wide and running swiftly, its waters sparkling under the bright morning sun. A shadow fell across the water, and she turned.

Trey stood a few feet away, arms crossed, expression again one of utter annoyance. Well, she could almost understand that. Having the woman who was supposed to be your bride turn tail and run as soon as she heard the news probably wasn't all that flattering.

"Exactly where did you think you were going?" he asked.

Since she'd asked herself pretty much that same question only a moment earlier, about all she could do was shrug. "I don't know. Away from that evil old woman."

His mouth, faintly shadowed by a stubbly beard, thinned. "Our *prima* can have that effect on people."

Had he just cracked a joke? Hard to say, since his hazel eyes were still narrowed and he certainly didn't look amused.

"And you're okay with letting her run your life like that?"

"Like what?"

Sloane crossed her arms and lifted an eyebrow. "Oh, please tell me that you didn't know what she was planning."

He didn't reply right away, but instead came closer to the creek. To her relief, though, he didn't approach her directly, only knelt down and picked up a smooth, flat rock from the ground and skipped it across the water. Without looking at her, he said, "I knew. Believe me, I'm not any more thrilled about all this than you are."

She knew she should be relieved…but she also found herself vaguely insulted. What, he didn't think she was good enough for him?

Which was ridiculous. She didn't want to be with Trey. She wanted to be with Jeremy. Trey's opinion of her was immaterial.

He turned toward her, a faint smile on his mouth —a mouth that should have been wide and friendly, but somehow wasn't. "Not because you aren't pretty," he said, appearing to correctly interpret her continuing silence. "But because I want to be with someone else."

"Oh," Sloane said, an unexpected spurt of sympathy coming to life inside her. "I'm sorry. Who?"

"A civilian," Trey replied, still wearing that ironic smile. "A girl from Sturgis."

That definitely would complicate things. "Let me guess—Liz isn't big on Walkers marrying civilians."

A too-casual lift of his shoulders. "She allows it from time to time, just because we need to have some diversity in our gene pool. But she thinks my gift is way too important to waste on someone like that, especially when she believes that combining my magic with yours will create a null." He paused then, giving her a speculative look. "You probably don't even know what a null is."

"Actually, I do," Sloane replied, trying not to sound

arch and failing miserably. "Jeremy told me about them. It sounds like a horrible gift."

"I can't say I'd want to have it, but I suppose it would be useful for keeping your clan well under your thumb."

Sloane started to think that maybe she'd underestimated Trey. He'd clearly came to the same conclusions she had as to why Liz Walker would want a null to rule as *prima* of the Walker clan one day. And since he obviously didn't have any designs on her, possibly she could try to make him see her as an ally.

"Neither one of us wants this," she said slowly. "So maybe we should try to figure out how to convince Liz that forcing the two of us to be together is a very bad idea."

Those words were met with a derisive chuckle. "If you knew your grandmother better, you wouldn't be saying that. She lays down the law, and that's it."

"And no one tells her to shove off?" Sloane asked. "What, does she mind-control all of you or something?"

Trey stared down at the ground and pretended to be absorbed in kicking one of the rocks that lay there.

His silence told her the awful truth. "Wait...that's her power?"

A nod. "The only reason she let me come out here and talk to you was that she thought she'd let me give it a try before she brought the big guns to bear. So to speak."

"And if anyone gets out of line—"

"She shoves them right back in," Trey finished for her. "It's pretty awful. I've only been on the receiving end of it once or twice, but it's sort of like having one of those nightmares where you think you're awake but can't move, like some other power has taken over your body and mind. If she wanted to, she could make you jump off a ten-story building and force you to smile while you were doing it."

Sloane stared at him in horror. Bad enough that she'd had to take even that small peek into Liz Walker's thoughts. She couldn't imagine what it would be like to have that evil mind forcing you to carry out her every whim.

"Luckily, she doesn't use it all that much," Trey went on. "I think it tires her out. But she doesn't have to. Everyone is so used to doing whatever she asks that no one has the guts to stand up to her."

A shiver passed over Sloane, even though the sun shone down brightly and the day was warm enough. "So…what do we do?"

He gave a helpless shrug. "I don't know."

Great. Obviously, Trey was not going to be the ally she'd hoped for. Or maybe it was just that he'd spent his entire life being cowed by the Walker *prima,* and so he had no idea how to fight back.

"What if we ran?" she asked, knowing how desperate she sounded. "We could pretend to be spending the day together, getting to know each other better. Then we could just…leave. Keep driving. You could take me back to Wilcox territory. I bet they'd give you refuge there. Then you could send for your girlfriend."

For just a moment, hope flared in his eyes, but then he once again lifted his shoulders in another of those despairing shrugs. "She'd catch us. Or rather, she'd figure it out soon enough and make sure we never got out of Walker territory. I have plenty of relatives who'd be more than happy to sell me out if it meant getting them in the *prima's* good graces."

Great. This was just getting better and better. Sloane shifted and risked a quick glance back toward the house. As far as she could tell, everything seemed quiet there. For the moment at least, it appeared that Liz Walker was allowing Trey to handle things.

"I refuse to believe there's nothing we can do," Sloane said. "Maybe you've spent your life getting kicked around by that terrible woman, but I haven't. We just need to get ourselves some time to think."

Once again, she looked over at the house, at the bank of windows where the dining room was located. It might have been her imagination, but she thought she detected movement near the center window, as if someone standing there had just twitched aside the curtains.

Spying on them?

Probably.

"Liz doesn't read minds, does she?"

"No," Trey replied. "She uses her mind to force people, but she can't see what they're thinking."

Well, thank God for small favors. Sloane had no idea yet what she planned to do to get out of there, but she knew she needed to buy some time. This was going to be difficult, although she supposed it could have been worse.

At least Trey was relatively good-looking.

She looked him squarely in the face and said, "I need you to kiss me."

His eyes flared wide in surprise. "What?"

"I don't *want* you to kiss me," she told him. "I *need* you to do it because either Garrett or Liz is spying on us from the dining room window, and we have to make them think we're going along with their plan. People always get sloppier when they think you're already on their side."

Trey shoved his hands in his pockets and regarded her for a long moment, his expression shifting to one of grudging respect. "You're really something, aren't you?"

"I try to be," she said lightly. "Now, go ahead—and make it look real."

For one nerve-wracking moment, she was pretty sure he was going to balk. He only stood there, watching her without moving, and she swallowed. If he didn't go for it, she'd have to think of something else. What that was, she had absolutely no idea.

But then he took a step toward her, and another. He removed his hands from his pockets and wrapped his fingers around hers, pulling her close. A very small pause before he reached with one hand to push a wavy lock of hair away from her face, the gesture far more tender than she would have believed him capable of.

He bent and pressed his mouth against hers. There was maybe just the faintest hint of the coffee he'd drunk on his lips, which were warm and strong. No point in deepening the kiss, not when they were doing this for an audience, but she'd kissed enough guys to know that his technique was pretty decent.

Not that it mattered. She'd been kissed by Jeremy Wilcox, and so she knew what a real kiss felt like, the kind that made it seem as if a delicious, bubbling warmth had flooded through her to the very tips of her fingers and toes.

Still, it wasn't a bad kiss, and she sent a mental thank-you winging out into the universe that he'd stayed the course and hadn't chickened out at the last minute.

The embrace lasted a few seconds more, and then he let go of her hands and sent her a look that was half puzzled, half surprised. What that meant, she didn't know. She hoped he wasn't second-guessing his attachment to the girl in Sturgis—that could make matters much more complicated than they already were.

"You think they bought it?" she asked, hoping to dispel the mood.

Trey blinked. "I guess we have to hope so. I still

don't know what you think that was going to accomplish."

"It bought us some time, if nothing else. They're going to think we've accepted the situation. Since they can't read our minds, they won't know we're lying to them."

To her relief, he seemed willing to abandon his protests. "Okay. What now?"

"I suppose we'll have to go back inside." Sloane wasn't too thrilled by that prospect. Liz Walker's house was beautiful, but it also seemed oppressive somehow, as if the very walls had absorbed something of their owner's negative energy. It felt infinitely better to be standing out in the sunlight and talking to Trey while the creek burbled away in the background.

Unfortunately, they couldn't stay out there forever.

"Probably," he agreed. A brief pause, and then he ventured, his tone almost shy, "I suppose we should hold hands as we go back."

"Good idea," she said, making sure she sounded brisk and unconcerned.

He reached out and twined her fingers in his. Those fingers felt different from Jeremy's, rough with calluses, as if Trey did a lot of work with his hands. Maybe he did. After all, she knew very little about him.

And she didn't need to know more. She'd do what she could to help him, but he also needed to help himself.

As they walked, she asked about something that had

been tickling the back of her mind. "If Liz is so into making sure she has an heir, why didn't she force Garrett to get married and have any kids other than me?"

Trey's fingers tightened on hers. "She did. He was married a long time ago, but...."

"But what?" Sloane said, somehow knowing even as the question left her lips that she wasn't going to like the answer.

"She killed herself," Trey replied. "I don't know why —I was just a little kid when it happened."

Good lord. The sun beating down on them might have been warm enough, but she was cold in that moment, mind already busy with speculation. Had Garrett's wife been in love with someone else but entered the marriage because Liz forced her into it? Had she hated him and taken the only way out she could?

"That's terrible."

"I know."

He seemed to realize there wasn't much else they could say on the subject, not when neither of them had any real details, because he was quiet the rest of the walk back to the house. They went up the stairs and through the kitchen to find Liz and Garrett sitting at the dining room table, sharing a cup of coffee and looking very pleased with themselves.

"Well," Liz said as they entered the room, "it seems you two have worked things out."

"We talked," Trey said. He bent and gave Sloane a

quick kiss on the cheek, and she made herself smile. The flush that touched her face was real enough, however, and she supposed it could only help to bolster the impression that she'd had a change of heart about him and didn't quite know what to do about it.

"He's, um…he's very nice," Sloane put in, feeling like an idiot but knowing she needed to say something.

Garrett gave them a pleased look, a broad grin touching his lips. He seemed so cheerful, it was hard to believe that he'd lost his wife under tragic circumstances. Or maybe they hadn't been all that tragic to him. If their marriage had been arranged by his mother, it would be natural to think he hadn't been all that emotionally involved.

"You two sit down, have a roll and some coffee," he said. "Or tea," he amended as he looked at Sloane.

She realized she was pretty hungry. Trey let go of her hand, and they both sat down and helped themselves to the basket of pastries and their now nearly cold beverages.

"Trey, you can show Sloane around today," Liz said, looking so pleased with herself, she might as well have been a cat that had swallowed a whole flock of canaries. "I'm sure she'll want to see more of Spearfish, especially the house you'll be sharing. I have a meeting later this morning, but we can all sit down and talk this afternoon, get everything worked out. The weather should still be fine enough a month from now for your wedding, and so we'll plan on that. Does that sound good?"

Sloane guessed it was a rhetorical question; she doubted very much that anyone had contradicted Liz Walker in the recent past. "Um…sure," she said. "I don't know much about the weather in this part of the world."

"I don't think it will be much different from what you were used to in Utah," the *prima* replied. "And of course, Trey's house is very comfortable."

In contrast, Trey looked very uncomfortable. He didn't say anything, however, only picked up another pastry and set it on his plate. Sloane knew better than to have a second one, since she wasn't a big fan of sugar. Odd how there hadn't been any offer of something with protein, like eggs or ham or bacon. Was Liz a vegetarian?

The trill of an incoming phone call interrupted the conversation. Liz paused and picked up the silver-gray iPhone lying on the table next to her place setting, giving the screen a brief glance before she put the phone to her ear.

"This is Liz Walker," she said. A long pause, during which her silvery eyebrows drew together, deepening the lines between them until they could almost have been canyons in the contours of her face. "It what? No, there has to be a mistake." She stopped there, mouth pursed in annoyance. "I'm quite sure it's a mistake. No, I'll be right over."

She ended the call there and slammed the phone down on the table with an audible crunch. Sloane winced, thinking for sure the delicate glass of the screen must have cracked. But no, it seemed intact, although she only had a moment to take a look before Liz gathered it up again and rose from the table, her lean form practically vibrating with anger.

"I have to go out," she announced.

Garrett looked up at his mother with some concern. "What's wrong?"

"I'll handle it," she said crisply, which obviously wasn't an answer at all.

However, he only nodded, as if he knew that challenging her when she was in such a mood wasn't a very good idea. She stormed toward the door, leaving the remaining three to sit at the table and look awkwardly at each other.

"Well," Garrett said, tone falsely hearty, "I guess I'll leave you two kids to keep on getting acquainted."

And he rose from the table as well.

"What the hell is going on?" Trey remarked, staring after the departing form of his cousin.

Sloane had been wondering that as well…until she decided to shove scruples aside and take a quick dip into her grandmother's thoughts before she was out of range entirely. Some kind of mix-up at the bank, something about all the funds having mysteriously disappeared from her bank account. She knew it had to be a terrible mistake, but….

Except Sloane guessed it wasn't a mistake at all. She didn't claim to know everything about Jeremy's magical computer-hacking gift, but she had a feeling it wouldn't be that difficult for someone with his abilities to access bank accounts and all sorts of other personal information, and cause whatever havoc he thought would be appropriate.

And considering how upset he'd been when the Walkers took her away, she guessed those havoc levels would be pretty damn high.

A slow smile spread across her lips, and Trey gave her a startled glance.

"What's so funny?" he demanded.

The smile remained in place. "I think your *prima* is about to find out what happens when you cross a Wilcox...."

18

THE NEXT MORNING, JEREMY WAS UP BRIGHT AND early, mostly because he knew that South Dakota was an hour ahead of Arizona and he didn't want to miss a single second of the chaos he'd just unleashed on Liz Walker. Sure, he'd drained Garrett Walker's accounts as well, but as far as he could tell, Sloane's biological father didn't have any large transactions looming in the next couple of days. It might take him a while to figure out his bank balances weren't quite as plump as they used to be, unless he was the sort of person to check them every day. Since his login history showed that he only accessed those accounts every couple of weeks, Jeremy figured it was safe to believe he'd continue in blissful ignorance for a while longer.

Liz, on the other hand, was already feeling the pain. Because he had access to her phone number from her personal banking information, he'd tapped into her cell phone signals as well. As he sipped his morning coffee, he listened to an apologetic official from her local bank call her and tell her that the funds she needed to access for her cashier's check simply weren't there.

She'd been disbelieving, of course, and had hurried off to correct the "mistake."

Normally, Jeremy would have gone to take a shower once he was done with his coffee, but he didn't want to miss a single second of that particular interview. He'd turned Liz's phone into a recording device, just to be safe. However, he also worked his way into the bank's security camera feed, thinking he might as well cover his bases. It would be so much fun to see her fury as she confronted the bank officials over her missing money, even if the sound and the visuals might not be entirely synced up.

He did have time to fetch himself a second cup, and settled down just as the security camera at the Pioneer Bank and Trust's Spearfish branch showed a furious Liz Walker stalking in the front door and going immediately to the office of the branch manager. Once there, she slammed the door behind her.

Damn it. The security cameras didn't show the inside of the individual bank officials' offices, only the lobby and the open area where the tellers' desks were located. Still, at least he'd gotten to see how angry she was, and that provided enough of a visual for the ensuing confrontation.

"Someone needs to tell me why those funds weren't

available this morning!" she said, controlled fury in every syllable. "I transferred the money from one of my brokerage accounts on Friday, so there's no reason why it shouldn't have been there today."

"I'm very sorry," came a man's voice, a nervous-sounding tenor. He didn't sound like someone in charge, but then again, he probably had never been forced to confront an infuriated *prima* before. "I don't know what to say, Mrs. Walker—two of your accounts are down to a couple of cents, and your main checking account only has"—a pause as apparently the man stopped to look something up on his computer—"one thousand and thirty-eight dollars and fifty-two cents available."

"That's impossible."

"Could you possibly have transferred the funds to another bank?" the man asked, sounding more timid than ever. It wasn't that implausible a scenario, but it also intimated that she might have had a senior moment, and that sort of insinuation probably wouldn't sit very well with Liz Walker.

"No," she snapped. "I was transferring funds *to* this account, not from it. And even if I had, wouldn't such a transfer show up in my transaction history?"

"Yes, yes, it would," the man said. "Let me check on that for you."

Another pause. Jeremy swallowed some mocha java and grinned, wishing he had Sloane with him to savor the moment. That poor banker wasn't going to find a damn thing. All those transfers Jeremy had performed the night before hadn't left a single trace. There was no way to tell where that money had gone. About the most they could do was determine approximately when it had disappeared, but he was okay with that. In fact, he wanted Liz Walker to take a moment and put two and two together, to realize that the collapse in her finances had coincided pretty much exactly with the time when she'd decided to take Sloane away from him.

After a minute passed, the banker said, "This is... very strange."

"What's strange?"

"I checked the transaction history, as you asked. The transfer from your brokerage account posted on Monday afternoon, just as you said it should have. The money was there. But sometime last night, it just...disappeared."

"How can hundreds of thousands of dollars just 'disappear'?" she demanded, sounding angrier than ever. "That money was mine, and it was there. It must be something your bank did."

Although Jeremy couldn't see the man's face, he had a feeling the bank manager must have paled at that accusation. No one wanted to be on the hook for that amount of money, let alone a small local bank in the middle of nowhere.

"We'll do what we can to investigate," the man said. "I'm sure there must be a logical explanation."

"What about my cashier's check?"

"I'm very sorry, Mrs. Walker, but since the funds aren't currently available, we can't cut that check. I'm sure if you call your buyer and explain—"

"Explain that you and this bank are monumentally incompetent?" she broke in. "Those funds need to be restored by close of business today, or you'll hear from my attorney."

A tense little silence. Then the man said, his tone not quite as polite, "That's your prerogative, Mrs. Walker. As I said, I'll have my staff look into it. Right now, though, it looks as though someone snapped their fingers and made those funds disappear into thin air."

"What did you say?" Liz Walker asked, her voice sharp.

"I said, it seems like someone snapped their fingers and made that money disappear. Of course, I know that's not what actually happened. But I've never seen funds get withdrawn from an account and not leave some kind of a transaction record."

"Figure it out," she said. "Or else."

A sound that was probably her opening the door, followed by a slam which seemed to reinforce that impression. The security cameras in the lobby picked her up as she stalked away from the bank manager's office, head held high but eyes as narrow and squinty as someone doing a Clint Eastwood impression from *The Good, the Bad, and the Ugly*. She went out the front door, and a few minutes later, there came the obvious growl of an engine coming to life, something big and throaty like the V8 in his Dodge Ram.

However, it didn't appear that Liz Walker planned to go anywhere right away, since it seemed as though she was making a phone call as she sat there in her vehicle. A man's voice came on the line.

"Shep Murdoch here."

"Hello, Shep," Liz said, sounding much more pleasant than she'd been with the bank manager. "Something's come up, and I need to reschedule our meeting this morning. Could we meet instead on Thursday?"

The man didn't answer right away. When he did speak, concern was clear in his voice. "I'm not sure if that's going to work, Ms. Walker. You know I have other parties interested in that parcel, but I was willing to sell it to you because you said you'd have the money for me today. If that's not the case, then I'm going to have to go with someone else."

Was that odd noise Liz Walker grinding her teeth together?

Jeremy sincerely hoped so.

"Look, Shep, this is a small hiccup and nothing else. I'll have the funds to you tomorrow. That isn't so huge a delay, is it?"

"Well—"

"Excellent," she said, clearly wanting to take advantage of his momentary hesitation. "Why don't we meet at eleven tomorrow instead? I think you owe me that much consideration."

A second or two passed. Then Shep said, "All right. Tomorrow at eleven. But if you don't have the check for me then, I'm going to let the other interested parties know they can submit their own bids."

"I'll have it. See you tomorrow."

The call ended there, but obviously, Liz Walker wasn't quite done yet. She made another call, and a half-familiar voice came on the line.

"Hi, Mom."

"Don't you 'hi, Mom' me," she all but barked at him. "Where's that daughter of yours?"

"She and Trey went out a little while ago," Garrett Walker replied, sounding startled by his mother's attack. "He said he was going to show her around Spearfish. I think it's nice the way those two are getting along together, don't you think?"

"Yes, very sweet," Liz said, her tone indicating just about the exact opposite. "I think that girl is playing us for fools, Garrett. I don't know how she managed it, but she's somehow managed to set the dogs on us."

"'The dogs'?" he repeated.

"Those damn Wilcoxes, or someone else she's working with. I just went to the bank, and the money's gone—all that money I transferred to purchase that parcel, plus all the other accounts at Pioneer Trust. I haven't checked yet, but I have a feeling that's only the tip of the iceberg."

"They took your money?"

"Try to keep up, Garrett," she said. "Yes, my money. Probably yours as well. You can check after you hang up. But you need to find that girl—she's the only leverage we've got."

"I'll see what I can do."

Garrett sounded chastened...and very, very worried. As he should be.

At the same time, Jeremy couldn't quite hold back a wave of disquiet. While he'd wanted Liz Walker to figure out who'd been meddling with her money, he honestly hadn't thought she'd be able to put two and two together quite that quickly. It sounded as though Sloane wasn't around at the moment, which he supposed was a blessing. On the other hand, he didn't like the idea of her getting the nickel tour of Spearfish from that Trey guy. And what was that comment about them "getting along so well"?

No, he really didn't like the sound of that.

Obviously, he needed to get to Spearfish, stat. Problem was, more than a thousand miles separated him from Sloane. Not for the first time, he wished he had Connor and Angela's gift of teleportation. Just imagine your destination and blink, and then you were there.

But he didn't have that gift...and he had a feeling if he asked for Connor's help, the *primus* would tell him he needed to stay out of it. All that crap about not meddling in other clans' business. Jeremy supposed that was all well and good when you were just looking at a situation in the abstract, but this was different. This involved someone he cared about.

Which on its own was crazy. He shouldn't be having feelings like this for someone he barely knew. Sure, he could blame it all on the wild witchy chemistry that seemed to flare to life whenever the right person finally crossed your path, but he didn't like being that simplistic about the situation.

And yet, here he was.

All right. Asking Connor for help was out of the question. Maybe Lucas could have been cajoled into taking him on another Sloane-related mission, but Jeremy kind of doubted it. Lucas's wife Margot had gone along with the scheme the first time, but it seemed unlikely that she would go for another trip so close on the heels of the last one…especially considering how all that had turned out. No, she'd probably give Jeremy a load of grief for even contemplating sending her husband into harm's way a second time around.

That left chartering a flight. As he'd pointed out to Sloane, that sort of venture would cost big bucks. Very big bucks.

She was worth it, though. And it wasn't as if he didn't have the funds on hand. No, probably the biggest hitch would be finding a charter pilot in the area who could leave on almost a moment's notice.

Well, that was what the internet was for.

To his surprise—and relief—he located a company

that flew out of Flagstaff Pulliam and could get him to Spearfish in around two hours on one of their light jets. And the rates for a roundtrip weren't that much more than one-way, which meant the prices he'd quoted Sloane a few days earlier had been a bit inflated. True, flying with Lucas hadn't cost them anything, but still, Jeremy now wished he'd done a little more investigating and therefore kept his cousin out of the whole mess.

But he couldn't change the past. About all he could do now was act quickly and hope he was able to salvage his and Sloane's future together.

It felt kind of strange to be driving around with Trey, but at the same time, Sloane was damn glad to be far away from Liz Walker's house. And actually, just knowing that Trey was interested in a girl from Sturgis helped a lot as well. She didn't have to worry about him having designs on her, not when he clearly wasn't any more interested in his *prima's* matchmaking than she was.

He'd asked her if she was hungry, and she'd said yes. A few bites of a sweet roll wasn't quite enough to satisfy her appetite, especially with everything that had been going on. So he'd brought her to a cute restaurant on Spearfish's historic main drag, a kind of gastropub place that felt a lot hipper than she would have expected from such an out-of-the-way location.

Just as they were sitting down, Trey's phone buzzed. He pulled it out of his pocket, looked down at the screen, and made a face.

"It's your father," he said.

"Don't call him that," she replied with a grimace, and he acknowledged the request with a nod as he touched the button to ignore the call, then did something with the phone's settings before slipping it back in his pocket.

"Sorry. Anyway, I put it in airplane mode, just to be safe."

Sloane nodded, even as their waiter came over and asked if they wanted anything to drink.

Boy, did she. But since she guessed that having a glass of wine or a margarita probably wasn't a very good idea right then, she instead asked for some iced tea, while Trey requested a Coke. Once that business was handled, she remarked, "They're probably trying to track us down because she wants to grill me about what happened to her money."

Trey's eyes widened. "Her money?" he repeated.

"You know that scene at the house just before she took off? Well, I took a quick peek at her thoughts and saw that the bank had called her to tell her she didn't have the funds available for her big real estate transaction today."

"No wonder she flipped out," he said. Then he raised a brow. "You had something to do with that?"

"Nope. But I'm pretty sure Jeremy did."

"Your Wilcox friend."

Maybe she was taking a risk, telling Trey what was really going on, but she had to count him as an ally. Unless they were all playing some sort of elaborate game with her, making her think he was a friend so she'd be disposed to think more kindly of him.

Abruptly, she asked, "Do you have any pictures of your girlfriend?"

That question made him blink. She couldn't really blame him; her request had come from way out in left field. "Of Liane?"

Pretty name. Maybe it was even attached to a real girl. "Yes."

Still looking puzzled, he got his phone back out, unlocked it, and then went to his camera roll. A bit of scrolling through its contents, and then he paused and handed the phone over to Sloane. "That's her."

She glanced down at the screen. The photo looked as though it had been taken out in a wilderness area somewhere; wooded mountains and a gorgeous water-fall served as the backdrop for a woman who looked to be around Sloane's age, with long honey-colored hair and a pretty heart-shaped face. She was smiling at the camera, although almost self-consciously, as if she wasn't really sure whether she wanted to be the focus of the picture. It definitely wasn't a professional photo, and didn't look staged, so Sloane had to believe it was the genuine article.

As she handed the phone back to Trey, she said, "She's really pretty."

"Thanks," he replied, looking almost embarrassed by the compliment. He returned the phone to his pocket, then remained silent as their waiter came by with their drinks.

"Are you ready to order?" he asked.

Of course, they weren't, but Trey covered for her, ordering a burger for himself so she had time to figure out what she wanted to eat.

Actually, a cheeseburger sounded really good. She scanned the menu quickly, then requested a burger with mushrooms and caramelized onions and jack cheese. That important business handled, they waited for the waiter to leave before they resumed their conversation.

"How did you meet her?" Sloane inquired.

Trey picked up his Coke and took a long pull through the straw. "I was riding down to Sturgis and stopped in at one of the bike stores there. Her family had just bought the place, and she was working at the counter."

From the way he spoke, she guessed he was talking about motorcycles and not bicycles...or horses. "So," she said with a grin, "you met her like two ordinary people meet each other. No witches involved."

He cast a quick, worried glance around them after Sloane uttered the "w" word, but since it was early for lunch, the place wasn't very crowded yet, and all the tables near them currently unoccupied. "Yeah, exactly like that," he replied. "It was nice, I guess."

"And no one knows about her?"

"No. We've only been seeing each other for a few months, so it hasn't been too hard to keep her away from the family, but sooner or later, she's going to start wondering why I haven't brought her to meet my parents." His mouth turned down, although whether from disgust at himself for his cowardice, or at the situation in general, Sloane couldn't tell.

"Why don't you just stand up to her?" she asked.

Somehow, Trey was able to guess that she wasn't talking about his secret girlfriend. "I told you how awful it is when she takes hold of your mind. It's not an experience you want to repeat. So…people just sort of roll over and do what she says."

"That's messed up, Trey," Sloane remarked, then reached for her neglected glass of iced tea.

Anger flared in his hazel eyes. "It's easy for you to sit on the outside and judge. You don't know what it's like to be caught up in a world you can't escape from."

She couldn't help smiling at the irony of those words. Obviously, he didn't know anything about her childhood, only that she'd been raised far away from Walker territory. "Actually, I kind of do," she told him. "My adopted parents were Mormon. Talk about restrictive. Except I did escape. I got away and made my own life for myself. Maybe that's what you Walkers need to do."

"A clan turn on its *prima?*" he returned, both his tone and his expression incredulous. "That's just…not how this works. You'd know that if you'd been raised in a clan."

"Well, thank God I wasn't," she said. "At least that way, I didn't get turned into a mindless robot."

Probably not the most tactful thing to say, but she couldn't take the words back now. And as she sat there, watching the shifting expressions on Trey's face, she got the feeling that he was actually weighing what she'd said, was wondering if there was some truth to her words…even if he might not be quite ready to admit that truth.

He drank some more Coke, then said, "All I'm trying to tell you is that none of this is simple. And I don't know what your Wilcox friend is up to, but Liz Walker is not someone you want on your bad side."

"Neither is Jeremy Wilcox," Sloane said calmly. "He makes those hackers you see on TV or in the movies look like, well, hacks. I don't know what he did with your *prima's* money, but I can guarantee you she isn't getting it back until she lets me go."

Something that might have been a spark of admiration flickered in Trey's hazel eyes. "He can really do stuff like that?"

"Oh, yeah. And I have a feeling the disappearing money is just the first shot fired over her bow." She paused there, wondering what else Jeremy had up his sleeve. All sorts of tricks, most likely, all of them calculated to make life miserable for Liz Walker and anyone else stupid enough to think they could try to bend Sloane to their will. "I doubt she'd be too happy to have the IRS going up her ass with a microscope."

That comment made him give an unwilling chuckle. "No, probably not. So, that's his talent? Computers?"

Sloane nodded. "Not just computers, though. Cell phones and stuff like that, too."

Trey appeared to absorb that piece of information, then nodded. The waiter showed up with their burgers right then, and the conversation was shelved for a time while they dived into their food. With each bite, Sloane felt a bit better about life. Yes, she was still stuck in Walker territory, and she honestly didn't know when or if Jeremy was going to show up to extricate her, but at least now her stomach had stopped griping and she could feel her energy levels improving.

"Do you think Garrett will come looking for us?" she asked after she'd devoured a little over half her burger.

"Probably," Trey replied. "I mean, if Liz really has figured it out and knows that your friend Jeremy is behind all this, then she's going to want some answers."

Great. Some of Sloane's enthusiasm for the food waned, but she made herself take another bite of burger and wash it down with a swallow of iced tea. Her imagination was already conjuring images of Garrett busting through the restaurant's front door and dragging her bodily out of the booth where she sat.

"Maybe we should get going, then," she said, but Trey only shook his head.

"I think we're okay for now. There are more restaurants in Spearfish than you'd think, and this isn't one of my usual hangouts. That's part of the reason why I brought you here."

This reply reassured her somewhat, but she still found herself rushing as she ate the last few bites of her burger and sweet potato fries. Although he didn't look worried, Trey also made short work of his remaining food, and put a couple of twenties down on the tabletop rather than waiting for their server to return with the bill.

Thank God. Sloane got up from the table and followed him out to his truck, a big dark blue Ford F-250. Garrett had driven one that was similar, only black. As she fastened her seatbelt, she asked, "Does everyone in the Walker clan drive a Ford?"

"No," Trey said, pulling the truck away from the curb. "But Garrett owns the Ford dealership here in Spearfish, so most of us who live in town or somewhere nearby buy our cars there."

She supposed that made sense, although she still thought it made the Walkers seem as if they were just a little bit too lockstep.

Then again, she kind of knew that already.

They drove a little bit, and then he cut down on a road that identified itself as Highway 14. "I thought I'd take us through Spearfish Canyon," he said. "It's a pretty drive, and it'll keep us out of town for a few more hours." A pause, and then he added, "Although we're going to have to come back eventually. It's not like we can stay away forever."

No, she supposed not. Although.... "Where does this highway end up?" she asked. "I mean, does it intersect with a bigger highway farther down the road?"

"If you keep going, it hits Highway 85," he replied. "And if you head west on it, then eventually you'll cross the border into Wyoming."

Perfect. "There aren't any Walkers in Wyoming, right?"

"No witch clans at all in Wyoming," he told her. "It's kind of neutral territory."

Right. Jeremy had told her something about that. Better and better.

Before she could speak, however, Trey said, "I know what you're thinking. You want me to drive down there and take you across the border where you'll be safe. But there are Walkers out that way, too, and you know the *prima* is going to put the word out for people to keep their eyes open. We'd never reach the border."

"Then what's the point in going into Spearfish Canyon at all?" Sloane asked, trying to ignore the sinking feeling in her stomach. She would not give up. She just wouldn't.

"It's somewhere to go," Trey replied. "It'll get us a little breathing room. Besides, it's the kind of place I would take you if all I was doing was showing you around the area. If Garrett or someone else does catch up with us, it makes a good cover story."

That made some sense, but she still didn't like it. Although Trey had made it sound as if he was more on her side than he was on his *prima's,* Sloane couldn't help thinking that he was being a little too defeatist. So what if there were Walkers everywhere? They could blow through one of their settlements in his truck and just keep going until they hit the Wyoming border. Exactly how much of a barrier it would provide, she honestly didn't know. Yes, there weren't any witch clans in that state, but what did that mean, exactly? It wasn't as if the border was a big electrified fence that would repel any unfriendly witches and warlocks.

She supposed she could understand why Trey was trying to play it safe…although she also hoped he wasn't playing both sides.

Hedging his bets.

Otherwise, she had a feeling she was going to get uncomfortably squeezed in the middle.

Time to push those doubts aside, however. She gave a small nod, trying to let Trey know she understood what he was doing. After that, they fell silent for a time as the road wound up through the canyon, traveling through some of the most beautiful country she'd ever seen, with a creek running parallel to the road and lime-stone cliffs rising above growths of pine and oak and sycamore. Here and there, an ambitious leaf had sprung into autumnal gold or scarlet, a bright contrast to the more subdued hues of the evergreens.

Sloane couldn't exactly allow herself to relax, but she found herself falling under the spell of her surroundings, glad of a chance to breathe in some natural beauty and try to forget the evil she'd left behind her. She couldn't be completely successful—not with Trey as a constant reminder in the driver's seat—but she knew she felt much better than she had when they'd fled Liz Walker's house earlier that day.

After they'd been driving for a while, Trey pulled off in a place called Savoy, an old mining camp. They followed the signs to Spearfish Falls and hiked their way down to the canyon floor for the best view. The way was rocky and a bit slippery at times, and Sloane wished she was wearing something a bit more substantial on her feet than a pair of ballet flats. Still, she made it down without incident and allowed herself to stand for a moment and just watch the falls, hearing their roar and feeling a faint mist of moisture on her face.

"It's beautiful," she said.

"I've come here with Liane a few times," Trey replied. "It's a good place to get away."

"Thank you for this," she told him, and she meant it. While she would much rather have had Jeremy as her companion, she couldn't deny the beauty of the place, the sensation of peace that seemed to fill her as she breathed in the cool, fresh air. Tranquil as they were, her surroundings couldn't quite keep her from asking a question that had been tickling at her mind for some time, something she'd known better than to ask back at the restaurant where they'd had an early lunch. "So…how *did* you find me?"

He shrugged. "My talent lets me track members of the Walker clan. I'd get a pulse from time to time that told me there was someone with Walker blood out in the world somewhere, but you were so far away, I could never get a true read on exactly where you were. I just knew it was someplace way south of our territory. Eventually, it bothered me so much that I told Liz about it. She told me to head south, going through Wyoming and Utah so I wouldn't be stepping on any other clans' toes. Once I was down in Utah, I was able to get a better read on you—but I also realized you were heading off into Wilcox territory, and there was no way I could follow you there." For a moment, he went silent, looking pensive. "Honestly, I didn't know who you were. Maybe Liz had a hunch, but she didn't tell me anything. All I knew was that you were a Walker. Anyway, I went back into Utah and waited, and then when you went to Laughlin, the ping was strong enough that I could find you there. You know what happened next."

That was for sure. Sloane now regretted the way she'd attacked him in the parking lot of the Riverside casino, but what was she supposed to do? Trey acted very threatening, although she guessed he'd addressed her as "witch" because he truly didn't know exactly who she was, except apparently a lost member of the Walker clan.

"Who was the girl in the casino?" she asked then. Not much of the woman's appearance had stuck with her, but she seemed to remember the person in question been much darker than the photo of Liane that Trey had showed her earlier.

Another lift of his shoulders. "Just someone I met in Laughlin. I figured having a companion would give me some protective camouflage while I tried to size you up. It's not that hard to find someone to hang with if you're paying for drinks and dinner."

Since Sloane had spent plenty of time in casinos over the past few years, she knew what Trey had told her was only the truth. She'd generally avoided hooking up with random guys, but she'd encountered plenty of other women who had no problem hanging with a man for a while if she'd get some booze and food and fun out of it.

"Anyway," he went on, "when you took off like that, I didn't have much choice but to call Liz and tell her about what I'd seen. I knew you were a witch, and it seemed pretty clear to me that you were using some kind of psychic ability to win at the poker table, and I passed that information along. She was not happy I'd lost you, but she was also very excited—said you were her granddaughter who'd been missing all these years. I didn't even know Liz had a granddaughter."

That revelation didn't surprise Sloane very much;

Liz Walker was clearly the sort of person who would do her best to hide anything that might look like a sign of weakness. "So, when did she let you in on her little plan for you and me?"

Trey's mouth tightened. "During that same conversation. She asked if you were pretty, and I said yes, you were…and then she said that was good, because she wanted me to be your consort. Not exactly what I wanted to hear." He shot her a quick glance, as if to gauge her reaction to those words. "No offense."

"None taken," she responded, which was only the truth. Trey was in love with someone else, and she…

…well, she didn't know for sure whether she was in love with Jeremy Wilcox, but there was definitely something going on between them, a connection that would have precluded a hookup with Trey even if his heart hadn't already been given elsewhere.

The conversation petered out after that, and they wandered a bit, getting their fill of the welcome tranquility of their surroundings. Sloane wished more than ever that Garrett hadn't confiscated her phone, just so she could get some pictures.

Or maybe not. Did she really want to remember her time here in Spearfish?

Eventually, they hiked their way back up to the parking lot by the Latchstring Restaurant where they'd left Trey's truck. As they approached, however, two men emerged from behind the big Ford, Garrett Walker and an older man Sloane didn't recognize. However, the uncomfortable tingle at the back of her neck as the stranger approached told her he must be another Walker warlock.

"Hi, there," Garrett said in that deceptively easy-going way of his. "I thought I might find you here."

19

CHARTERING A FLIGHT DIDN'T TAKE AS MUCH effort as Jeremy had thought. He transferred some money from his savings account to the checking account associated with his debit card, made a call, got confirmation that the transaction had gone through, and headed out to the airport, all in less than half an hour.

The pilot was a slim, middle-aged man named Dave Lewis. He greeted Jeremy in a no-nonsense sort of way, as though he was used to twenty-five-year-old kids chartering jets every day of the week, and said they should be in Spearfish in a little over two hours. Much better than Lucas's Piper Seneca, but then again, while a good plane, it wasn't a jet.

Jeremy had also made arrangements to pick up a car at the local Enterprise in Spearfish, so he knew he wouldn't have any trouble getting to Liz Walker's house on the outskirts of town. No, the real trick would be deciding the best angle of approach. He guessed that Liz Walker would know when he was in her territory… maybe. It was always a crap shoot as to how sensitive a given *prima* was when it came to interlopers on her clan's lands. But he supposed he should assume the worst, and try to move quickly before anyone could stop him. Still, should he head straight into the thick of things without worrying about the consequences, or should he try to analyze the situation once he was on the ground and see if he could come up with some sort of plan to get to Sloane?

Both approaches had their merits. He had a feeling he was probably going to do this balls out, mostly because it wasn't as though his particular gift offered him any real advantages when it came to an actual confrontation. All he really had was his leverage over the Walker clan's finances.

He had to hope it would be enough.

While he was on the phone with the charter company, he'd told the rep that he didn't plan to be in Spearfish for more than a few hours, and so the round trip would take place on the same day. That meant they'd be getting back to Flagstaff after dark, but he knew it shouldn't be a big deal. This was a jet with a professional pilot, not somebody out tooling around in their Cessna.

They landed in Spearfish at a little before three in the afternoon. Jeremy thanked Dave for the smooth flight, then went over to the terminal, where someone from Enterprise was waiting for him with the Ford Escape SUV he was renting. A bit more time was wasted as they went back to the car rental office for him to finish up the paperwork, but still, he was behind the wheel and on the road before it was barely a quarter after.

All right. He'd studied the maps, and so he knew Liz Walker's imposing stone beast of a house was located off a private lane on the northern edge of town. As far as he could tell, the lane wasn't gated. If it was, well, he'd leave the Escape at the side of the road and climb over the damn gate if he had to. Whatever it took to get to Sloane.

However, when he reached the lane that was his destination, he found it to be unprotected by any physical gates. There was a small sign that said "Private Property—No Trespassing," but a sign certainly wasn't enough of a deterrent to prevent him from entering. If Liz Walker had set up any wards to keep out strange witches and warlocks, he couldn't sense them.

Which was probably the point.

The land here was beautiful, rolling, with oak and sycamore and poplar trees that dotted the property and provided shade as they bordered the private lane. Jeremy drove down it slowly, wondering as he did so whether

Liz Walker had any kind of intruder-warning hexes planted along the way, like the McAllisters once had in various places around Jerome to warn them if any witchy interlopers—namely, the Wilcoxes—were attempting to trespass on their land.

If those sorts of wards existed here, oh, well. Sooner or later, he was going to come in contact with the Walker *prima* and her goons, and he'd just have to deal with the confrontation as best he could.

Still, that didn't mean he was going to be completely reckless. The lane turned, and beyond the trees that formed its border, he caught a glimpse of a huge gray house. He slowed his rented SUV to a crawl, and saw what he'd been hoping for—a small break in the trees, big enough for him to leave the Escape behind and continue on foot.

A fresh breeze played with his hair as he exited the vehicle. The air smelled good, of dry, sun-warmed grass and distant pine and fir. He wouldn't allow himself to be lulled by his surroundings, though. It might be beautiful, but that didn't mean the property wasn't still the home base of a pretty nasty witch clan.

The lane widened into an open gravel-paved space that fronted a large multi-bay garage. Parked in front of that garage were a couple of big Ford trucks, one black, one a metallic royal blue. Clearly, someone was home, although Jeremy couldn't see any immediate signs of life within the house.

Trees had also been planted in strategic spots around the place, providing shade and a bit of cover. He did his best to move from one to the other, attempting to mask his presence—and also feeling vaguely foolish, like someone in a parody of an action movie.

Well, he was a hacker, not a fighter.

Somewhere off in the distance, a creek burbled away. With any luck, the sound of the water passing over its stony bed would help to mask the sound of his footsteps. At the rate he was going, he might be able to get all the way up to the back door without —

"Stop right there, kid."

Damn it. Fighting a sense of inevitability, he slowly turned. Standing a few yards away was a man Jeremy didn't recognize, probably at least a decade older than Garrett Walker, maybe more. His bright blue eyes stood out against a deeply tanned, lined face, and the gray in his hair glinted in the sun.

Trying to sound calm, Jeremy said, "I'm here to see Liz Walker."

The man didn't look overly impressed. "That a fact."

"It's about those funds of hers that went missing today."

A single blink, but it was enough to tell Jeremy that his words had registered. A moment crawled past, and then another. Then the man gave a very faint nod, although in regard to what, Jeremy couldn't be sure.

"Come inside," he said. "No funny stuff."

"No funny stuff," Jeremy repeated. Not that there

was much he could have pulled even if he wanted to. He wasn't armed, and his talent wasn't something of much use in a fight.

The man jerked his chin toward the house, and Jeremy started walking. They mounted the steps on the front porch and went inside, into a cool interior that smelled faintly of something aromatic. Maybe Liz Walker smudged with sage, or burned palo santo wood. He wasn't sure what good that would do her, considering she was the evil presence there. Was she trying to banish herself?

And while he was used to nice houses—the Wilcoxes didn't believe in false modesty—he had to admit that his surroundings were pretty ritzy. With the gray-toned faux wash on the plaster walls and the expensive art everywhere, he found he had to remind himself he was in Spearfish, South Dakota, and not Beverly Hills or Scottsdale or something.

They entered a room that appeared to be Liz Walker's library—bookshelves covered one wall, and a large, overstuffed chair had been placed against one window to provide natural light for reading. It should have been a cozy space—except Liz Walker sat in that chair, eyes narrowed as she watched him enter. Standing off by the bookcases were Sloane and that guy Trey, while Garrett Walker apparently had the place of honor at his mother's side.

To Jeremy's infinite relief, Sloane looked just fine. Maybe a little tense, which was to be expected. But her gorgeous deep blue eyes lit up as soon as he walked in, although almost at once, her happiness at seeing him appeared to slip into worry. It seemed pretty clear that she was anxious about what Liz Walker would do to him.

Well, he had to admit that he was worried, too. He'd already experienced firsthand what a terrible magical talent her son possessed, and there was no reason to think her own gifts as *prima* would be any less strong…or less horrible.

"Ah, the Wilcox hacker," she said. She didn't bother to get up from her chair, only remained there with her bony hands clasped in her lap, the glare of her eyes hardly less blue than the gleam of the heavy turquoise necklace around her neck. "It's very brave of you to come beard the lion in her den, boy. Exactly what are you trying to prove?"

"Let Sloane go," he replied at once. "She comes with me, and I'll return all your money."

The Walker *prima* didn't look too impressed by his offer. Still watching him with narrowed eyes, she said, "So, you admit stealing it."

"I didn't steal it," he retorted. "I just…hid it. I don't need your money."

"The Wilcoxes are so rich?"

"We do okay."

A pause. Although Jeremy kept his gaze fixed on Liz Walker, he did his best to observe Sloane out of the corner of his eye. So far, she'd remained silent, as though she understood there wasn't much she could do except watch and wait for the outcome of this particular battle of wills.

"I'm afraid," the *prima* said, "that I can't let Sloane go. She's very valuable to this clan…and to me. My granddaughter, you know."

"Yeah, I know."

His casual acceptance of that fact seemed to rattle Liz Walker; surprise flared in her eyes before she got hold of herself and grasped the arms of the velvet-upholstered chair where she sat. Voice calm, she said, "Then you understand why she must remain here. I can see you have feelings for her—and that's understand-able…she's a very pretty girl—but your feelings cannot interfere with my clan's business. And that business is for her to remain in our territory…and to marry her cousin Trey."

Oh, *hell* no. Now Jeremy understood why the guy had been tagging along with Garrett Walker, why Trey and Sloane had been thrown together. Judging by the expression on Trey's face, he didn't look all that thrilled to be chosen as the *prima*-in-waiting's consort. Ordinar-ily, Jeremy would have been encouraged by his apparent reluctance, but right then, he found himself irrationally annoyed by the man's reaction. What, Sloane wasn't good enough for him?

"And she doesn't get any say in this?" Jeremy demanded.

Liz Walker gave him a condescending smile. "Silly

boy. What say do any of us have in the duties we must fulfill for our clans? I suppose you've shown some degree of bravery—or foolhardiness—in coming here to joust for your lady love, but all you've really done is drawn your clan into something that doesn't concern you." The smile faded, and her thin mouth pursed, making the lines that surrounded it jump into sharp relief. "So, I'll thank you to release my money. Now."

As if he could simply snap his fingers and make the money appear. Well, he supposed he could, if he was allowed to go back to his rented SUV and retrieve his laptop from where he'd stowed it under the passenger seat. Or actually, he could probably do the same thing on his phone…although he wasn't about to tell Liz Walker that. No point in making this easy for her.

He set his jaw and replied, "Just as soon as you let Sloane go."

Without speaking, Liz rose from her chair. For some reason, Jeremy hadn't expected her to be so tall…maybe because Sloane wasn't. Her spine was as straight as that of a woman forty years her junior. "I'm not joking here."

"Neither am I," he replied, inwardly marveling somewhat at his bravado. The woman was scary, he wouldn't deny that, but he also wasn't going to back down. Not when the alternative was slinking away like a kicked dog and leaving Sloane to be forced into marriage to a man who didn't even want her.

"Fine," the *prima* said. Her eyes seemed to bore into him, drilling their way straight into his head.

Give me back my money, she seemed to tell him, although her lips didn't move.

No, that was her voice echoing inside his own damn brain.

Sloane shook her head, expression terrified, and for a second or two, he couldn't understand why. Then he realized it was because her own gift allowed her to observe his thoughts, to look into his head and see how Liz Walker had invaded it.

That was the *prima's* gift. The power to coerce others using their very minds.

The men in the room—the Walker warlocks—weren't doing anything, only standing there and watching. They had to know exactly what she was doing to him, and they sure as hell wouldn't interfere.

Give me back my money.

"Okay," he said, his tongue thick, as though something other than his own will was commanding it to move. Still, he was able to employ a single delaying tactic. "Gotta get…laptop from my car."

Do it.

His feet began to move of their own volition, sending him back through the house, down the front steps and through the yard. The small part of his brain that still felt like his was yelling at him to stop, but he couldn't do it, couldn't do anything except keep walking.

The laptop was right where he'd left it. He pulled it out, marveling at the same time that Liz Walker's control would extend this far, that her hold on his mind hadn't snapped like a rubber band drawn too tight.

Then it was back to the house, back to the library. Liz Walker had sat down again, but none of the others seemed to have moved. Maybe she was forcing them to remain where they stood...or maybe they were just afraid of what she'd do if they tried to interfere.

The *prima* pointed at his laptop. "Fix it."

Jeremy went to a small side table placed up against one wall, and took the vase of flowers sitting on it and set it down on the floor. He put the laptop on the table and opened it up, then logged in. From that point, it was simply an issue of letting his gift take control, of allowing it to retrace his steps and access the holding accounts where he'd placed Liz and Garrett Walker's money so he could return those funds to the accounts where they belonged.

Only...he couldn't seem to perform those simple tasks. It was as though he understood what he needed to do, but with the Walker *prima* maintaining an iron grip on his mind, his own talent couldn't force its way through to perform the necessary steps.

"I—I can't," he said, again with his tongue so thick, it felt as though it was about to get permanently stuck to the roof of his mouth.

"What?" Liz Walker demanded.

"It's…you…you're blocking my talent. I can't do this without my own gift."

Her mouth thinned, and she glared at him as she once more got up from her chair. "No tricks, boy."

"Not…a trick." Although the room was cool enough, sweat trickled down his back, down his temple. He reached up to wipe it off his forehead, somewhat surprised he still retained enough free will to do even that much.

For a long moment, she remained silent, staring at him with those sharp blue eyes, the ones that looked as though they wanted to slice him to bits. "All right," she said at last.

The cold grip of her will began to relax. Almost as soon as he began to feel something like himself again, however, another voice intruded on his thoughts.

We can fight her together, Jeremy!

Sloane. At least, that sounded like Sloane's voice, although her lips hadn't moved and her expression remained stony as ever.

What was she doing inside his mind?

I don't know, she said. *It's like—it's like something inside me woke up when she used her power on you. Maybe she activated something. I don't know—I don't know how any of this is supposed to work.*

What do you want me to do?

Imagine a wall, she told him. *A tall brick wall. A wall she can't get past.*

Dutifully, he visualized a wall like the one Sloane

had described, even as he input a few meaningless keystrokes to make it look as though he was doing something. *Okay,* he said.

Good. Hold it in place. Keep typing—just don't do anything that actually releases those accounts.

Got it.

Another bead of sweat dripped down his forehead. This time, he ignored it. He didn't know what the hell Sloane was doing.

All he could do was pray that she did.

As soon as Jeremy was marched into Liz Walker's library, Sloane's stomach dropped to somewhere roughly around the floorboards. What the hell was he doing there?

Rescuing you, she thought then. *Just like you wanted him to.*

No, she hadn't wanted this to happen. She'd wanted his help, true, but she'd never thought he would boldly march onto the *prima's* property like he owned the place. And okay, he'd actually been hauled in by Lionel Walker, Liz's younger brother, but still, he hadn't looked terribly concerned as he confronted the woman and demanded that she release Sloane.

He should have been, though. He should have been very, very worried.

Her own fear for him ratcheted up at least twenty

notches as she watched that terrible old woman use her equally terrible gift to place him under her control. Jeremy's eyes had gone glassy, and he'd walked out of the library to fetch his laptop as if that had been the plan all along.

Something had happened during those few terrible moments, however. Sloane couldn't explain why or how, but she'd actually felt the dark shimmer of her grandmother's gift as it reached out to surround Jeremy and compel him to follow her commands.

And once she'd felt it, she suddenly understood how it worked.

How she could turn it back on itself.

But first, she needed to make sure Jeremy was free, so he wouldn't get caught in any blowback.

Luckily, his own gift had stepped in there. He couldn't do what Liz demanded as long as he was under her control. Now he was free and pretending to do as she'd asked.

They didn't have long, though. Sloane had a feeling that the *prima* might not have understood every keystroke and command, but soon enough, she'd realize he was stalling and would reach out with her power once again.

Time to nip that in the bud.

She slid into her grandmother's mind, saw her worry and anger...but also a growing fear that she might have damaged Jeremy in a way that couldn't be repaired. That had happened in the past with a few

Walkers who hadn't been quick enough to accede to her demands. The blunt force of her will bludgeoning theirs had been enough to turn them into mindless husks of the people they once were…before they dropped dead, their brains so burned out, they couldn't even keep her victims breathing anymore.

Not that Liz cared about Jeremy…only that if she'd damaged his mind, he might not be able to restore her accounts. Even if he did, she'd make sure he didn't survive this encounter. Couldn't have him interfering with her plans for her granddaughter, after all.

Rage boiled within her. Sloane didn't even stop to think. She only knew she had to stop Liz Walker, had to keep her from hurting the man who had stolen so unexpectedly into her heart. That anger turned her thoughts into a weapon, one that struck hard and fast and purely by instinct, beating against the dark, malevolent power at the center of the *prima's* soul. Liz let out a gasp and staggered backward, falling into the chair behind her. At once, Garrett let out a shocked sound and sank down to his knees as he reached for her hand.

"Mom? *Mom!*"

His own thoughts told Sloane he believed she was having a stroke. In a way, that was nearly the truth. The cells in her brain were imploding under the onslaught of her granddaughter's psychic assault. She had no defense against such an attack, had never believed anyone would have the necessary strength to do such a thing.

Karma can be a real bitch, huh, grandma?

Liz Walker's eyes closed, and her face went slack. Sloane felt the exact moment when her will left her body, when the woman she had once been was gone.

"Oh, God," Garrett moaned, holding on to his mother's hand.

For just the barest second, a sickening wave of remorse swept over Sloane, and her stomach clenched, making her wonder if she was about to vomit. What in the world had she done?

You just rid the world of a monster, she told herself. *She killed members of her own family. She forced people into loveless marriages. She made her own son lie to your mother so she'd have the genetically designed granddaughter she wanted.*

She was going to kill Jeremy.

Maybe God would judge her one day. For the moment, however, Sloane decided she wouldn't judge herself.

Trey was the first to speak. "What happened?" he asked, face pale beneath its suntan.

"A stroke," Sloane said. "I—I felt it hit her mind."

There. Only half a lie…or maybe three-quarters. She had a feeling if there was an autopsy, that was exactly what the medical examiner would find. The only real difference was that in this case, those ruptured arteries hadn't occurred from natural causes.

Garrett got to his feet and passed a hand over his face. Something in his expression made Sloane think of a little lost boy, not a man in his forties who had a grown-up daughter. But then his gaze sharpened, and he stared at her like a man who'd suddenly been thrown a lifeline.

"You're the *prima* now," he said, and she shook her head, wanting to deny his words.

"No, I'm not." Or…*was* she? She had absolutely no idea how these things were supposed to work. About all she could tell was that she didn't feel any different.

Jeremy came to her rescue then. Leaving the laptop sitting on the table, he went over to her and took one of her hands in his. "Did you feel anything?" he asked, his tone urgent. "When a *prima's* power passes to her heir, it's like a—a zing or something. You can feel the power enter you. At least, that's what I've heard."

Oh, thank God. "No," she replied at once. "I didn't feel anything. So, I can't be the *prima*…right?"

The two Walker warlocks, uncle and nephew, looked at each other in consternation.

"Liz must have had a *prima*-in-waiting already, didn't she?" Jeremy asked. If he found it at all strange that he was being forced to be the voice of reason to a witch clan that had kidnapped the woman he cared about and tried to get her to marry someone else, he didn't show it. Actually, he looked almost relaxed, as though now that the *prima* was gone, he knew the two men he faced weren't any kind of a threat. "After all, she wasn't even sure of Sloane's existence until a couple of days ago."

"Meredith," Lionel said, sounding slightly dazed. "My daughter."

Well, that made some sense. Lacking a granddaughter, Liz would have selected someone as close to her as possible, provided her powers were strong enough. "I guess you'd better call her," Sloane ventured. "See if she felt the powers go to her."

Lionel reached in his pocket and pulled out his cell phone. Before he could make the call, however, the phone began to ring, and he lifted it to his ear. "Meredith? Yes—I know. Just a few minutes ago. A stroke, we think."

Once again, Sloane let a prayer drift heavenward that the *prima* powers appeared to have been passed to their designated heir. She had to hope that this Meredith would be a better person—and *prima*—than her aunt, but she wasn't about to stick around to find out.

"I'm sorry," Jeremy said in a low tone to Trey and Garrett. "My beef was with your *prima,* not you. Let me finish what I was trying to fix."

He went back to his laptop and began typing rapidly, with none of the hesitation Sloane had noticed earlier. Obviously, his gift was back in full swing, which meant all the Walker bank accounts would be restored to their full strength in no time.

Garrett's eyes were red and burning as he said, "I suppose you'll be leaving now."

"Yes," she replied. "This isn't—this isn't where I'm supposed to be."

Don't look in his mind, she told herself. *You don't want to know.*

To her relief, he only gave a very brief nod. "I think I knew that all along. I just wanted to believe otherwise."

And he turned from her and went back to stand by his mother's side, taking her lifeless hand in his.

Sloane had to swallow against the lump in her throat. Maybe Liz Walker hadn't deserved her son's devotion, but it was still painful to watch.

Trey was silent for a few seconds. His hazel eyes were shadowed, almost wary, as if he didn't know for sure whether he could allow himself to hope again.

On an impulse, she put her hand on his arm. "If you really care about Liane," she said in an undertone, "go to her today. Go get married somewhere. Do it before someone else decides to stop you."

He didn't protest, only gave a grim nod. His jaw tightened. A sign of the resolve hardening within him?

Sloane hoped so.

Jeremy came back over to them, laptop stowed under one arm. "It's done," he said. "And you won't hear from us ever again."

A corner of Trey's mouth quirked. "That's probably a good thing."

A hug would have been horribly awkward, so Sloane only said, "Take care of yourself, Trey." Then she took

Jeremy's free hand and began to walk out of the room, knowing she needed to go upstairs and get her things before she could truly be free of that house. Her spine stiffened as she went, and she wondered what on earth she would do if Garrett called out to her, tried to get her to stay in Spearfish, if only until her grandmother was buried.

To her infinite relief, he did not.

20

Jeremy had a feeling he knew exactly what had happened to Sloane's grandmother, but he knew better than to ask. Or at least, he wanted to make sure they were far, far away from Walker territory before he gave voice to the suspicion that was preying on his mind.

Sloane seemed calm enough as she climbed into the charter jet and glanced around. Too calm, probably. He couldn't read her mind, of course, but he got the impression of someone trying their hardest to hold it together because the alternative just wasn't realistic right then.

"You seriously chartered a jet to come get me?" she asked, sounding almost amused. "Wasn't that insanely expensive?"

Jeremy shrugged and fastened his own seatbelt.

"Turns out you get a pretty good discount on a round-trip rate. So, it's not quite as bad as what I quoted you."

"Hmm," she responded, but that was all she said.

A few minutes later, they were taxiing down the runway and leaving Spearfish, South Dakota, behind. And good riddance, even though he knew that wasn't quite fair. The countryside around there was really beautiful. It wasn't the town's fault that a particularly nasty witch clan had decided to make Spearfish its headquarters.

The flight went smoothly, as he'd hoped it would, and a few hours later, they touched down at Flagstaff Pulliam. Jeremy thanked Dave, the pilot, who responded it was all in a day's work and that he hoped they would have a good evening. What he actually thought of that lightning trip to South Dakota, Jeremy had no idea. Probably better that way.

After opening the passenger-side door of his truck for her, he put Sloane's suitcase in the back seat. Silence filled the cab as he pulled out of the parking lot.

"We'll be at the cottage in no time," he told her.

To his surprise, she shook her head. "Could we—could we go to your place instead? I think that would feel better."

"Um, sure," he replied. What was going on with that request? Not that he had any intention of turning her down, but…. "I think I might have left some takeout containers lying around the kitchen," he confessed. "I was sort of distracted when I bailed earlier today."

"That's okay."

Was that just the barest trace of a smile touching her gorgeous lips?

He thought it might be. That was a good sign, right?

His townhouse was closer to the airport than the cottage, and so it only took a few minutes to get to his neighborhood, a minute more to pull into the garage and press the remote to close the door behind them. For some reason, doing so made him feel better, as if they were now enclosed in a protective bubble that would keep out the rest of the world.

As he'd feared, the kitchen was something of a mess. He murmured an apology to Sloane as he tidied up as best he could, tossing empty takeout containers in the trash, rinsing off the plates and glasses that sat on the sink so he could put them in the dishwasher. During this flurry of activity, she stood off to one side, watching him as he worked. Something in her face was still and remote, and he hoped he'd be able to reach her. It would be horrible to think that she'd managed to free herself from the Walkers, only to have the encounter scar her forever afterward.

"Do you want a drink?" he asked. "I've got a couple of bottles of wine in the pantry."

For a second or two, she didn't respond, as though she had to let the question work its way through her brain a couple of times before she could figure out how to answer him. At last, she said, "Sure. That's probably a good idea."

"And food?" Jeremy added. All right, it wasn't even six o'clock yet, but he had no idea whether she'd eaten much of anything when she was in Spearfish. And he was hungry; all he'd had was a hurried breakfast of some toast hours and hours ago.

She offered him a smile that didn't seem terribly natural. "Um, sure," she said. "You can choose."

"Pizza?" Then again, maybe he should have suggested something a little less prosaic. He'd just thought pizza was safer, since his favorite pizza places had their own delivery people and he wouldn't have to worry about Randall Lenz showing up on his doorstep once again. While he was beyond grateful to the man for the advice he'd offered, Jeremy would prefer to not have that kind of interruption at the moment.

"Pizza sounds good." A slight gleam entered Sloane's eyes, and suddenly, her expression didn't look nearly as stilted. "Canadian bacon and pineapple?"

Jeremy couldn't help rolling his eyes. "Seriously?"

"I like girl pizza. Sue me." Then she seemed to relent, adding, "Okay, on half. You can get whatever you want on the other half. Well, except anchovies."

Since he considered anchovies the work of the devil, that request wouldn't be too difficult to fulfill. "No anchovies. Just pepperoni and black olives."

"That works."

He made the call, then went to the pantry and got out a bottle of merlot that had been languishing there for several months, a leftover from one of the planning parties he and Laurel and Jake had held at his house while they were getting Trident Enterprises together. In fact, Jeremy vaguely recalled it was Laurel who'd brought over the wine. Oh, well...he had to hope she wouldn't mind that he'd drunk it without her.

A couple of wine glasses in one hand and the bottle of wine in the other, he took Sloane into the living room, since he figured they didn't need to be formal with pizza and actually sit at the dining room table. Besides, he'd always liked the living room in his town-house, with its gas fireplace and the built-in bookcases on either side. It was probably a little warm to have a fire burning, but he turned it on anyway, hoping the coziness of having it going in the background might help to relax them both.

Sloane settled herself on the couch while he uncorked the wine. "I like the fire," she said.

"Just let me know if it gets too warm, and I'll turn it down."

Such an ordinary exchange, considering what they'd just gone through in South Dakota. However, Jeremy got the distinct feeling they'd need to ease their way into that particular topic of conversation.

She nodded, and he poured some wine into each of their glasses and sat down on the sofa next to her.

No toast; it didn't feel right. They both sipped quietly, and then she said, "It's good."

"Thanks," he replied. "I can't really take credit for picking it out, though—I think my cousin Laurel brought it over a while back."

"Then I guess I'll thank her when I meet her," Sloane said.

A simple enough comment, but it allowed another of those tiny tendrils of hope to unfurl inside him. If Sloane was talking about meeting Laurel, then that must mean she wanted to stay in Flagstaff, didn't it?

Or maybe he was reading too much into things.

"You'll like her," he said. "She knows all the good places to shop."

Sloane actually chuckled. "Oh, well, then we already have a lot in common."

"Really?" Jeremy asked, even though he worried he might be venturing into sensitive territory. "It didn't seem like you brought that much stuff to the cottage."

"True," she responded. As far as he could tell, she didn't seem offended by his comment. "I had to make sure all my stuff always fit in a couple of suitcases. But I tended to switch it out a lot—I'd donate my old clothes to Goodwill on a regular basis. I didn't want to have anything so memorable that casino security might recognize me when I came back around after I was gone for a while."

That strategy made some sense. The combination of

the various wigs and the ever-changing wardrobe prob-ably ensured that no one would notice she had been to a particular casino before. After all, the only reason why he'd been able to figure out those different women were the same person was because he had his facial-recogni-tion software to help him.

She went quiet then, sipping her wine. Jeremy sat next to her, intensely aware of her presence, of the way the dancing light from the fire shimmered along the luxuriant waves of her malt-brown hair and picked out enticing shadows in the neckline of her blouse. He wished he could think of exactly the right thing to say that would put her at ease, that would let her know he understood why she'd done what she'd done.

If his suspicions were even valid.

With a clink, Sloane set her glass down on the coffee table. Since it had a glass top, a coaster wasn't necessary, but the sound still made him startle slightly.

"She was going to kill you," she said, her voice clear and distinct, as if she wanted to make sure he under-stood every word. "That's why I did it."

Damn. Jeremy set down his glass as well and reached for Sloane's hand, wrapping his fingers around hers. They were warmer than he'd expected, and he hoped that was a good sign. "It's okay."

"Is it?"

"You were trying to protect me."

She released a breath and stared into the fire for a

moment, clearly unwilling to meet his eyes. Still looking away from him, she said, much more softly this time, "I didn't think it would kill her. I was just hoping to… knock her out or something. Whatever would give us the time to get away."

"I know." He squeezed her hand. "It's awful…I get it…but you didn't have any choice."

"Maybe." Again, she was quiet, although she shifted on the sofa so she faced him squarely. The worry in her eyes made him ache for her, made him wish he could reach out and touch her and take all her pain away. "It's just…I don't know how to move forward from this."

He lifted her hand to his mouth and kissed it gently, barely brushing his lips against her fingers. Exactly why he did that, he wasn't sure. It could have been simply that he didn't know whether she was ready for a full-on kiss, but he wanted to show her that what she'd done hadn't changed how he felt about her.

"Well, you don't have to figure out your entire life right now," he told her. "Just take it a step at a time."

The doorbell rang then, and she managed a smile. "And the first step is having some pizza."

"Exactly."

Jeremy untwined his fingers from hers and got up to answer the door. The transaction only took him a few minutes, but when he returned, Sloane had moved from the couch and was now sitting on the rug, shoes kicked off and feet tucked up under her.

"I wanted to sit closer to the fire," she said.

"That looks like fun, actually. I'll meet you down there."

He put the pizza box down on the coffee table, then settled himself on the floor next to her. The maneuver was a little more awkward for him than it probably had been for Sloane, just because she didn't have nearly as far to go to be sitting on the rug. Still, he managed it without too much fuss. Since it seemed the right thing to do, he untied his tennis shoes and pulled them off.

"Better?" she asked, and he nodded.

"Much."

The next couple of minutes were taken up by pulling out their chosen pieces of pizza and munching on them in a silence that somehow felt much more comfortable than the one they'd shared just a short time earlier. Pizza had its own particular magic...even pizza with Canadian bacon and pineapple.

He snagged a second piece of pepperoni and black olive for himself. There were so many things he wanted to say to her, and yet the brain that was so good at compiling code and finding every weakness in a firewall couldn't seem to come up with the one sentence that would be exactly right for the situation.

The words came blurting out. "What was with that Trey guy?"

Sloane had just taken another bite of pizza, so she had to finish chewing it before she could answer. "My grandmother wanted me to marry him."

"Yeah, I know. But what were you saying to him at the end there, while I was finishing up transferring those funds on my laptop?"

The question brought an actual grin to her full mouth. "What, Jeremy…are you jealous?"

Oh, hell. "Maybe," he allowed.

Still smiling, she said, "He's in love with someone else. A civilian. I was telling him to hurry up and marry her before anyone else tried to interfere. I have no idea whether he'll take my advice, though."

Relief rushed through him. Not that he'd really thought there was anything going on between Sloane and Trey, but she'd also seemed friendlier toward the man than the situation warranted.

"Full disclosure, though," she went on. "I did kiss him."

"What?" Jeremy demanded, then wished he'd stomped on his tongue. Talk about sounding like a jealous boyfriend.

"Liz was spying on us," Sloane explained. "I was trying to make it look like we were going along with her plans, trying to buy some time to figure out what the hell I was going to do next."

Oh. Jeremy supposed that explanation made some sense. And how creepy was it to have your own grand-mother watch you make out with the cousin she wanted you to marry?

Distant cousin, he hoped—that was sort of how it worked in witch clans—but he didn't trust Liz Walker to have followed any normal standards of behavior when it came to getting the super-babies she wanted for her clan.

"Of course," Sloane added, "I would much rather have been kissing you."

"Oh?" Jeremy managed, knowing how strangled he sounded.

"Oh," she repeated softly. Her eyes met his, and her mouth parted, so lush, so inviting.

He put down his piece of pepperoni, praying that he was reading her correctly. If he wasn't, well, he'd apologize for his stupidity and try to go back to eating pizza as though nothing had happened.

Her lips were the softest thing he'd ever felt. He pulled her to him, deepening the kiss, and in the next moment, they were lying on the rug, bodies pressed together as they embraced almost feverishly, as if they both needed the other person's touch to erase what had happened to them in South Dakota.

He kissed her, and tasted wine and the sweet-tart tang of pineapple on her mouth. Maybe he'd have to revise his opinion of "girl pizza."

Rational thought fled after that, because she was reaching down to undo his belt, to work the buttons of his Levi's underneath. Some part of his mind protested that this was all going too fast, but he also knew he didn't have the will to stop her, that he needed to let her do what she needed to do.

Off came his T-shirt, and her hands moved over his

skin, her fingertips warm and sensual as they traced their way down his chest, reached inside his underwear to take hold of him. A groan tore its way out of his throat, and he let himself surrender to her touch, to the sensation of her hands gliding up and down his length.

Then she paused to undo the buttons of her blouse, to unhook the lacy white bra she wore beneath. Her breasts were full and rounded, the skin creamy in its perfection, and he thought he'd never seen anything so beautiful.

Time to caress those breasts, to suckle them like the divine treat they were. It was Sloane's turn to moan then, to surrender herself to the sensations that must have been coursing through her body. Jeremy undid the button and zipper of her jeans and slid them down, his fingers slipping underneath her panties to feel all her warmth and her wetness, to know then that she clearly wanted him just as much as he wanted her.

They kissed again, and again, and then he was at her entrance. He hesitated, wondering if this was really what she wanted, but she breathed in his ear, "It's okay…I'm on the pill," and he knew then there was no reason to stop, no reason not to let her lie down on the rug so he could finally slide into her, could be with her in a way he knew he'd never been with anyone else. Not this kind of closeness, not this realization that the person he held was the piece of his life that had been missing up until that moment.

He was making love to her because he loved her.

Simple as that.

The fire was warm against his bare skin, but her flesh warmer still. And when the climax swept through him, she cried out at almost the same time, her legs wrapped around him, driving him deeply into her, their breaths mingling and their hearts beating with the same glorious rhythm.

Afterward, they held each other for a long while, as though neither one of them wanted the moment to end. At last, though, he slipped out, but he didn't move any farther than that, his arms still holding her close.

The air was thick with words unspoken.

He knew he needed to say them, though. He didn't want her to think this was just about sex. If that was all he cared about, then he would have gone into her hotel room in Helena, would have slept with her that night.

"I love you, Sloane," he said.

Her eyes widened—eyes that shone in the reflected firelight, that stared up at him as though he was the only thing in the room, the only thing in her world. "Even after…?"

"It doesn't matter," he said firmly. "I think you're the bravest person I've ever met."

A flutter of her eyelashes. He realized why in the next moment—it was because she was trying to blink back tears.

"I love you, too," she whispered. "It's—oh, this whole thing is crazy. But I know I'm crazy in love with you."

He pulled her toward him and kissed her again, and again, and again. Eventually, though, they picked up their discarded clothes and put them back on, then settled down to finish the rest of their lukewarm pizza and their bottle of wine. And when they were done, they went upstairs and to his bedroom, where he pulled her down on top of him so they could make love all over again.

It was perfection, just like her.

Sloane had fallen asleep in Jeremy's arms, and when she woke up the next morning, she had to blink for a second or two, had to remind herself of where she was. But no, this was Jeremy's bedroom, with the spare black-painted furniture and the bare white walls, as if he'd been so wrapped up in his computers, he couldn't be bothered to hang any pictures. The bright sun glared in through blinds they'd forgotten to close.

His dark hair stuck up every which way, and his chin was covered in stubble, and she thought he was quite possibly the most gorgeous thing she'd ever seen in her life. Deep within was still the ache of what she'd done in South Dakota, but it didn't hurt quite as much this morning, and she knew that had everything to do with the miracle that was Jeremy Wilcox…and knowing that she'd come to the only place she was meant to be.

He rolled over and smiled at her, and she smiled

back, even as her hand stole into his and squeezed it gently. That felt right, too. Was it strange that this should feel so right? Everything that had happened between them the night before seemed as though it had come from some deep well of knowing within her, as if her soul had recognized something her mind was still trying to figure out.

Well, she'd have to go with her soul, and with her gut. So far, they hadn't led her astray.

"Can I ask you something?" she said, her tone almost hesitant.

"Anything," he replied.

She hesitated. His words came back to her. *I think you're the bravest person I know.*

No time to stop and think. "Is it okay if I wake up beside you tomorrow?"

She knew she was asking about something much bigger than the next day…even if she wasn't quite ready to admit it to herself. But that was fine. Jeremy just had to answer that single question. They'd figure out the rest as they went along.

And she'd figure out where she finally belonged in the world.

"Yes," he said. "And the day after that…and the day after that. Whatever you want."

"Thank you," she said.

It was all she said, but she thought he understood her, even if he couldn't read her mind.

They would face all their tomorrows together.
Forever.

The End

~

The Witches of Wheeler Park series continues in *A Wheeler Park Christmas*.

ALSO BY CHRISTINE POPE

THE WITCHES OF WHEELER PARK

(Paranormal romance)

Storm Born

Thunder Road

Winds of Change

Mind Games (September 2020)

A Wheeler Park Christmas (November 2020)

PROJECT DEMON HUNTERS*

(Paranormal Romance)

Unquiet Souls

Unbound Spirits

Unholy Ground

Unseen Voices

Unmarked Graves

Unbroken Vows

THE DEVIL YOU KNOW*

(Paranormal Romance)

Sympathy for the Devil

Charmed, I'm Sure

A Wing and a Prayer

THE WITCHES OF CANYON ROAD*

(Paranormal Romance)

Hidden Gifts

Darker Paths

Mysterious Ways

A Canyon Road Christmas

Demon Born

An Ill Wind

Higher Ground

Haunted Hearts

THE WITCHES OF CLEOPATRA HILL*

(Paranormal Romance)

Darkangel

Darknight

Darkmoon

Sympathetic Magic

Protector

Spellbound

A Cleopatra Hill Christmas

Impractical Magic

Strange Magic

The Arrangement

Defender

Bad Blood

Deep Magic

Darktide

THE DJINN WARS*

(Paranormal Romance)

Chosen

Taken

Fallen

Broken

Forsaken

Forbidden

Awoken

Illuminated

Stolen

Forgotten

Driven

Unspoken

THE WATCHERS TRILOGY*

(Paranormal Romance)

Falling Dark

Dead of Night

Rising Dawn

THE SEDONA FILES*

(Paranormal Romance)

Bad Vibrations

Desert Hearts

Angel Fire

Star Crossed

Falling Angels

Enemy Mine

~

~

The Refugee Ruse

STANDALONE TITLES

Hearts on Fire

Taking Dictation

Night Music

Golden Heart

* Indicates a completed series

ABOUT THE AUTHOR

USA Today bestselling author Christine Pope has been writing stories ever since she commandeered her family's Smith-Corona typewriter back in grade school. Her work includes paranormal romance, fantasy romance, and science fiction/space opera romance. She makes her home in Arizona's beautiful Verde Valley.

Don't miss out on any of Christine's new releases—sign up for her newsletter today!

Christine Pope on the Web:
www.christinepope.com

www.ingramcontent.com/pod-product-compliance
Lightning Source LLC
Chambersburg PA
CBHW021133260626
47169CB00005B/1597